D
U
ENTANGLED
L   *THE RESISTANCE*
I
T
Y

Jeremy Hughes

Table of Contents

CHAPTER I: MARKET

Look, I have no idea where "here" is. Much less do I know how I got here. And no, I don't have any papers. So, stop asking. My answers won't change. All I can tell you is everything about this place is vastly different from what I'm used to. Everyone here is incredibly short. All of your clothes are weird. And you keep clearing your throat and moving your mouth when you talk. It looks like you're eating air. All of this is weird to me.

Which is ironic, because as a child, I was always the weird one. The outcast. Pretty much ever since I can remember, the other children treated me like I had some sort of disease. But I didn't. The Shaman made sure of that. He said I would just be smaller and grow slower than the other children. But that didn't keep them from picking on me and calling me names. I think I finally gave up trying to make friends around age six or seven. Right after I met the bully.

All of the children my age were already much taller and bigger than me, but this boy was the largest of all of us. One day, I tried to make friends with one of his friends and, apparently, he didn't like that very much. I was simply talking to his friend and he stepped in between us, towering over me. I backed up a few steps to put some distance between us in case he wanted to fight.

He liked to call me names at every opportunity he got. Freak was basically his name for me by this point. He warned me to stay away from his friend. I didn't really have anything to respond with, so I just stood there. A few moments passed before he shoved me backwards. I tripped over something and hit the ground. I couldn't breathe. And, of course, they all had a good laugh from it. From then on, encounters like this were rather common if I wasn't careful where I went and when.

But there was one place that always offered somewhat of an escape. After my mundane chores of feeding and cleaning the stalls of all of the smelly goats, sheep, and chickens, I always went down to the Market. It was the little bit of excitement that I had. They brought in trinkets, clothing, and food from far-off lands. Stuff we never saw outside of the Market. But the food was by far the best part. These traders would bring in wild game they caught or hunted and roast them over a fire or put them in a stew. Unique and foreign spices permeated the air, sometimes spicy, sometimes savory, and every variation in between.

There were fowls of some sort, stripped of their feathers and extremities, roasted over the open fire, and served with a spicy dipping sauce. I remember the first time I had it. I wasn't sure what was happening with my mouth, just that it went numb almost immediately. Then the sweat beading down my forehead and the mucus coming out of my nose. But it was so good. The trader just laughed at my reaction. Another trader had wild tusk pigs, which smelled horrible before cooking by the way, but the meat was so tender and juicy after cooking it all day. They would also bring in only the freshest of vegetables, fruits, and nuts. We had farms that supplied all of the vegetables used to feed the Hive, but for some reason, those brought in by the traders were so much better.

Traders were exiles from their Hive. They engaged in this barter trade system in order to use what skills they had to obtain what they didn't. For example, if one of them was really good at hunting, but wasn't good at cooking, he or she would trade meat to one of the traders who would cook it. The hunter would either get food in return from the cook, or sometimes the cook would trade some of the cooked meat to another trader for something the hunter needed. It could get pretty complex at times.

A few of the traders were from our Hive, but most of our exiles moved far away. Some of the traders from the Market would travel with the weather, so we'd only see them in the warmer months. The rest lived in nearby makeshift housing. We weren't allowed outside of the Hive for any extended period of time. Anyway, the Market was the only reason I ever got excited.

Most traders weren't very friendly to me either. I can't say that I blame them, but they did appreciate when I would help them out. A quick brush of the area around a stall or bringing them tinder for their fire would usually net me enough food to make it to evening meal. I wished I could eat their food all day.

The slosh we ate in the Hive was such a conglomerate of tastes, it tasted like everything and nothing, all at once. I hated it, but it was all we had to eat outside of the Market. And when you're hungry, well, you eat whatever you have.

I remember one particular chilly day in autumn, he and his friends surrounded me in front of one of the stalls in the Market. I glanced around at the traders for some sort of intervention of the beating that I knew was coming. Instead, they just ignored me and continued about their routines. Traders in our society were pretty much the lowest of the low and their ability to participate in the Market hinged on not drawing attention to themselves. As such, they avoided interaction with anyone that wasn't going to buy something.

As I looked around at the traders for help, the bully grabbed me by my neck and threw me to the ground behind him. It happened so quickly. I couldn't breathe. I could feel my hands turning hot. I was so dizzy and the back of my head hurt. The other two giggled to each other. I rolled over to get up, which was when I felt a sharp pain in my side. I collapsed again, feeling the dust cake to my hands and side of my face as I struggled to take a breath. I rolled again to sit away from them. I could see all three of them were really enjoying torturing me.

As he walked towards me, I grabbed dirt and slung it at his face. He parried the dirt, but it gave me a moment to get up and run. I knew I couldn't outrun them, but I had no other choice.

I had never been this deep into the Market before. I must have taken a wrong turn somewhere. I was beginning to panic. By this point, I was sweating profusely. I desperately tried to find an exit when I finally reached the back of the Market. I had run into a dead end.

I turned around just in time to catch a massive blow to my chest, knocking me square off my feet. I felt my head hit something hard and everything went dark. After what felt like a few moments, I opened my eyes to someone standing over me that I didn't recognize.

The stranger asked me immediately if I was okay. I said I was, even though I was hurting pretty badly from all of the abuse. But I didn't need to unload all of that on her. I didn't even know her. She helped me sit up and checked the back of my head. As my eyes began to focus again, I could tell she was much older and frailer than the rest of the traders I had met at the Market. Her movements were slow and inaccurate at times, but still deliberate. I watched as she shuffled over to her small cauldron and drew a bowl of something from it. Slowly, she turned and shuffled back over and handed me the bowl with a smile. I sat up a little straighter against the wall and took a sip.

All of my taste buds at once started singing. My eyes grew wide with wonder as I stared into the dark broth. It was quite unbelievable how rich and flavorful it was. She turned back to me as she collapsed onto her makeshift chair and introduced herself as Tes. I was so entranced with the soup that I almost didn't hear her. As I slurped the remainder of the bowl, I explained that I was only a few weeks away from Commencement and that I didn't have a name yet.

When I looked up after the explanation, she had another bowl ready for me. She asked me to use the spoon this time and chuckled at my enthusiasm. I smiled widely and started on the second bowl. I'm sure she was reveling in the fact that I was enjoying her soup. She didn't seem to have any customers this far back in the Market.

After about a minute, she asked if I knew the children that chased me to her. It was such an odd question. Of course I knew them. I mean, I didn't exactly have any friends, so I guess I knew everyone about the same. I could have offered some sort of explanation, but I just nodded and sipped.

I didn't really like talking about the bully. Mother never took me seriously when I talked about him. So, I was always scolded when I brought him up. She must have read the apprehension in my eyes. After a few tense moments, I gave her a brief history of the bully and his friends and how they treated me.

This is the first time it had gotten really violent. Granted, the last time they pushed me into one of the stalls, knocking over a table of delicate trinkets that shattered on the ground. That incident got me banned from the Market for three days. The time before that, they followed me around for half the day, picking up random things from tables and throwing them at me. Regardless of how hard I tried to avoid them, they always managed to find me.

Tes shuffled over to her tiny pile of sticks, retrieved a few, then shuffled back to her cauldron, stoking the fire. She suggested I tell Mother about the bullying. I scoffed at first, thinking she was joking. But she reiterated her advice stating that Mother's job was to look after all of the children, not just some. I'm not sure what her experiences were in her Hive, but it's different here. Even Mother didn't like me. She'd probably just dismiss my claims again or implicate me in provoking the bully. The uneasy feeling in my stomach was barely quelled by the warm soup. I thought I was going to be sick for a moment.

After a few minutes of this discussion, I looked to the sky and realized just how late it was. Brilliant oranges and pinks were starting to form to the west, signaling that I should be leaving soon. We weren't allowed out after dark. I dropped the spoon and turned the rest of the second bowl up while thanking Tes for her hospitality and the fantastic soup. I may have been a bit short with her now that I think about it.

I needed to hurry home so I wouldn't get into any more trouble. I had already had my rations cut twice this season and I didn't want them to be cut a third time. I was already so hungry and my body was starting to show the signs of my lack of nutrition.

I ran back to the entrance of the Market and up the southern slope. The torches were already lit on the path and an uneasy feeling settled in again. I knew I was late, but if I were lucky, I could sneak into the hut without anyone seeing me. Just as I was about to crawl into my nook, a guard grabbed me and spun me around. Mother had been looking for me all afternoon and wanted to see me in her chambers.

The other children giggled and whispered about what I was in trouble for now. The bully flashed me a grin as I followed the guard. He really didn't have to enjoy my misfortune so much. I felt my face get hot and a lump form in my throat. She's the last person I want to speak to today.

It was much darker in her chamber than normal but this was a room I never wanted to be in. It always ends with me losing something. Perhaps she was about to retire for the evening and would let me off easy. The guard pushed me in and stood outside. In the blink of an eye, she grabbed me, pulled me directly in front of her desk, and looked me sternly in the face.

She remained silent for a short while. Silent, but not idle. I watched her face twist and turn as she contemplated what she was going to say. She finally asked where I had been all day, her eyes casting her curiosity in the flickering candlelight. I recapped my experience at the Market with the other children and Tes. She interrupted me and told me that lying to her was not a good idea. My eyes locked back with hers. I attempted to pick back up on my explanation when she slammed her hand down on her desk and commanded my silence. Any hopes I had that she would let me off easy this time were out of the question after that.

She said that I should have been studying for Commencement, not coming up with lies to get the other children in trouble. My anger got the best of me as I stepped toward her desk and slammed my fists down, yelling that I was not lying and she could ask the traders if she doubted my story.

She towered over me, propping herself up with her hands on her desk. She exclaimed that traders weren't allowed bond of word since they were exiles. The remaining slight glimmer of hope I had was now gone, as was any trust I had left in her. She halved my rations for the third time that season. I was already hungry most of the day.

Mother then tried to softly explain that Commencement was nearing and that I needed to focus on studying for it, if I were to get a good profession. Then she told me not to lie to her again and dismissed me.

Thoroughly embarrassed and angered, I turned to walk out of her chambers. I was almost across the threshold when she warned me not to cause any more trouble before my Commencement. I had never attended Commencement, as children aren't allowed to participate. Mother informed me that if I was not chosen for a profession, or if I refused my profession, I faced exile or worse.

I'm almost certain my heart skipped a beat. The lump crept up a little higher in my throat and chills rode my skin as the cool night air induced a sharp inhale. The walk back to my nook was uneventful and unescorted, but full of questions. I didn't understand why Mother didn't believe me, yet again.

I had a hard time falling asleep that night. I kept reliving the scenario with Mother to see if there was a way that I could have avoided getting my rations cut again. No matter which way my visualizations went, it always ended the same way. I just couldn't win with her.

Suddenly, I caught three sets of eyes in the reflection of the dying fire. I guess I had been thinking out loud again. I rolled over and tried to think of nothing as best as I could. That failed miserably within a few minutes. I found myself trying to imagine what some of the other Hives were like. If they had someone like me who was different. I wondered if their life was as troublesome as mine.

Dawn came incredibly early the next morning. I struggled to get myself awake and dressed for morning chores. By the looks I was given at breakfast, I must have kept more than one of the other children up last night. I didn't care. It was mostly their fault anyway.

I shoveled the meager portion down as quickly as I could handle it. I knew if I went to the Market again today, the bully would find me. Commencement was the single, most important time in my life. I didn't want to be exiled. And I certainly didn't want to find out what was worse than exile.

I hastily poured the feed into each of the troughs for our livestock and discarded any out of place foliage not meant for their bedding. I contemplated rummaging through the feed for something edible. I was so hungry. But I knew I needed to leave before the bully and his friends finished their breakfast.

I ran back to my nook and grabbed my extra sweater. Since I didn't want to risk going back to the Market, the only other place I could go was into the forest. It was strictly forbidden, but I had a plan to make sure I was back before sunset. And if questioned,

I would simply say I was in the Market all day. I just needed to make sure no one saw me leave.

On the east side of the Hive, I carefully descended the steep hill, attempting to not make any noise. About halfway down, I heard two voices up above discussing something to do with a fight that happened the night before. I knew they were guards and I panicked. I quickly turned to face the incline, hoping the light brush was enough to camouflage me from their sight. That's when I felt a boulder the size of my head shift under my feet and fall loose. As quickly as I could, I spun back around and grabbed it in mid-air. Crouching, I dared not move a muscle until I was certain the guards heard nothing.

A few moments passed and, finally, so did they. A flood of relief came over me and I almost dropped the boulder. Putting it back in its original place, I continue to creep down the rest of the way without incident. Once at the bottom, I scurried through the tree line as fast as my little legs would carry me. After I was sure I was out of sight, I slowed down to catch my breath and get my bearings.

I traveled towards the sun in the sky to make navigating back to the Hive easier that afternoon. It was such a nice day. Brisk, but nice. Most of the leaves had already changed to bright oranges, yellows, and reds. Some had even begun to litter the ground. In the distance, I could hear the sounds of white tail moving through the low brush. The birds chirped overhead.

In the midst of my appreciation of nature, I smelled him. I looked around for what smelled like a bear. It didn't take long. I'm not sure how I missed him to begin with. He was easily the biggest bear I've ever seen. I crept quietly past him, making sure to stay downwind. I begged my stomach to postpone its angry monologue until we were past the bear. I had no intentions on becoming this monster's last meal of the season. Not that I would have much of a meal at that time. More like a snack.

I made it about two hundred meters past the bear when I stumbled upon what I assumed was a small, abandoned village. It looked like no one had been here in a really long time. The buildings had significant damage from the winter and spring storms and even the rooves had fallen in on a few of them. The overgrowth throughout the village was lush and unhindered by the remnants of humans. Nature simply found a way around the man-made obstacles.

I searched through a few of the huts, finding little other than dirt. Suddenly, I heard voices approaching and an odd stench permeated the air. Something was burning, which out here, was an awfully bad sign. I crouched down and crept to the window of the hut I was in. I saw two warriors talking and passing something that was smoking between them. What were they doing this far from the Hive? More importantly, how do I get out of here without being detected? I decided the best option was to sneak out the back door and down the small hill. Once I was out of sight again, I needed to put some distance between us. They seemed unaware of me and were also completely unconcerned with the village itself.

I slowly and quietly made my way parallel to my original path, careful to avoid the loudest foliage. Last thing I needed was to get caught outside of the Hive. I still had a few hours to burn before I needed to head back. Hopefully, these warriors wouldn't be there on the way back. I didn't want to have to sneak by them twice.

Snap! The small limb crunched under my foot. I froze in place and listened for the warriors. I didn't hear anything. No talking, nothing moving through the foliage, even the wildlife didn't make any noise.

I knew I had to get out of there as quickly as possible. Each passing second that I was there increased the chance I'd be found. I felt something watching me. I knew they had to have heard the branch snap and were looking for the source. I started to tip toe directly away from their location as quickly and quietly as I could. I quietly professed my undying hatred for every piece of foliage that all of a sudden decided to make noise under my feet.

Out of nowhere, I see one of the warriors appear in my path from behind a tree. He inquired why I was outside of the Hive, his alert and curious state evident by his stare that peered at me from behind his long brown hair.

I tried to pass it off as just taking a walk. He wasn't buying it. I panicked and did the only thing I could think of. I threw dirt and leaves in his face and ran as quickly as I could past him down the side of the hill.

Tons of thoughts flooded my brain at the most inappropriate time. Dodging trees and questioning everything about my life at the same time. I thought about the bully and wondered why he hated me. What did I do wrong? I'm sure I'd be exiled for this. Attacking a Warrior is an offense punishable by exile. I hoped it wasn't enough to find out what "or worse" meant. In hindsight, I really could have picked a better time for reflection.

Daylight turned pitch black in a split second. The ground I had moments before been running on suddenly gave way, throwing me a couple meters down face down on a really hard stone with a loud thud. I sat up, trying to catch my breath and figure out where I was. From what little I could see, I was in a cave of some sort. The only light emanating from the hole I had just created. My leg and chest hurt slightly, but no major damage. At least there was some good news.

I stood up and brushed myself off. I tried several times to get the warriors' attention from inside the cave. I didn't see a way out and I would need their help. I yelled for help over and over again. Nothing. No laughter. No prodding. No "look at the freak stuck in a hole". Figures. I guess they didn't even follow me. After all, they can run much faster than I could and they should have caught me with little effort.

After a few minutes, my eyes started to adjust. Raising my hand to block the blinding light, I could see the rest of the cave I fell into. There were weird paintings on the back wall with faded colors and odd shapes. Part of that far wall was sunken in, like something hit it really hard.

As I approached, I heard something growl from behind the wall. Some of the smaller rocks on the wall started to glow. I decided that exploration of this cave would be best left for another time, particularly when I had a weapon to defend myself with. My first priority was getting out of there. If night fell and a pack of wolves found the cave, I'd be easy prey.

I leaned down to rub my leg where it hurt as I stared at the hole in the ground above, determining the easiest way to escape. I backed up to the far wall, got a running start, leapt up using the wall as a launch point, and was almost able to grab hold of the ledge.

Every jump, I got a little closer. I could still hear the growling from behind the wall. It offered a worthy incentive to get out of here as quickly as possible. I really didn't want to fight whatever this thing was.

On the third or fourth jump, I was just able to grab the inside ledge of the hole I fell in. It was weaker than expected and immediately collapsed, creating an even larger hole. The dust and blinding light created by the last jump sent me squinting and coughing into a corner of the cave.

Once everything settled, I could see that I had managed to pull down a larger section of the roof. Luckily, it fell in such a way that allowed me to climb up it and leap up to solid ground. As I climbed out, the growling stopped. He'll have to find something else for dinner tonight.

I knocked the dirt and dust off of me and looked around for the warriors, half expecting them to be propped against a tree and laughing at my misfortune. But they were nowhere to be seen. I'd rather be scolded for attacking them and running than this. They really couldn't have cared less what happened to me.

The incident with the cave took more time out of the day than I had allocated for my journey. I could tell the sun was already setting and that it would be dark very soon. I knew I wouldn't make it back to the Hive in time to avoid being caught, and that's only if the warriors didn't report my absence. I sighed and accepted the consequences that wouldn't come to fruition until tomorrow. That's only if I made it through the night.

I focused on finding shelter. I had no idea how to survive out here. I'd never been outside the Hive at night. The best idea I could come up with was to try to back track to the abandoned village and hope it didn't rain.

My stomach started to make noises again. I had hoped the warriors were camped out at the village around a fire cooking something delicious. Not that they cared about me, but maybe I could convince them to share.

As I briskly walked back the way I came, the sounds of dusk flooded my ears as darkness started to take its hold on the forest. I knew I needed to hurry up. Wolves would soon be out and we don't exactly get along. I must have run much farther than I thought I had.

I headed towards the sunset. Dusk was now settling in and the heavy tree cap negated any lingering light the sun offered. Lightning bugs were everywhere. The sounds were almost deafening. It seemed I posed no threat to any of these creatures, and they flaunted their knowledge of it by bombarding my eardrums with their calls.

Finally, I could see the outline of a broken-down hut on the outskirts and a wave of relief came over me. At least I would have shelter from the larger predators in the area. Well, as much shelter as I could get from old, dilapidated stone huts like this.

But if the bear from earlier came looking for a snack, he could probably just lay across the hut and bury me alive. One of them should, at least partially, mask my scent for the night. Maybe that will be enough to keep me safe until morning.

As I walked nearer, I noticed light coming out of one of them and the sound and smell of a fire. I called out to whoever was camped in the hut. A few tense moments pass before I see a head poke out from the door and then a full figure. She calls out, wondering why a child was out after dark. I explained I got trapped in a cave and needed shelter for the night if she was able to accommodate. I finally realized I had stumbled upon Tes' home at the same time as she realized who I was. We both relaxed as we embraced. She invited me inside.

I followed her inside to the crackling sounds and warmth of a small fire. The chill from the air here was non-existent. As quaint and minimalistic as her home was, it was cozy. I just wanted to curl up on one of the beds and sleep for days.

She asked me to have a seat around the fire and explain more about what happened. She took the seat opposite of me as she tended the soup in the kettle. I described the meeting with Mother as the motive for why I left the sanctuary of the Hive. I explained I had intended to return before dark. That was, of course, until I fell into the cave.

The frustration from her eyes contrast against her heavily wrinkled face reminded me of Mother. But I was not afraid of this woman. In fact, it was just the opposite. She was concerned about me. She was upset that I was in this predicament. But why? She didn't know me from the next child. Why did she care so much about me?

Tes drew stew from a pot over the fire and listened carefully as I explained every detail of the day's journey. She warned that it was hot as she passed me the heavily decorated blue and white bowl.

The fire had taken most of the evening chill, but the bowl of stew finished it off. It was like holding the sun. The smell was so intoxicating. I drew a spoonful of various vegetables and some sort of meat, blew on it a few times, and shoved the spoon in my mouth. I can only describe the taste as nothing short of pure bliss. The meat and vegetables simply melted in my mouth. It was like eating fire if that was possible. A tasty, succulent fire that warmed every part of my body. If I weren't so hungry, I would have savored the first bite longer.

Tes drew herself a bowl and sat back down across from me. She seemed to have much more patience around food than I had. I guess you can afford that when you eat food like this every day.

We sat listening to the ebb and flow of the fire crackling between all the forest sounds, eating the best food I'd ever had.

After a minute or two, I set my bowl down to take off my extra sweater. When I looked up, I saw two yellow eyes peering at me from the shadows outside. I grabbed the spoon in a futile attempt at preparing to defend myself. Tes noticed the tension and looked outside. Then she made some sort of throat noise that coaxed the eyes closer to the doorway. I kicked the bowl over, nearly tripped over the stool, and backed against the wall as an absolutely massive wolf slowly walked in. Tes shuffled over and petted the wolf's chest.

She introduced Shadow as a friend, but I could do nothing but breathe heavily and stare into her golden eyes. I thought to myself,

This is it. This is how I die. Surviving a whole day out of the Hive, only to be eaten for dinner by a giant wolf.

Tes took the spoon from my hand as she put her arm on my shoulder. She giggled for a moment and told me to relax.

Shadow leaned her head down and sniffed my face. I closed my eyes, afraid of what would come next. Then I felt the weirdest, wettest stone wipe my face from my chin through my hair. Tes busted out laughing as I slid down the wall trying to figure out what had just happened.

Tes coaxed Shadow to back up from me. When I had cleaned my face off as well as I could, I looked up to see an equally giant tongue sticking out of Shadow's mouth. She seemed amused at the event.

Tes explained that everything was ok and that Shadow liked me. I thought that was odd. Not that I was an expert on wolf body language or anything, but I didn't get that impression. Shadow told me I tasted bad though. I sat there for a few more moments trying to make sure I heard what I thought I heard.

I could hear Tes giggling as she shuffled across the hut to retrieve Shadow's much larger bowl from the shelf. I couldn't help but think this was some sort of elaborate prank. Shadow came back over, licked my face again, and curled up on the ground on my legs. She was so heavy! Amidst the fear of provoking her, coupled with the loss of feeling in my feet, I got Tes' attention. She giggled again and called Shadow over to eat.

I thought she was going to break my legs as she stood. I moved around on the ground in order to feel my legs again as Shadow made loud lapping and gulping sounds as she ate. As beautiful as she was with her jet-black coat, she was just the clumsiest eater. That delicious soup Tes prepared came flying out of all sides of Shadow's bowl. I felt so bad that she was wasting it. Then again, I had already knocked over my bowl of soup when Shadow came through the door. So, it's not like I could say much.

Shadow suddenly stopped eating and looked toward the doorway, sniffing at the night air. After a long pause, we heard the unmistakable growl of a bear. My pulse raced and my breathing quickened. Tes gave me a sidelong glance to see what I would do. She tried to stay calm despite the obvious concern on her face. I was petrified and standing behind the largest wolf I'd ever seen. Shadow crept slowly into the darkness. Only the sounds of the night and the flickering of the fire remained between carefully guarded exhales. We dared not move for fear of alerting the bear to our presence.

A low growl permeated the hut, shaking small objects and settling some of the embers in the fire. It felt like an eternity, frozen in place, waiting for the bear to find us.

And then we heard the bear roar again as it came into view outside the door. Luckily, he was too big to fit through it. Tes and I slowly and quietly crossed to the corner opposite of the bear. I blinked and the bear's giant head was gone, replaced with the most ferocious and terrifying growls, yelps, and thuds. Tes grabbed me and we quickly shuffled out of the hut and away from the bear.

Shadow had gotten a hold of him and slung him to the ground by the neck which sent him into the hut next to hers. Our eyes started to adjust and we could make the outline of the bear standing on its hind legs in the place where a hut once stood. He was easily four and a half meters tall. Shadow leapt at his throat as the bear embraced her and they both tumbled backwards, rolling into another hut, and demolishing it. But this time, the bear ended up on top of Shadow and snapped at her throat.

Shadow bit his nose hard and blood went everywhere as he shook his head. This seemed to only make him madder as he roared loudly and took another lethal shot to her neck. The fighting went on for a few more seconds before I realized just how badly outmatched Shadow was. Tes couldn't help her and if I didn't do something, we would all be dead soon.

But at the same time, I'd never fought a bear, especially not one that big. I wasn't sure exactly what I could do to help the situation, but I ran up to the bear's side and threw the hardest punch I could muster into his exposed side. I heard a loud crack and a painful growl. The bear's swipe knocked me about ten meters away into the side of another hut.

Almost whimpering, he turned to look at me as Shadow took the opportunity and launched again for his throat, connecting flawlessly, and sinking her teeth deeply in the thick fur and flesh. The bear roared, gurgled, and lunged backwards in an attempt to remove her teeth from his neck. He landed on his back, with Shadow still attached to his neck. Several long moments go by until the bear stops breathing and she releases, stepping back from the large puddle of blood that accumulated at the bear's neck.

I slowly stood up and a wave of relief came over me as I realized the threat was gone. Shadow walked over to me and put her forehead against my chest. I wrapped my arms around her head and hugged her oversized face. She was much gentler with Tes, simply allowing her to pet her head as Tes gave her thanks. Tes ushered us back inside to finish dinner. We would deal with the bear's carcass in the morning.

We spent the rest of the night dining on the remainder of the delicious stew and listening to the forest. Afterwards, Shadow curled up next to me on her bed. Tes fell fast asleep and had the cutest snore. I almost couldn't hear it over Shadow's heavy breathing behind me.

As I watched the brilliant flames dance around the pit, I reflected on the day's events and how it all ended up with me punching a bear. I never would have imagined in my wildest dream that I'd do something like that. But Shadow needed help at the time and it was the only thing I could think of.

Of all the ways it could have played out, I got really lucky running into Tes and Shadow. I probably should have died a half dozen times that day, but I was even more concerned with how I was going to explain all of this to Mother. That gave me the most anxiety.

I woke up in the early hours to Tes stoking the fire up and Shadow's heavy breathing. I reached for my extra sweater, folded nicely on the end of the bed.

As I pulled it on, Tes asked me if I was still hungry. Honestly, I was still full from the night before, which doesn't happen. The sky was starting to lighten up, so she suggested we get moving back to the Hive. Tes put out the fire and got her things together for the trip.

We started walking as day broke. I was rarely up this early, so the bright colors in the sky took me by surprise. I kept glancing back over my shoulder every so often to catch a glimpse of how the colors had changed since the last time I looked. By the time we reached the base of the Hive, the sun was already high in the sky and I had to remove my extra sweater again.

We circled around to the front entrance of the Hive and were immediately met by two warriors who simultaneously grabbed me by the arms and dragged me inside. I looked back to see Tes in the doorway and told her "thank you".

The warriors delivered me to Mother's chamber. She was waiting for me. She was furious that I didn't return to the Hive the night before. I didn't know how she was going to react with this, to be honest. Sometimes it's like she cares and other times it's like she doesn't want anything to do with me.

I explained how in order to avoid confrontation with the bully, I slipped down the eastern slopes and went off into the forest. It was just supposed to be a short hike but being caught by the warriors and falling in the cave prolonged the journey.

I told her about Tes and Shadow and how they saved my life. Between the shelter, fire, food, and the bear, they both had a big hand in keeping me safe overnight. I could tell she was still a little worried about me, but more curious than anything else.

At the end of the story, she sat in her chair in silence for what seemed like a few minutes. She raised her head and apologized to me. Her eyes alluding to the realization that I had been telling the truth all along and that she had missed it. She was very remorseful and vowed to correct the issue, provided I never do that to her again. I agreed.

Mother spoke with the other children that morning and instructed them to leave me alone. It was odd seeing her anger not directed at me. From that moment on, I was bully-free. I had already spent half my life dealing with bullies. It's not like I had any friends after that either, but at least I wasn't living in fear of the other children. Sometimes, I would catch them staring at me in the Market only to disappear after a few minutes.

I visited with Tes every day in the Market and dined on her delicious food. I even got permission from Mother to stay with her overnight sometimes, even though it was normally strictly forbidden for children to even leave the Hive.

Shadow and I took a liking to one another very quickly. I would throw large sticks and she would retrieve them. It was so much fun for both of us. Sometimes she'd bring it back, knock me over, and lay on me for fun. We'd laugh as I'd push at her and tell her to get off me. She'd roll over on her side, still laughing as I struggled to push her the rest of the way and move the stick off my chest. Tes liked to watch us play.

As Commencement neared, the Hive changed into a festival. Commencement was the only time Traders were allowed inside the Hive. Traders were tasked with suppling Commencement in exchange for their ability to operate in the Market the rest of the year. I helped Tes move some of her supplies and set up for the big day. She would bring three different stews to be given to the population during the ceremony. The sled was loaded down and very heavy to drag through the thick forest, much less up the hill to the Hive.

I was so excited for Commencement. I was at a peak of happiness in my life. Everything was just starting to come together. And for once, I had something besides food to look forward to. In fact, I couldn't stop thinking about it. Tucked away in my nook, I imagined scenario after scenario in rapid succession. Each visualization basked in its own glory.

CHAPTER II: COMMENCEMENT

I woke shortly before daybreak to the bustling sounds coming from the Commons Chamber in the center of the Hive. Everyone was setting up for the Commencement ceremony. I almost couldn't contain my excitement. I daydreamed again about being a Warrior. I imagined what it would be like to sit around a fire with other warriors, sharing good food and good conversations. Just the thought of it made me smile.

I was startled back to reality by Mother, who had brought all of the children fresh clothes for the Test and Commencement ceremony. She smiled widely as she stated how big of a day it was. I beamed back at her in anticipation. I couldn't wait!

After a few more minutes of contemplation, I got dressed and walked to the east side of the Hive. The sky was covered in all sorts of colors from the impending sunrise. It was as if even the sun knew what day it was. I closed my eyes and enjoyed the soft warmth it offered and smiled as I took a deep breath. It was time.

I returned to my nook, grabbed the first set of clean clothes, and darted down the west slope to the creek. Stripping down, I waded into the small but deep stream, trying to hold my breath in to keep it from being stolen by the chilly water. I ducked under the water, quickly ran my hands over my body, knocking off any dirt or debris, and then nearly jumped out of the stream. It was so cold! I felt my skin tighten all over my body which ended with me shivering as I picked through the stack of clothes.

Once dressed and warming up, I couldn't help but to take in the surroundings. All of the different colors of the leaves, both on the trees as well as on the ground. Different types of flying insects buzzing around. Overhead, the birds were singing songs of celebration. Nature was celebrating with us. I tried to enjoy my last time as a child, since I'd never be here again.

I tugged at the new clothes, trying to get comfortable. They felt rough and a bit awkward. But they would do. I wouldn't let that affect me today. Today was the day I was going to become a man and be assigned a profession. Well, of course, if I pass the Test first and avoid being exiled in the process.

Out of all the possible professions, I wanted to be a Warrior the most. They were strong and no one messed with them. Even the other Hives were afraid of our warriors. If I were a Warrior, no one would mess with me either.

But the most attractive thing about warriors were they were all friends with one another. I would always find them in pairs if not more. When not on duty, they could always be found encircling a fire somewhere in the Hive, telling stories and such. It would be really nice to have friends.

The options confused me at times. Tes knew how to make really good food. If I became a cook, I could make better food for the Hive. Maybe I could help her get back into the Hive again and we would cook the best meals for everyone. We would hold festivals every week and cook more food than we could eat.

I knew I didn't want to be a farmer. I hated dealing with livestock already. They're smelly and messy. And tending the fields just seemed like a waste of time if all that work turned into the slop they fed us.

Guards were an even weirder bunch. They had all of the best combat training, but they had their man parts removed since they were also charged with guarding the breeders. The Overlord and Barons were deadly serious about mating. If you were even suspected of fathering an illegitimate child with a breeder, you and your offspring faced certain death. It wasn't something I cared to get involved in.

I was horrible at hunting. I was neither quiet enough nor coordinated enough to hunt game that could hear and smell you from a hundred meters out. And without the element of surprise, hunters couldn't get close enough to get the kill.

Quite honestly, builders just sat around until something broke. What a boring life. I wanted excitement and danger, but I wouldn't find it waiting for one of the livestock to break a trough or the warriors to throw one another through the side of a hut.

The starting horn sounded loudly in the distance, snapping me back to reality. Realizing I was late to the Test, I pulled my old clothes to my chest and hurried back to my nook to drop them off before descending the south slope to the field in a dead sprint.

By the time I got there, all of the other children were already in line. I ran up to the end of the line and stood, catching my breath. I felt the eyes of nearly the whole Hive on me. I stood straighter and tried to control my breathing to dispel the attention I'd earned with my tardy appearance.

The proctor stared at me for a moment and then began his speech as he turned to walk to the other end of the line. He explained how Commencement was a transition from childhood to manhood and how the Test would help the Barons decide which professions each of us was best at. He droned on for several more minutes about how important this tradition was to the Hive and the history of those before us, or something like that. I preferred my daydream instead. It interested me much more than his speech.

I wondered if I would be any good as a tamer. Shadow and I worked pretty well together. Maybe I could find another animal like Shadow, one that would be my companion and keep me safe.

The proctor interrupted me again as he stepped in front of me to end my obvious distraction. He explained how important it was to make sure we completed our best challenge first, since it was likely the Barons would focus most on it. He pointed to and described the stations set up all around the field for the different skills desired by the Barons.

Some of the tests were beneficial to more than one profession. Like the Stone Throwing and Brute Force challenges appealed to both guards and warriors alike. The game tracking challenge required skills that both tamers and hunters desired. And the fire building challenge highlighted a skill that both cooks and builders needed. I needed to carefully consider all of the skill stations before deciding which challenge I accepted first.

As soon as the proctor told us to move to the skill station of our choice, the bully and a friend of his sprinted over to the Stone Throwing challenge. This challenge was the main focus for the Barons of both guards and warriors. I wasn't the greatest at throwing stones anyway, but with the additional emphasis on passing the first challenge coupled with where the bully went, I decided the Brute Force challenge should be the first one I attempted.

As I walked over to the tree line for this challenge, several of the Barons were standing off to the side, discussing amongst themselves and looking at me. I was the only one that chose Brute Force first. Apprehension got the best of me and I started to back away when I saw Mother standing off to the side. She smiled slightly at me and gave me a nod of assurance.

As my indecision quelled slightly, the station proctor approached me and asked me if I wished to complete the Brute Force challenge. I peered back at Mother, who simply nodded and smiled at me. A surge of confidence welled up in me as I confirmed to the proctor. The idea for the challenge is to be able to uproot or knock a tree down, displaying Brute Force.

I slowly walked up to the biggest tree in the line and stared at it for a moment. I could hear the Barons discussing bets as to whether I could actually do it. One suggested to another that I should have chosen a much smaller tree. Another implied I should have chosen a sapling off to the side. The laughter was deafening. Great. Short jokes again.

An anger rose in me that I hadn't felt since the night the bear was about to kill Shadow. I reared back and swung as hard as I could at the middle of the tree. There was a loud crack that swept over the field like thunder as the tree split from the roots at the trunk. It twisted awkwardly as it toppled to the ground, bouncing off another tree and landing with a thud.

I turned around to find no one was talking anymore. Everyone was just staring at me. I was confused for a moment. I thought maybe I did something wrong or taboo. I asked the proctor for clarification, but his reply with his mouth agape was simply "well done".

As I walked back to the line, I looked for the bully at the Stone Throwing challenge. He was still there, waiting for his friend to make his attempt. I could tell he had thrown his stone near a hundred meters, by the proctor's mark. I knew I had made the right choice.

The remainder of the Test was not as spectacular as the first challenge was. I manage to throw my stone less than eighty meters. A good throw, but not even close to the best. It didn't help that my stone was bigger than my head. The fire building challenge was fruitless and I swear the cattle were determined to not listen to me. Apparently, I didn't plant the seeds properly, even though I followed the proctor's guidance exactly.

Finally, the ending horn sounded and we headed back up to the Hive. The bully purposefully bumped into me during the walk back. We started arguing and calling each other names. He made me so angry. I started to feel it well up in me again when Mother stepped between us. She said nothing but pointed at the Barons who were observing our spat.

I angrily sighed and resumed my walk, distancing myself from him. I could still feel his hatred on the back of my neck as if his stare were burning holes in me. It didn't matter. With any luck, I'd be a Warrior soon and he'd have to respect me. I mean unless he got Warrior too. That wouldn't be good.

I played situations in my head over and over again of me punching him. In one, he flew into the sky, never to return. In another, I hit him so hard he just disappeared into a pink mist. Before I knew it, we were back at the Hive.

While changing into the second set of clothes, my mind wandered again. I thought about all of the warriors I had seen before. Even though they were all intimidating, I thought about one or two I would try to make friends with first. My visualization didn't offer a definitive answer and that frustrated me.

Walking to the Commons Chamber, I started to get nervous again. On one hand, I knew the bully would be there. I had to make sure I wasn't near him. Last thing I needed was to beat him to a pulp in front of the whole Hive. On the other hand, I started to doubt my performance was enough to convince the Barons to appoint me as a Warrior. I was already at a disadvantage being so much smaller than the others. At this point, I'd take anything. Even though living with Tes would be awesome, I really didn't want to live outside the Hive.

Again, the starting horn sounded, this time amplified by the Commons Chamber's acoustics. We formed a line directly in front of the Barons' thrones, a few meters back. Shortly thereafter, the Overlord's horn sounded. The Guards had control of the only horn used for his entrance. It was a giant horn from a beast of some sort. I've never seen the animal that it comes from. Everyone bowed as he slowly shuffled into the chamber, aided by a Guard, and took his throne behind the Barons.

It took forever, but his horn finally sounded again. We all stood back up. This was it. It was time! I was so excited I almost couldn't stand still. First to make his pass was the Baron of Hunters. He was kind of a joke. He couldn't hunt and only had the title passed to him after his father died in a mysterious accident in the woods. I secretly blamed him for the lack of decent food. He wanted nothing more than to hang around with the breeders all day.

I tried to make as little movements as possible to minimize the chance that I would draw his attention. I did not want to belong to this man. Not only that, but I was not the greatest hunter that ever lived. I could do the basics like tracking and covering my scent, but when it came to determining the number and size of the specific prey by its tracks, I was pretty lost. And that's in addition to being slower than everyone else. I didn't even correctly guess half of the answers in the Tracking challenge.

I breathed a sigh of relief as he passed me and picked two of the children further down the line. The audience chanted and stomped in approval at his choices. One of the new hunters was so unhappy at being picked. I think he said he wanted to be a cook at some point. He was crying silently, but he joined his new family regardless. I was only glad it wasn't me.

There were whispers down the line to my left as the Baron of Cooking took his place and began evaluating each of us. I don't know how someone who eats slop all day can get that big. Maybe he eats different food than the rest of us. I think he already had his mind made up on who he was going to select because he waddled directly to him and grabbed him by the shoulder. The rest of us could have not been there and the outcome would have been the same.

The Baron of the Guard was next. Besides hunting, this was the other one I definitely didn't want. The Guards were a very odd bunch. They never interact with anyone outside of the Guard and almost never go outside the Hive. Sometimes the Barons would go down to the Market and one of the Guards would accompany him, but it was always the same Guard.

Their skin was so light, they blended in with the walls of the Hive. There were even rumors that their man parts, at least some of them, were removed shortly after Commencement. But they did have the best training. They could easily take three or four warriors by themselves. Still, I didn't care to have my man parts removed or listen to Barons with the breeders all day. Ugh, what a boring life. No, I wanted a life where I felt wanted and respected. One where I could learn to fight properly and be a part of a group that had the camaraderie that I had seen them display before.

I held my breath when he paused in front of me. My heart beat faster as he stared down at me. Then, suddenly, he continued on. I felt light-headed. After a few moments, he selected two of the strongest boys. One was the bully and his friend from the Stone Throwing challenge.

I held back a smirk as they passed back in front of me. They both looked so proud to have been chosen to be a Guard. Walking as tall as ever, my hopes that he would get chosen for something menial were dashed. But I guess I should have expected that. The Baron of the Guards was all over them both during the challenge. My smirk turned to a frown as I realized no matter what profession I was chosen for, he'd still be higher class than me. My disgust turned to anger.

The Baron of Warriors stood from his throne. My anxiety went to maximum level. He was a truly massive man. His thunderous strut was one of pure strength. I think he could take on the entire Guard at the same time. This man was simply legendary. Well before I was born, one of the northern Hives tried to invade us, which was all too common. Their spear throwers were so deadly accurate, they could hit a moving target from outside of five hundred meters. The Baron was the only Warrior that survived. He was just barely commenced at the time, maybe a couple of months into his training. One of the spears thrown at him during this battle managed to brush his face, leaving a deep gash. As if this behemoth needed any more distinguishing features, he also had this awesome battle scar.

His saunter down the dwindling line was much slower and methodical than the other Barons. Even though he was still up the line from me, I could feel eyes looking at me. Finally, his heavy footsteps stopped in front of me. He towered over me as his heavy breath served as the only sound in the chamber.

I could almost feel the internal debate he was having with himself. I really wanted him to select me. The only Barons left after him were Farming and Taming, and let's face it, I was not likely to be selected by either. He slowly placed his left hand on my shoulder and made some kind of loud throat noise. It startled me and I jumped in place, held securely to the ground by his hand. I wasn't expecting that part. Then the echo of the other warriors in the chamber sounded with the same grunt.

I had been chosen! And to be a Warrior! The chanting and stomping echoed again as I walked over to join the rest of the warriors. Each of them grunted again as they took me in arms, happy to have another brother. I went from excited and uneasy to feeling home by the time I had embraced three or four of them. After greeting each of them present, I turned to look at Mother. We smiled at each other. I was happy and she was proud.

The last few boys were picked either by the Baron of Farming or Taming. I wasn't really paying attention. I was busy imagining what was in store for me next. What snapped me back was the ending horn. There were two boys still in line. They weren't chosen by any of the Barons. I was confused. Maybe someone sounded the horn too soon.

The Overlord stood and his horn sounded again. Everyone bowed as he descended past the Barons to stand in front of the boys. I glanced up to see what was happening. The Warrior to my right grabbed my head and pushed it back down.

The Overlord's horn sounded again and we stood back up. He reached out and put his hand on one of their shoulders. A tear rolled down the boy's cheek. The Overlord had selected him for chamber duty. Basically, he waited on the Overlord and handled errands. Definitely not the greatest profession in the Hive, but at least he wasn't exiled.

The Overlord spoke in his feeble, broken voice and told the boy to join him. He stood and moved behind the Overlord, wiping his eyes. The Overlord then turned his attention to the last boy. He explained that he hadn't been selected for citizenship with the Hive and that he was to immediately gather any personal belongings and leave the compound.

The boy burst into tears. The chamber was awkwardly silent, except for his crying. After a few moments, he addressed the

Overlord, asking what he did wrong and begged for reconsideration.

The Overlord stood silently reiterating his command. The boy just stood there. I don't know if he purposefully denied the command or whether he was simply waiting to see if the Overlord would reconsider.

The Overlord raised his hand. A Guard stepped out and walked in front of the boy. The Guard's tone was much graver as he reiterated the Overlord's command to leave. The boy argued with the Guard, tears falling like rain. The boy had nowhere to go and knew no one outside of the Hive. The Guard gave him a final ultimatum, but the boy was not swayed and continued to plead his case.

The Guard looked at the Overlord who simply nodded. In a flash, the Guard quickly twisted the boy's head. I felt lightning sweep through my body as his awkward face met mine. All at once, his weeping was replaced with a series of loud cracks that echoed through the chamber, followed shortly by the sound of his body hitting the ground. A brief silence ensued until one of the breeders in the back cried out, sobbing loudly.

My heart stopped for a moment as I tried to realize what just happened. The Guard just killed that little boy! I looked at Mother to see her reaction. Aside from a single tear on her cheek, she showed no emotion.

I couldn't understand how this is what "or else" meant. Why wouldn't Mother tell us this would happen?! If we had to choose between exile or death, we'd definitely choose exile! I was so angry with the whole Hive. I was angry at the Guard for being merciless. I was angry at Mother for keeping this secret. I was angry at the Hive as a whole for accepting it. I was angry at the Barons for not choosing him. I was angry at the Overlord for ordering it. I had no idea what I had gotten myself into.

The Warrior to my right grabbed my arm and whispered for me to calm down and control my emotions. I tried to catch my breath as the tension in my muscles slowly rescinded. The Guard picked up the boy's body and carried him outside. The Overlord's horn sounded again as he returned to his throne. We all bowed. My angry breath pushed the dirt in front of my face aside as I was still trying to make sense of why we would allow this to happen.

I knew the boy, sort of. He was kind. Shy, but kind. The bully picked on him too. He was like me in that sense. Only he apparently didn't have any skills that the Barons wanted.

The ending horn sounded followed shortly by the starting horn. A line of girls walked in and stood where we once were. Again, the Overlord's horn sounded, we bowed, and he approached the girls. One by one, he stood in front of them, looked them over and either put his hand on their shoulder or moved to the next.

Those he touched joined the breeders in the back. Those he didn't remained in place. After the last girl was looked at, he returned to his throne as the horn sounded and bowing ensued. The remaining girls joined the cleaners off to the opposite side from me.

Luckily, none were rejected by the cleaners. I didn't want to see a repeat from earlier. The Overlord's horn sounded as he rose from his thrown. We bowed again as he retired from the chamber. Shortly thereafter, the ending horn sounded and loud chanting and stomping filled the hall as we started conversing with one another.

My brothers turned and congratulated me in succession. I mumbled replies, the boy's face still fresh in my mind, twisted and painful. And they didn't even flinch. I guess they had seen this before. I debated on whether I should let it go too. It seemed normal. But I couldn't. It seemed so heartless.

The Baron approached in the midst of congratulations. His heavy footsteps booming throughout the chamber. He offered me congratulations as he stood, towering next to me, his scar flexing as he grinned. He stated he was happy to have me and then grunted again loudly, echoed by the remainder of the warriors that surrounded us. For the first time, I felt truly accepted.

We ate so much! There was some sort of drink there too. It was different from water. Flavored with berries and nuts and something else. I couldn't figure it out. At least that was how it tasted. It smelled absolutely horrible though. Like rotting meat.

Every time the Baron or the warriors spoke, everyone would grunt and drink. It was very awkward. And the more I drank, the weirder I felt. At first, I became happier. But then I became dizzy and even fell down once. The Baron laughed heartily at this, to which I instantly became reclused and then, for some reason, I laughed along with him. I was really confused at this point, but I was happy. I had been accepted and we all celebrated together.

Sunset came and passed as we continued to eat and drink. I don't know if my body liked the drink too much because it came back up later. We discussed all sorts of things from recent training exercises, how one of the warriors beat another in a duel, to more serious topics such as one of the northern Hives who had killed the breeder sent to them as a gift and sent her body back in pieces. We were all over the place.

I woke up in a part of the Hive I hadn't been in before. It felt as if I had fallen out of a big tree and hit my head. The sun was already high in the sky and the room I was in was empty except for me. I rubbed at my head to try and ease the pain. Everything was so bright. I shielded my eyes from the abuse as I sat up, wherever I was.

That's when I felt my belly get angry again. Last night's drink came spewing from my mouth and all over the ground beside the nook. Ugh, it smelled the same, horrible smell from the drink last night. This happened several more times. I had fallen down on my hands in reaction by the last one. One of the warriors rushed inside and helped me up to my feet.

He laughed heartily at, what I'm sure was, a fantastic sight with me on the ground heaving drink everywhere. He grabbed me by the arm and swiftly pulled me to my feet, which only made it worse, and asked me if I was ok. I just looked at him with a dumbfounded expression. He threw his head back and laughed heartily again. At least I knew the culprit was the drink now. I didn't much care for it the night before, but I despised it that morning.

He let go of me, making sure I was steady. As he turned to walk back to the doorway, he said we had training and that I was already late. The Baron sent him to check on me.

I kicked dirt on the spew and stumbled toward the doorway. As I walked toward the doorway, the sunlight kept getting brighter and brighter. I shielded my eyes as I walked outside to see the rest of the warriors in the southern field with the Baron. I slowly made my way down the hill, careful not to anger my belly anymore.

The Baron extended a welcome as I approached. He was louder than I remember. And then the grunting. Everything was so loud! I grabbed my head to ease the pain and continued blinking and squinting.

Everyone started laughing for some reason and the Baron handed me a flower. I was thoroughly confused at this point. I just stared at him.

He chuckled and told me to put it under my tongue. The little orange flower was so bitter. My face bunched together as another round of laughter ensued. Then, everything returned to normal as if nothing happened.

Still reeling from the confusion of the sickness and sudden relief, the Baron took me by the shoulder and pulled me in front of the rest of the warriors. His tone changed from lighthearted to serious. He said they couldn't call me little one anymore and needed to devise a name for me. Some of the warriors took turns yelling random names at the Baron.

After a few moments, the Warrior that helped me this morning stepped forward as the yelling died down for him to speak. He offered the name Tac. The Baron agreed with a grunt to which the whole group echoed.

My name is Tac. I had almost forgotten that I would get my name. I liked it. It was short and strong. Introductions followed.

The Baron was called Klik, but only by the warriors and the Barons. The rest of the Hive referred to him by title only.

The Warrior that helped me was known as Frejic. He took my arm strongly with a wide grin and welcomed me officially. I couldn't help but to grin back at him. This continued until I had been introduced to everyone with my new name. It was both awkward and invigorating to have a name. I kept saying it over and over again to myself.

Our training for the day was to practice making and throwing spears. I had never done either of these, but I managed to make my own crooked spear and hit one of the trees with it. Well, by hit I mean it glanced off at an odd angle and made an odd hollow sound. Might have been enough to make an enemy angry at me, but that's about it.

Frejic took me to the side and showed me how to use the knife correctly against the wood. He made a completely straight and smooth spear in almost no time at all. I was quite amazed.

Mirroring him as he began working on a second spear, I held the blade at the correct angle and worked by pushing it away from me as I held the soon-to-be spear at eye level. This helped me make sure the blade didn't dig too deep into the wood. After fashioning the tip of the spear, I glanced up at him.

He was amazed at how quickly I had picked up the skill. I think he may have given me more credit than I was worthy of.

The spear was still very crooked and the tip wasn't very sharp. It was better than the last one, but not near as good as the one he made.

We stood up and rejoined the group, Frejic showing off my spear, mentioning that I got it on the second try. There was plenty of grunting to go around. Klik instructed me to throw it at the tree as he pointed to a very thick tree about 30 meters from me.

I took a deep breath, pick the spear up to eye level and hurled it as hard as I could. It bounced off the tree again, end over end. I was instantly nervous again. I didn't want Klik to think he'd made a mistake by choosing me. Frejic stepped in and took the brunt of the anxious energy. He made it known that it took him almost a full month to hit a tree when he was younger. That definitely made me feel better.

But I wasn't done yet. I wanted to try again. I retrieved the spear and faced the tree again. Frejic stood behind me and coached my form. I took another deep breath and launched it again at the tree, making sure to keep a loose grip on it. It stuck!

I spun around to see Frejic's stunned face. He simply grunted loudly as did the entire group. I grunted back at them, which only made them grunt even louder. The rest of the warriors gathered around me taking turns grabbing me by the shoulder or rubbing my head.

Klik was incredibly proud, it seemed. He grabbed my head under his massive arm and grunted so loud my ears started ringing. Grunting loudly in response, we all turned to walk back to the Hive. The sun was getting low and it was time to start heading back for evening meal.

When we reached the Hive, Klik instructed me to retrieve my belongings from the children's chamber and bring it to the Warrior's chamber. I grunted in confirmation and ran off to do as I was told. I entered the children's chamber to find a new group of children had joined them. My belongings had already been gathered and Mother held them up for me to take.

She teared up as I approached, expressing her joy for my success. I thanked her and told her my new name and how I made a spear and stuck it in the tree on the first day. She smiled and said I'd make a great Warrior. I smiled back as I turned and walked out and headed towards the Warrior's chamber. As I got closer, there was a mouth-watering scent coming from the chamber. As I entered, the sounds of grunting permeated the entire room, welcoming me home.

Frejic shuttled me to the left side of the chamber and pointed out my new nook. I set my belongings down for the moment and joined the rest around the fire.

Fresh vegetables roasted on thin sticks along with chunks of juicy, charred meat. There were stories that night along with more drink and plenty of laughter to go around. As we sat around the fire, watching it die down, I felt home. Accepted. Like I finally belonged somewhere. It was the best day of my life.

CHAPTER III: COMPLICATIONS

Winter was usually rather harsh, but this year, the wind and snow battered us almost constantly. Each time a storm would pass, the snow would recede just enough in the following days so we wouldn't be completely buried when the next storm came through. Snow fell on the Hive like waves crashing on the shoreline during a hurricane. It was an extremely dangerous time, not only because of the winter storms, but also due to how scarce food was.

The Market was all but shut down. Even Tes managed to stay home during the dreariest of the season. The hike she usually made each day was daunting for someone her age. But during the winter, there was no way she could make it to the Market each day. Plus, she barely had enough food to get her and Shadow through to spring, much less enough to spare at the Market. And if a storm came through while she was away from home, she risked enduring it without shelter, which would surely end her life. But she made do as best she could.

The wind howled at all times but seemed to be even louder during the night. The wind and snow were relentless. If only food and morale were around in such quantities, maybe it wouldn't have been such an issue. Klik had heard some of the other Barons calling it The Great Winter.

Brok, one of the youngest warriors, almost incessantly berated us with how hungry or cold he was. As if he were the only one starving and freezing. A few of us would argue back and forth whenever someone mentioned either. One particular time, Klik chimed in, telling us about the last time he heard the phrase "The Great Winter". He said it was just after the war with the northern Hive that he was known for, the darkest of times for the Hive. Silence befell the room after his sentence, even the normally fierce wind and small fire died down a little to listen to his story.

He told us that when the snow got high enough, the wolves could tunnel through the snow and were less likely to be caught when attacking livestock. He described how the snow would fall in on itself behind the wolf and to be mindful of that when we were on patrol. We all grunted in acknowledgement.

Brok whined again, inquiring if there was any food in the chamber. I asked him how he could be so hungry if he had just eaten. Some of the others started giggling and Brok turned and flashed a disgusted look at me. This served only as encouragement and I continued to insult him, wondering how he was still my size with how much he ate. He'd had enough by this point, grunted loudly, and charged at me.

Before he even crossed the room, Klik swept his feet out from under him and he landed on his stomach with a thud. The room burst into laughter.

Klik commanded silence as the ever-present howling of the wind took control of our ears again. He towered over us all, telling Brok not to let his emotion get the best of him. Then he turned to me and reminded me that I knew what it felt like to be picked on by a bully.

My smile faded immediately as memories of my childhood flooded my mind. The five years since my Commencement had passed quickly between all of the training and fighting with the various Hives. In all of the excitement, I had all but forgotten about the bully. But the scars reappeared, fresh as yesterday, whenever I would have flashbacks of my childhood.

I looked down at Brok struggling to get back to his feet and I grabbed him by the arm to help him up. I apologized to him. He flashed me a grin and said I should be glad Klik stopped him. Klik smacked him in the back of the head for his pride.

We all snickered for a moment before drifting back to the cold, harsh reality. My thoughts settled back on my childhood and the bully. He had been chosen for the Guard. I hadn't seen him since Commencement. I wondered if they cut his man parts off yet. Most Guards become reclusive soon thereafter. Not that I cared either way, but I secretly hoped that it hurt him like he hurt me. I was glad to be rid of him.

Nik broke our concentration, stumbling through the doorway towards the fire. Klik turned to face him, eager to hear his report. Nik panted heavily at the cold, thin air with both hands on his knees. There was nothing to report but more snow. Klik thanked him and told him to rest. Then Klik turned to me and told me I had the next shift. We couldn't stay out long due to the cold and wind, but we still had a duty to check the perimeter to make sure there were no enemies within the Hive, human or not.

I grunted as I turned to go through the doorway. My man parts clung to me as the cold seeped into my body. I guess the bully didn't have to deal with this part. Following the carved path through the shoulder-deep snow kept most of the wind out. My shoes were soaked very quickly. I wasn't sure which was worse, the snow or the wind. I wrapped another sweater around my face and tried to keep the snow out of my eyes, looking for any tracks or signs of an intruder.

I used the blunt end of my spear to help me down the hill to the southern fields. There wasn't much out there, but it was a good vantage point, should anything decide to attack the Hive from the south. I stood halfway down the hill for a good while, partly because the wind was from the north and the hill provided some shelter. Also, because I was checking to make sure the snow in the fields wasn't disturbed, like Klik said. Tracking in snow was extremely easy, so long as you found the tracks before the snow could cover them up. It was the best part about patrols in the winter.

All was quiet except for the ever-present wind and then my teeth started chattering. It was so cold and the wind was so strong, I might as well have been wearing no clothes. My hands were almost completely frozen, so I put them over my mouth and blew "hot" air to try and thaw them out. It did almost nothing, so I shoved them under my armpits and embraced myself. I had just about had enough of this. There's nothing out here. I turned to go back up the hill to the patrol route, using my spear again to keep my footing.

Resuming the patrol, I moved along the ridge around to the eastern slope. I couldn't even really see anything as I was now walking almost directly into the snow and wind. I don't know how anything could survive in this without shelter of some kind.

Something caught my attention out of the corner of my eye. A flash of movement in the snow down the eastern slope. I squinted and shielded my eyes from the wind to get a better view. Snow, falling in on itself parallel to the base of the hill. It's just like Klik said. I waited a moment to see how many of them there were. I only saw one trail, so it should only be one wolf.

As I made my way down the slope, a familiar voice came from the bottom. It was Shadow. I scolded her slightly, stressing the fact that I could have killed her if she hadn't spoken. She giggled in amusement, licked my face, and told me that would have been hard to do with such a small stick.

Shadow hadn't come to check on me. Tes had fallen gravely ill and required my assistance. Shadow had done all she could for her, but she's just not getting any better and now she feared for her life. I was in absolute shock. Tes, even as weak as she was when I met her, was always a strong woman. It was hard to imagine what she had become.

Shadow snapped me back to reality and stated that we needed to start moving now. I told her I'd need to grab my supplies from the chamber and make sure Klik was ok with it.

I sprinted back up the hill and along the remainder of the patrol route, scanning the rest of the snow for tracks. I burst in the doorway, knocking over a few bowls and such that should really be placed somewhere more secure. Panting and trying to catch my breath, I stood with my hands on my hips and told Klik basically the same report Nik did. Nothing but snow.

I told him that a very dear friend of mine, who had helped me through the worst time in my life had fallen gravely ill in the small village to the east and that I needed to attend to her, if at all possible. Klik walked over to me, placed his massive hand on my shoulder, and looked me straight in the eyes. I knew he could feel my apprehension in the situation I'd just been made aware of. He had to have seen it written on my entire face.

He asked if I were sure I could make it in the storm. I told him that the majority of the trip was through heavy tree cover and that should help. But even with the weather begin what it was, I had to try. She risked everything to help me when no one else would even lift a finger. And now I must return the favor.

As his hand rescinded, I knew he understood the predicament. I packed up my supply stash in my bag. Klik told me to be extra mindful of wolves, since they're desperate in this season. I told him they'd have to get by my own wolf just as Shadow stepped in the doorway. I laughed at their shocked faces as they began reaching for weapons.

I told them to relax and that she wouldn't hurt them. As I finished packing, Shadow hurried me along. I told her that I understood and I was moving as fast as I could. Klik asked who I was talking to. I looked up and explained briefly that Shadow could hear Tes and I, as well as vice versa. It didn't seem to help, and with the issue at hand, I simply told him that it was a story for another time and I would be back as soon as I could. Klik grunted, followed by the whole group. I echoed their call and took one last look at them all, just in case.

Shadow darted out of the Hive and down the eastern slope before I could get my bag fastened and out of the doorway. I grabbed my spear and ran as fast as I could, following her trail down the eastern slope and into the forest. As expected, the heavy tree cover blocked some of the wind and snow, so that part of the trek was much easier. But it was still incredibly cold. The air felt like breathing snow, but running kept me warm.

It was a long time to Tes' hut in the abandoned village. When I got there, Shadow was already inside lying next to her. It was in the middle of the night, so I knew the first thing I needed to do was to get a fire going. There were only a few pieces of dry wood stacked beside the pit, but after a long and arduous process, I finally got it to start a small fire. I found a few dead standing trees just outside and knocked them over, breaking each one into smaller pieces to fit in the fire.

I stacked the wood next to the tiny fire to dry and put two of the smallest pieces on the struggling fire. The hut began to light up and I could see Tes' fragile body lying on her bed. I walked over and touched her freezing skin. She wouldn't have made it much longer in this cold. The wind whipped through the hut, threatening the infant fire's life.

I tried speaking to Tes to see if I could get her to wake up. Shadow said she could hear me, but she was too weak to respond. She said she had been laying behind her to try and keep her warm, but it wasn't good enough and that the fire went out two days ago when she collapsed, which was also the last time they ate.

I knew we needed to get her warm with some food and water in her belly first. But after that, I really wanted to take her back to the Hive to have the Shaman look after her. I knew it was risky, since Tes was not a citizen of the Hive. Our kind doesn't take kindly to exiles trespassing within the boundary. But I knew if we could just get her to the Shaman, he could dismiss any Guards or warriors who protested her presence.

I debated with myself and Shadow as to when or if to move her and take her to the Shaman. We weren't sure if she'd even make it until morning, but I knew if we went out in this storm, she'd freeze to death before we could get there. We would need to wait until sunrise before we could move her. The best I could do was get her warm, get her some food, and keep the wind out. Hopefully, she would pull through the night.

I stacked three more pieces in the fire as it hissed at me from the wet wood. Outside, I punched three larger trees and fell them down the slope. Dragging them up the hill and putting the bigger pieces in the windows and the biggest piece to the north side of the doorway to keep out some of the wind and snow.

When I stepped back inside, the fire had finally started to warm the hut. I removed the sweater from my face and tested to see if I could see my breath in the air. I couldn't, which was another good sign that the hut was warming up.

I pulled Shadow's bed closer to the growing fire. Then I carefully lifted Tes and set her down in the middle of Shadow's bed. Shadow curled up next to her. I brushed her snow-white hair from her face. She looked so peaceful. I picked up a large clay pot and got some of the fresh snow for soup. Setting it in the fire, I pulled some of the winter vegetables from my bag and began to break them up in the pot.

Shadow suggested I add some of the tree bark to the soup for Tes. I looked at her funny. Tree bark? In a soup? That was pretty odd. Shadow affirmed that Tes did it all the time to help with aches and pains of getting older. Skeptically, I walked over to some of the firewood and started stripping the bark. Shadow told me that was the wrong kind of bark and that I needed to find a thorncone tree outside of the hut.

Ugh, I had just started to warm up too. As I walked toward the doorway, she informed me to make sure not to take more than a handful from the tree, or I'd kill it.

I nodded as I wrapped my face up again and trudged back into the deep snowbank to retrieve some thorncone bark. I found one close to the huts and stripped a small amount from the south side, making sure the tree's meat wasn't exposed to the wind.

Following my path back was painful as it was directly into the wind and blinding snow.

The now roaring fire cut through the cold quickly as I shook the snow from my body. I brushed the snow from the bark and moved toward the pot.

Shadow giggled at my inexperience with such things. She lifted her nose to point across the room at the mortar and pestle needed to grind the bark into powder before adding to the soup. I grabbed it and began to drop the pieces of bark into the heavy bowl. As I started to grind up the bark, Tes began to wake up.

She called to me. I set the bowl down and moved over to the bed. Her voice was weak and I could tell in her eyes that we might have just shown up at the right time. I told her about the soup that would be ready soon, to provide her some hope of alleviation, but she had already passed back out.

I looked up at Shadow's concerned expression and sighed heavily. Trying to focus, I continued to grind the bark as quietly as I could. She desperately needed good rest. Dumping the bark powder into the soup, I stirred it slowly with the big wooden spoon she always used.

Shadow's ears perked up which caused the hair on the back of my neck to stand on end. She peered into the darkness outside and we remained very still and quiet. Her snout pitching up in the air, attempting to get enough scent to identify it.

Shadow quietly said we had trouble as she slowly stood, avoiding disturbing Tes. My senses for this kind of thing were never that sharp, but with the storm it was almost impossible. I couldn't hear, see, or smell anything out of the ordinary. Shadow said there were wolves nearby. They had passed by earlier, but hadn't come close enough to the hut. It was likely the smell of fire that drew them in this time. This is something we'd have to deal with first, if Tes was to make it through the night.

I wrapped my face up, grabbed my spear, and followed Shadow outside. Luckily, they were upwind from us, so we had the element of surprise. We pushed north into the elements, careful not to move too quickly. The snow hides many things that can be harmful. I was glad the snow wasn't very deep here. But the wolves approaching probably weren't. I kept my eyes forward, blinking the snow and wind away, looking for snow falling in on itself again.

And then I saw one. I called him out to Shadow and she, in turn, called out two more on the right. Three wolves. Shit. I was good with a spear by this point, but wolves are not humans. They are much faster and very agile. I really wished some of my brothers were here for this. But I knew we were on our own.

The three wolves slowly emerged from the snowbank between two of the huts. Teeth showing and making their familiar guttural sounds, their bodies were lean and lowered to the ground in preparation to attack. I stood as tall as I could and Shadow growled fiercely in return. She was much larger than they were, even in the winter.

The one on the far left howled into the night and then charged at Shadow. I knocked him against the hut before he could get to her. The wolf lay limp at the base of the hut, partially covered in snow.

The other two, seeing this, slowly closed in and began to circle us in opposite directions. I called out to Shadow that I had the one on the right again. I held my spear pointed in the direction of the wolf. With a mighty heave, I launched the spear and struck the wolf mid stride directly in the heart. His body tumbled backward into the snowbank against one of the huts.

I turned to find Shadow draining the life from the third wolf, perched over his body with his neck in her teeth. It was over. A wave of relief came over me and I trotted over to Shadow to find her panting. I gave her a big hug.

Shadow told me the first wolf had called for the alpha before he charged. And since he hadn't called back, the alpha knew something was wrong and would likely investigate, with backup. I wanted to know how many we were expecting, but Shadow said it depended on the size of the pack and how far away each group of the pack was from the call.

My heart started to race as the fear of what was to come settled in. I asked her if there was any way we could avoid the confrontation. She said it was unlikely, even if we left, they would simply follow our scent. They would catch up to us well before we could get to the Hive.

Shadow's ears perked up again and she sniffed at the air. Just then, a larger wolf peeked out of the snowbank, followed by four other wolves to his flank. I quickly retrieved my spear from the lifeless body to the side, making sure the alpha saw it, maybe encouraging him to back down. Instead, it seemed to infuriate him and he let out a long, sorrowful howl at the sky followed by the other four in unison. I could almost feel their pain in that moment, but this was survival. And they threatened those close to me.

The alpha didn't waste any time and charged straight at Shadow. He leapt for her throat as she dodged and tossed him aside behind us. This was good, now the pack is separated from the alpha.

Shadow took after the alpha and the four wolves started towards me. I launched my spear at one, hitting him between the eyes and I threw another one against a hut. Just as I did, one of them leapt for my throat. I connected with the bottom of his jaw and sent him straight up in the air about ten meters. The final wolf sunk his teeth into my leg and tried to pull me to the ground. I grunted loudly as I pulled his jaw apart and teeth out of my flesh. I snapped his jaw and threw him into the tree line.

I grabbed my left thigh to keep the blood from running free and turned to see the alpha on top of Shadow with his teeth deep in her throat. I immediately grabbed him by the back of the neck and threw him into one of the huts opposite of Tes'.

I moved in between the alpha and Shadow, cutting off any finishing blows he had in mind. He grimaced to standing, shook his head, flashed his teeth, and growled loudly. I didn't take the threat lightly and picked up a large stone from one of the huts, launching it at his face. It connected and he bowled over into the hut again and down the other side of the hill.

I waited a moment to see if he would get up, only to hear the wind still howling. I turned and hobbled over to Shadow, who still laid on the ground. The snow around her soaked with her blood. A look of fear filled her eyes and I could tell she knew the wound was too deep. Regardless, I removed my extra sweater from my face and placed it over her exposed throat in an attempt to stop the bleeding.

She told me that I have to take care of Tes. She made me promise that I would look after her. I ignored her and continued trying to stop the bleeding. She lifted her massive paw and put it on my arms. My eyes met with hers and she simply said, "Promise me." I did, which only caused tears to readily appear, blurring her last moments. I felt her paw go limp and the blood slowed to a trickle. Shadow was gone.

My face was hot and I could feel the streaks of tears still freezing on my exposed face. But I didn't care. I put my hand on Shadows head and closed my eyes, letting myself feel all of the hurt and rage from her death. I let my throat call out into the night and I collapsed away from her body.

An unknown voice pierced the night. He said that I now knew how he felt. I turned sharply to see a pair of eyes disappearing into the snow. My rage boiled over and I darted towards the eyes, pushing snow and tree aside. I stopped briefly to listen and look for evidence of his retreat, but I could hear nothing other than the wind. Nothing moved. Had I imagined the voice?

And then I remembered I needed to get back to Tes. Walking backwards to make sure the alpha couldn't sneak up on me, I made my way back up the hill and across the plateau. I couldn't even look at Shadow's body. The pain and rage still burning deep inside.

I peered into the dimly lit hut and knocked the snow off of me. All the commotion must have woken Tes up. She sat at the edge of Shadow's bed, a single tear upon her wrinkled cheek. No words were said for a while. I built the fire back up and drew us both bowls of soup.

I forgot about my leg and was thankful enough that the cold caused the bleeding to stop. I walked outside to retrieve my extra sweater. Staring at Shadow's lifeless eyes, I reached down and closed them gently, thankful for having met such a wonderful creature.

I built a raised bed of wood and carefully placed Shadow's body on top. This would at least keep other wolves away from it until the wind died down enough to light it and send her spirit on. I went back inside to find Tes curled up on Shadow's bed, weeping.

She and Shadow had been together for a long time. They had helped each other survive many cold winters and predators. I could only imagine the pain of losing her closest and oldest friend. I felt sorry for her and angry at myself. I should have been faster. Shadow deserved better than that and in the moment when she needed someone to watch her back, I failed.

I wrapped my leg up with my extra sweater and curled up next to Tes, pulling the heavy blanket over us both. I said nothing as I held her close to me, her pain bleeding into me even more. I stayed awake until the weeping stopped and rhythmic breathing ensued. I kept replaying the situation over and over in my head, trying to find ways that I could have saved Shadow's life.

In the morning, the wind had died down and the sun shone brightly as we must have slept a long time. Tes was already awake and out of bed when I arose. Her feeble frame cast a shadow from the doorway and I could see she was still very sick.

I stoked the fire back up and took one of the burning logs outside to the wood pile. It lay undisturbed from last night except for the snow that had built up. I put the burning log under the base and began to build a bigger fire, placing smaller sticks and logs around it.

I turned to find Tes staring at the mound in silence. For the first time since Shadow's fall, our eyes locked gaze. I had never felt so ashamed in my life. I could feel her pain sharply and looked at the ground. She slowly walked up to me as I started weeping quietly, the crackling sounds of the newborn fire masking my own sniffling.

She told me not to blame myself. Yes, it was painful for her, but her one comfort was that I was there in her final moments. She didn't die alone. She said it was a debt she could never repay me for. I tried to explain the situation and how I did everything I could. She caught me mid-sentence and stated that it was simply Shadow's time and that I needed to understand that and let her and the situation go. And then she offered words of wisdom that I will likely never forget. She said that fate had chosen this path already, all we had to do was walk it.

That gave me more comfort than I expected. In fact, it sapped all energy I had put into mourning Shadow and regretting the previous night's events. Refocused, and slightly annoyed that I hadn't finished grieving, I mentioned we still needed to get her to the Shaman and that she was still very sick. She pointed to the wound on my left thigh as she said he'll need to look at me too. Infection is a very serious threat outside of the Hive.

The fire under Shadow's pyre had caught, evidenced by the intense heat that hit my back. Thick smoke rose, partially concealing Shadow's body at the top. I couldn't help but wish there had been a different outcome to this.

I told Tes about the voice I heard after Shadow passed and how I had maybe chased the alpha into the woods. Tes pondered my words shortly and then turned to walk back into her hut. I'm not sure if she dismissed my statement, but then again, I wasn't even sure it actually happened.

I walked back towards the hut, turning to take in one last glimpse of the majestic beast that I was lucky enough to call a friend. But the fire had already caught at the top and obscured my view. I closed my eyes, said my final goodbyes, and wished her a safe journey in the next life.

Tes was stacking her bowls and pots next to her bag when I got back inside. I coyly inquired as to what she was doing. Apparently, if the alpha were still alive, he'd come back with more of the pack next time. In our failure to kill the alpha had now served as Tes' eviction notice. As if there wasn't enough to deal with right now. I was about at wit's end.

She had lived there for over twenty years, ever since she met Shadow. But now that Shadow was gone, she said she didn't need all of the space. Plus with her age, she reasoned she needed to be closer to the Hive in the future. All of it made sense, but I couldn't help but feel guilty and responsible for all of this.

Tes began putting all her belongings into her bag. I stepped outside to pull her sled around. She met me shortly, dragging her oversized bag through the doorway. I told her I'd get it. It was far too heavy for her to carry and she needed to save her strength. She smiled at me and brushed the ice away from my eyes. I smiled in return and hoisted the heavy bag on my back. She climbed on the back of the sled and laid down.

Trudging through the deep snow gave us both plenty of time to contemplate both the events of last night as well as plan the future. Tes needed somewhere to live. I needed her closer to me in case she needed something. The small village was almost a half-day journey in the snow if you didn't run and took rest when needed. That's too far for someone so frail.

Maybe some of the other traders lived closer and she could stay with them. That would probably be the best chance she had at surviving. That and seeing the Shaman, of course.

The sun was already low in the sky and cast a silhouette of the Hive on the ground in front of us by the time we reached it. I was exhausted and Tes had been asleep for a while. I stopped to check on her a few times, only to wake her from a slumber.

I set her bag down momentarily to help her up off the stiff sled. Her slow movement indicated that whatever ailed her was getting worse. I'm sure the cold didn't help. I needed to get her inside.

I grabbed the bag and followed her slow movements up the hill, leaving the sled at the bottom. Holding my hand out in preparation to catch her, we slowly inched our way up the slope. Once we finally reached the top, the sun was almost gone and the torches that were above the snowdrift were lit.

We made our way to the entrance of the main chamber where the Shaman was. In the dim light, I could tell there was a Guard standing there.

He ordered us to stop where we were. I yelled out that I was a Warrior and that Tes was very sick and needed to see the Shaman. He retorted that exiles were not permitted within the Hive boundary. To which I said the Shaman cares for all, not just those you deem worthy. We started again toward the Shaman's chamber.

The Guard waved his hand and struck us both, knocking us to the ground about fifteen meters away. I opened my eyes repeatedly, trying to shake the heavy blow. I looked over to see Tes bent in an awkward position in the snow. I crawled over to her quickly. Rolling her over, her body was broken and lifeless. I watched to see if her breath showed, but none did. I felt the last bit of hope drain from me, replaced with an even deeper rage.

It filled me to the brim, warming my blood and skin. I stood over Tes' body, taking in the awkwardly peaceful look on her face.

Turning to face the Guard, I yelled that he had killed her. Even the flames in the torches seem to feed on my rage. He stood defensive of his position and called me a freak. It was him. The bully. The word sparked even more rage as all of my visualizations of fighting the bully came rushing forward as I knew this time they would manifest.

I grabbed a nearby torch and threw it at his face like a spear. He calmly knocked it away, extinguishing the flame in the snowbank to his left. I threw a large rock at him and he deflected it as well. I charged at him, grunting loudly in the cold, dimly lit entrance.

We exchanged many blows, knocking each other into different snowbanks. With blood flowing from much of our faces, I punched him square in the face, knocking him into another snowbank.

This time he didn't move. Upon closer inspection, he had landed on a boulder off to the side of the entrance, which was buried in the snowbank. His eyes were open, but had no movement. No breath came from him.

I walked back over to check on Tes. Her face was now blue and snow dusted her deep wrinkles. I knew she was gone. In less than a day, I had lost both of my oldest friends. The pain and grief I felt at that moment brought me to my knees. As I wept over Tes, I could hear voices inside the building and approaching me.

Guards surrounded me quickly thereafter. I stared at Tes' face as two Guards picked me up to my feet. They bound me in chains and held spears at my neck. My brothers stood helpless to the side. I yelled to them to make sure her spirit got to the next life.

A loud grunt resonated throughout the entrance as I was dragged into the back of the main chamber. I knew she would be taken care of and that's all I could hope for at the moment. Quite honestly, I didn't care about what came next.

I was chained into a small room that I had not seen before. A large boulder was placed over the entrance, blocking both my escape and most of the light. There was a small hole in the back, though just enough to let the room breathe. I pulled at the chains for a while to see if I could break them, but to no avail. A lot of emotions flooded my head that night, mostly in a random order.

I awoke early to the sound of the stone being moved. I stood up and tugged at my chains again for good measure. Two Guards reached in and pulled me out. They dragged me back to the front of the main chamber to where all the Barons and the Overlord himself were assembled.

After a short silence, the Overlord spoke boldly in his agitation. He announced that I was accused of killing a Guard, which was a direct violation of the oath I took when I became a citizen and a Warrior. He asked for an explanation. I told him briefly who the Guard was, how he had treated me growing up, and how I was attempting to get Tes help for her illness. I recounted the interaction with the bully and how the fight started and ended.

I glanced over to Klik, who seemed disappointed in my story and looked sternly at me. The Overlord spoke again, informing the chamber that killing a member of the Guard is punishable by death, but that, due to extenuating circumstances surrounding the nature of the event, he was going to exile me instead. I didn't care which he chose to do. Even my loyalty to my brothers was diminished.

He granted me a few minutes to gather my things and to speak with the warriors if they so chose to speak with me. But after that, I was to leave the Hive and never return. The horn sounded and I felt two spears at the back of my neck again. I watched the Overlord leave, but this time I didn't bow. Two more Guards picked me up and removed the chains.

I slowly walked outside to find my brothers gathered near the eastern slope. Frejic had Tes' bag set in front of him. He took me in arms when I approached and we hugged each other tightly.

I spoke mainly with Frejic. Klik didn't follow us. We said our goodbyes and stared into each other's face for memory sake since we would likely never see each other again. After a moment he smiled and grasped my shoulder. As the smile faded, I picked up Tes' bag and walked past the rest of my brothers. Brok took me in arms and cried. I held him shortly until I felt the nudge of a spear in my back.

I walked towards the eastern slope, turning to take one last look at my brothers. They all faced me and I smiled at them. Descending the eastern slope, the Guards stopped near the top. I grunted loudly in my brothers' direction, but I received no reply. I loaded Tes' bag on the sled and began pulling behind me as I made my way to the east. I was on my own now.

CHAPTER IV: EXILE

I decided to go back to Tes' hut, at least for the time being. I knew the alpha was still out there and would likely return. If he wanted a fight, bring it. I had nothing left to lose. I would hold nothing back this time. He had no way of knowing what had transpired and the pain I was in, but he would certainly take the brunt of all of my frustration and rage, warranted or not. And I was oddly ok with that.

The forest was eerily quiet on the journey back to the abandoned village. It gave me time to think about all the things that happened over the past few days. Shadow, Tes, the bully, and my exile. I found myself reliving the same sequence of events over and over, trying to change them. I was so deep in thought, I almost walked into a few trees. Well, that and it was pitch black out didn't help.

I finally stumbled back into the village sometime later. By then, the clouds had moved on and the stars helped illuminate the snow just barely enough to see outlines. Even without the wind, it was very cold and my feet went numb a while ago. I fumbled my way around Tes' hut and worked on getting a fire started.

As the small fire illuminated the walls, removing some of the chill from the air, I could see the pot was still half full of soup. I guessed the alpha hadn't been back yet. He would probably need a while to rebuild his pack to take me on. Maybe he wouldn't come back at all.

Either way, I knew I needed to figure out how to secure the hut better if I was going to be staying here. The heavy tree I put outside of the door to block the snow was working well, so I moved it over to block the doorway, just in case. Shadow usually warned us of any threats close to the hut, but now it's just me. I certainly didn't want to be surprised by a wolf or bear standing in the doorway.

I sat on Shadow's bed for a while in the dimly lit hut, listening to the sounds of the crackling fire. I had no more routines. No more patrols. It was kind of nice actually. But I also had no one else to share it with. No one to laugh at my jokes. No brothers to keep watch while I slept and vice versa. Things would definitely be different from here on and I wasn't sure if I liked the idea of being on my own or not.

The soup finally boiled. I picked up the bowl that Tes had given me when we first met. Tears welled up in my eyes as I thought of the day she took care of me in the Market so long ago. She was gone forever. Drawing the soup, I couldn't help but to talk to her. I didn't care if she wasn't there, I just needed to talk.

A lot of awkward and remorseful sentences came out as I ate the soup. With no one else to help eat, I drew another bowl and found myself regretfully full before I could finish it. I curled up on Shadow's soft bed and listened to the fire, still thinking about everything that had passed.

I was abruptly woken up by the wind howling again. It had gotten colder and the snow was falling again. I stoked up the fire and put more wood on. I needed to come up with ways to fortify the hut for when the alpha returns, or a bear. I'll need to defend myself. The night wasn't quite over yet. I spent the remainder of it contemplating ways to protect myself interlaced with random memories of Shadow and Tes.

I woke up again sometime later. The fire had died again and the soft haze of midday through the clouds and snow gently lit the room. I guess I took for granted how nice it is to sleep through the night with someone else keeping the fire going. I was going to miss that.

I hadn't changed clothes in three days. Shadow's blood still stained my extra sweater. I decided to wash my clothes and myself. It's not like I had anywhere to go, but it was something to do. Something to keep my mind from wandering too far.

I grabbed one of the smaller pots from across the room and filled it with snow from the window. After placing the pot in the fire to boil, I stepped outside. Most of Shadow's pyre was no longer visible. I just hoped Tes and Shadow were together in the next life and happy. They deserved at least that much. This life was cruel to both of them.

I spent the rest of the day washing my clothes, eating, and sleeping. I didn't feel like doing much else. Not that there was anything else to do. No friends, no brothers, no patrols, no duties. That day turned into a week and that week turned into a month. Before I knew it, the snow had melted.

The tree that I was using to block the doorway started falling apart shortly thereafter. Even with the amount of vegetables Tes had stored up, I knew I'd be out of food soon. I needed to learn how to hunt, and quickly.

Throwing boulders wasn't really an option. They're loud and inaccurate and I'd have a better chance of hitting a tree than actually hitting and killing any prey. So I crafted the only weapon I knew how to use. I cut down a sapling of some sort and shaped it into a spear with a sharp rock I found. I had no iron, so making a point of the spear was a little difficult. Thankfully, Klik had taught us about fire hardening.

In a pinch, you could burn wood until it just turned black, then file it down on a smooth rock to get a stronger and sharper point. This would keep the spear from chipping or splitting for the time being.

What he didn't say was how long that would take. It must have taken half a day for me to make and fire harden a single spear. And I knew I needed several of them in case one broke. But I was just happy to have made one. I really hoped I recreated the process correctly. It's quite dangerous out here to not have a reliable weapon.

After I was satisfied on the tip of the spear, I took it outside for some practice. To my pleasant surprise, it flew straight and stuck in the tree on the first throw. I stood there for a moment to make sure it actually worked. I was rather pleased with myself.

I took the next few days to make six spears just in case. Then of course I collected firewood and any of the spring berries that were starting to come in. Most were sour and tart, but I was so tired of soup that anything, even unripe fruit was a welcome deviation from the normal course.

But most of all, I missed meat. Succulent, juicy meat. My favorite was when Tes would use the bones to make soup. Those were the best kinds of soups. The kind you eat for several days because it just keeps getting better and better. And in order to make those kinds of soups, or at least try, I needed to hunt. Tes taught me as much as she could about cooking, but she was always better than me.

One chilly spring morning shortly thereafter, I set out to the south of the village. There was a small creek that ran between the Hive and the village, but I didn't want to go towards the Hive, just in case I ran into any of the warriors out on patrol or a Guard. They probably wouldn't hesitate to attack and I wasn't ready to face them.

I expected whitetail to be in the area since it was a stable water source. And boy was I right. I carried three spears with me and was able to kill one whitetail and injure another before the pack took off into the woods. I never did find the second one, but that's ok. I may have gotten overzealous. I still had to carry this heavy thing back up the hill to the village.

To my surprise, I easily lifted the kill into the air and carried it all the way back to the hut. That actually turned out to be the easiest part. Cleaning it was a much more difficult challenge. I didn't have the sharpest of rocks, so it took a long time to get a decent piece of meat. By that point, I was salivating all over the place. I impaled it with one of the cooking sticks and stuck it in the ground over the fire. Then I placed all of the remaining meat in the salt box to slow the decomposition process.

I made an absolute mess trying to clean the whitetail and harvest the meat. I also harvested some of the bones, hooves, and fur to make other things later. I took the carcass back down the hill and left it by the creek to decompose. Exposed carcasses tend to attract problems like vultures and wolves. Problems I didn't need or want right now.

I pulled the stick from the fire and stuck it in the ground near the bed to cool, even though all I really wanted to do was gnaw on it immediately. I had to find something to do to keep from being enticed to burn my mouth. So, I went outside to collect more firewood. I stopped for a moment to catch a glimpse of the sun setting behind the trees. Such beauty but at the same time, such carnage. The sun fought its daily death with the brilliance of pinks and oranges. And yet, every time, it's inevitable. My thoughts circled back to Tes and Shadow. I missed them both dearly. I hadn't spoken to a person in over a month. Or was it two? I was starting to lose count.

Frustrated, I carried the wood back inside and sat down. I sank my teeth into the chunk of meat. The juice burst from my mouth and I was immediately refocused. I closed my eyes and slowly chewed. Despite my near dire circumstances, this was definitely helping to take my mind off things. It felt nice to relax and let everything go.

I'd been so worried over what had happened and what would happen that I managed to forget that I'm still here. Tes and Shadow are gone. I can't change that. But I can still enjoy the fruits of my labor. I can still experience happiness. I promised myself to let go of the past and make the best of what was ahead. Like Tes used to say, this is the path that fate has chosen, all I have to do is walk it.

The meat lasted long enough to plant seeds in the spring. Although, the older the meat got, the drier and tougher it got. But it was still better than the soup I made with the winter vegetables. Soon I would have fresh vegetables. I planned to throw a feast for myself. I felt I should celebrate life and all it has to offer. Plus, it gave me something to look forward to.

Since it was now in between the winter and spring storms, I decided I should try to patch up the hut. Tes wasn't strong enough to do it when she lived here, but I am. I took some of the stones from the surrounding huts and replaced the broken or missing ones. I looked at some of the other huts and what I thought was a window in Tes', err, my hut was actually several missing stones. Replacing them closed the small gap at the top which let snow or water in during the storms.

I also replaced the tree I used to block the doorway. It wouldn't keep out the larger predators, but I would at least hear them getting in with enough time to wake and get a spear.

Now that I had fortified the hut and planted the seeds over the past week, I was starting to really dislike being in the hut all the time. I thought being outside tending to the garden would be enough, but I needed more. I needed to go on an adventure. Nothing crazy, just get out of the hut for the day.

And then I remembered that strange cave I fell in last autumn. It was curiously straight in some places. Like it was made from some weird, hollow stone. And the sound the floor made as I walked across it really puzzled me. The only caution I had was the growling I heard behind the wall. If there's something in there, I could get in there too. The question was how.

I started first thing in the morning, just as the sun was coming up over the tree line to the east. Squinting and blocking the overwhelming light with my hand, I made my way down the eastward slope. The last time I went this way, I was running from the warriors that caught me outside of the Hive. It was so trivial now that I think about it.

I carefully combed over the area as I got closer to where I remember the hole in the ground is that lead to the entrance of the cave. The ground was undisturbed leading up to where the entrance was. I had no idea how big this cave was. But I wanted to find out. It was exciting. Something different.

With the sun almost high in the sky, I started walking in circles around the entrance, going farther out with each cycle. I expected there was another entrance nearby, I just needed to find it. After searching for a long time, I gave up trying to find the second entrance and walked back to the big hole in the ground.

The weight of the snow must have broken off a lot more of the ground. The hole was bigger than I remembered and it was much brighter, allowing me to see more of the cave. The wall was covered in rocks that were painted with some sort of markings. Most of them had different colors and different markings than the ones next to them. There were even drawings of what looked like people. This must be a very old cave. I had never seen anything like this. All the lines were perfectly straight. It was very odd.

I slowly descended into the hole, trying to make as little sound as necessary. If the wolf was still inside, I didn't want him to know I was there before I had a chance to attack. I gently grabbed hold of the protruding rock and tried to move it. It creaked as I pulled harder. Finally, it came loose and all the force I used to pull on it slung it across the room, landing on the ground with a heavy thud.

Where the rock was revealed a hole in the wall. I pulled my spear off my back and pointed it in the direction of the hole. I threw a rock into the hole in case the wolf was still there. This time, the walls didn't scream, but something inside the hole screamed several times.

I slowly crept into the hole, letting my eyes adjust to the darkness. The weird moaning rocks on the floor descended around a small room. I could just start to see how far down when the walls of this smaller room lit up like the sun. I fell backwards towards the entrance, tripping over the steps. My eyes hurt. The light came from the rock above me as if it opened up and let the sun in. But even the sun wasn't this bright today. I wasn't ready for it. Once my eyes finally adjusted back to the light, I stood back up and looked around the room.

The rocks descended a long way down and I got really dizzy just by looking over the edge. I grabbed onto one of the rocks on the side. I wasn't sure if I wanted to explore this anymore. It wasn't anything that I had expected. I stopped to listen both outside and farther down in the cave to see if anything made sound. There was nothing, again. So, I slowly walked around the room and down into the cave, testing to make sure the rocks were steady before I stepped on them.

This took a long time. As I slowly descended, more walls lit up like the rock above. I could see the entire cave now and it was bigger than any cave I'd ever been in. The bottom floor was littered with bones, dirt, and dust. A wolf definitely lived here. I just had no idea where he was.

The rocks I stepped on continued to moan softly as I progressed towards the bottom. I kept my eyes on the floor, looking for any movement. I didn't want to become lunch, of course. Every now and then, I'd stop and listen to make sure nothing else was in here. It was quiet. Really quiet. No wind, no animals, no water, no nothing. It was very eerie and reminded me of the walk through the forest the night of my exile.

Once I was sure nothing was down here, I put my spear away and started looking around. There were more weirdly shaped rocks against the cave wall. Only, these glowed different colors. They weren't near as bright as the ones on the wall, but I could definitely see them. Most were steady like the sun, but some of them flickered like fire.

As I got closer to one of the rocks, the lights seemed to get brighter and one of them turned red. All of a sudden, the whole cave started growling loudly. I stepped backward swiftly and pointed my spear at it. As soon as I did, the growling stopped. This was so weird and I was thoroughly confused by this point.

I poked the rock with my spear. It made a softer scream and the lights resumed flashing as they were before I stood next to it. I moved closer and the rock turned red and the same growling came out. I kept my spear at the ready, just in case.

I stood over it and stared at the rocks for a while. Every now and then, the growling would start, sometimes catching me off guard. I couldn't tell if it was threatening me or not. It was almost pleasant growling, like how Shadow used to growl when I would hug her. I leaned on the wall with my hand to see if I could look into the rocks and see anything else, maybe a reason for why they glowed.

That's when a much louder growl came from the walls of the cave. This was so loud it hurt my ears. I dropped my spear and covered my ears. More rocks flashed from the walls, but these were red like the one on the rock. The screaming stopped as a lot of dust fell from the walls and ceiling. I covered my mouth and nose with my hands to keep from breathing it in and picked up my spear.

I noticed another big hole in the wall that wasn't there before. The dust finally stopped and a lower growl came from the walls. It came from all sides of the cave and there were more lights on the rocks than before.

I had enough exploring for one day and my stomach was growling at me, so I slowly made my way back to the top of the cave and out. The sun was starting to set behind the trees. I made my way back to the hut, happy with the day's adventure.

Exploring the cave gave me something to look forward to. I ate some of the berries I had collected on the way back. They were just turning ripe and still had a hint of sour to them. I ate the last of the whitetail meat I had and saved the rest of the berries for morning. I'd need to hunt again in the morning before I could go back into the cave.

When I closed my eyes that night, I kept seeing the flashing rocks. Part confusion and part curiosity, I wondered who made this cave. Maybe it was our ancestors before the great purge. I tried to figure out why they would build a cave like this. It must have taken them years to dig it out. And for it to just get covered up. It surely wasn't anyone from the Hives I knew of. It was purely magical.

I finally fell asleep a while later after many questions and not so many answers. The next morning brought the first of the spring storms. Rain fell angrily from the sky. I wouldn't be able to hunt today. No prey roamed during the storms. I spent most of the day staring at the fire and thinking about the cave. The berries kept my stomach happy for a while, but I had to finish off the rest of the winter vegetables I had stored up. They were almost rotten, so I made soup to keep from getting sick. I hoped the storm would pass quickly. I'll need more food in the morning.

Sometime in the afternoon, the tree blocking the doorway started moving. I grabbed my spear and pointed it at the tree. It worked! And then I realized something big was outside. I hoped it wasn't the alpha. It was hard to hear anything with the storm raging. But the tree was definitely moving.

A loud thud came from the ceiling and dust and water fell. I pushed myself against the side of the hut away from the sound. The ceiling started groaning and more dust fell. And then it caved in exposing a huge bear in the rubble. This bear was even bigger than the one Shadow and I killed before. He was so angry and hungry. He growled loudly and started moving towards me. I threw my spear and it pierced his shoulder.

Screaming in agony, he pulled back out of the hut and scratched at the spear trying to dislodge it. That gave me my chance to get out of the hut. I knocked the tree free from the doorway and ran out into the pouring rain. I turned around to see the bear had removed the spear.

In my haste, I forgot to grab the other spears. The bear now walked slowly towards me, still growling. I picked up a large rock and hurled it at the bear's face. This just seemed to make him angrier and he charged me. I punched him square in the jaw, knocking him on his back. He got back up quickly and shook off the blow.

This was not going well. I turned to run away as fast as I could. The bear gave chase, breathing heavily and growling on my neck. The cave! I knew he was too big to get in the doorway. I just hoped the wolves weren't there. As I ran, I darted between trees to keep the bear from catching me. I could hear the cracking and thuds of his pursuit as each tree sacrificed itself to keep me from arm's length. They kept him just barely out of range.

I jumped down in the cave and ran through the doorway as I heard the bear circling the entrance above. His growling was louder in the cave. I backed away from the entrance very slowly, hoping he'd just go away. After a few minutes, and to my relief, I heard him moving away.

I sat down in the corner for a moment to catch my breath and collect my nerves. Once I was sure the bear wasn't coming back, I moved slowly down the rocks into the bottom of the cave. I pleaded for the wolves to not be there.

All was quiet at the bottom except for the low growl of the walls. It didn't look like anything had moved since I left, so that was a good sign. I still didn't feel very safe with all the bones on the ground. I couldn't tell how the wolves got in, but they could come back at any moment and I had no weapons.

I slowly approached the other hole that appeared after the walls got angry. As I walked in, the ceiling lit up just like the last room. More rocks covered the walls of the smaller room and began flickering like before. In the middle of the room was another rock, but this one was different. The whole rock slowly flashed. As I got closer, the rock flashed faster. I touched the rock with my foot and it stopped flickering and glowed a bright blue.

A low growl came from behind me. I turned around to see the alpha standing in the doorway. I slowly backed away, stepping completely on the lit rock when a loud whine and growl came from the walls. The alpha seemed to be as confused and intrigued as I was. The rock lit up brighter and brighter until I couldn't see anything. The sound was deafening and all of it disoriented me a bit.

When my eyes finally adjusted, I was back outside. Well, somewhere outside. I wasn't really sure where I was. I stumbled to a nearby tree to help me steady. My head hurt really bad and I felt like I had run all day. I was exhausted. I sat down next to the tree and fell asleep.

When I woke, two men in weird clothes were pointing these rocks at me and growling.

"Who are you?!" one of them shouted and growled, thrusting the rock at my face.

I was too tired to speak.

"He said, who are you?! Do you understand me?" the second inquired, still growling.

I closed my eyes and started to fall asleep again when they grabbed me and lifted me to my feet.

They put me in chains. My head was still throbbing from the lights and I was too tired still to fight them. They put me inside this hut of sorts that wasn't there when I fell asleep.

Then the hut, or whatever it was, started moving! I fell down from the movement. I thought maybe they pushed this thing down the hill. I expected to be thrown against the walls and I braced for the impact. After a few moments, I realized I wasn't rolling down the hill. I sat up and saw openings on both ends.

Steadying my balance against the wall, I stood and looked through one of the windows to see the two men on one side. The side they were on was facing the way we were going. It was like a big, enclosed sled. It was made of the same rock the cave was made of. It groaned and whined as we moved.

The two men talked about me as we rode in the sled. Soon, I could see huge huts appear in the distance. We got closer and closer to them, so I guessed they were taking me back to their Hive. I'd never seen this Hive before or clothing so weird. I was thoroughly confused yet again. Was this the northern Hive that Klik spoke of? I still wasn't sure how I got outside the cave. And why did these warriors growl when they talked? And when did it stop raining? This didn't feel like spring to me. It was all very weird.

Finally, we came to a stop in front of a very large hut with even more of their warriors out front. They all had the same oddly shaped rocks. Even if I could have fought them, I didn't think it was a good idea. I was too tired to put up a good enough fight. There were too many of them now and they all had weapons.

Two more warriors opened the sled and pulled me out. Four more warriors surrounded me, pointing their rocks at me.

"Walk!" one of them growled as another pressed the side of the hut and a hole appeared.

I slowly walked inside the hut to find glowing rocks on the ceiling with more warriors standing to the far side of the room. One of them touched the far wall and yet another hole appeared.

I continued to walk farther inside and they sat me on this weird rock.

"And that's how I got here," I said.

CHAPTER V: INTERROGATION

"Are you on drugs?" Titus asks.

After flashing a puzzled look, Tac responds, "I don't know what that means."

Titus wipes his brow and rubs his left temple in frustration.

"Look, Tac, which is not even an approved name by the way, we've been here for over three hours. I want to know where your papers are, NOW!" Titus shouts as he slams his fist down on the table.

"I've told you already, I don't know what you mean by papers," Tac responds sternly. "I've already told you everything I know."

"Papers, Tac! Papers!" Titus shouts as he pulls his Imperial papers from his uniform pocket and shoves the opened document in Tac's face. "See? It has my name, address, birth date, and a bunch of other stuff that tells people who I am."

Titus throws his papers down in front of Tac and turns away from the table, rubbing both of his temples, "Got anything like that?" he asks softly.

"No," he simply replies.

"Aww, for fuck's sake!" Titus yells as he grabs his papers from the table and puts them back in his pocket.

"Can I go home now? I need to deal with the bear before sunset and fix my hut," Tac inquires.

"No, you're not going anywhere until I figure out where you came from," Titus replies, staring him down.

"But I've already told you that. I don't know…" Tac replies as Titus cuts him off.

"I don't know what's worse, the fact that you just wasted three hours of my life by telling me some fairy tale or the fact that you talk without opening your mouth." Titus states.

"I didn't realize I was supposed to," Tac says, opening his mouth. "Is this better?"

Titus sighs in defeat and walks to the door, placing his hand on the biometric scanner.

"I suggest coming up with a better story to explain why you don't have papers. The judge won't sit there and listen to your little story," Titus shouts over his shoulder as he leaves.

"And close your damn mouth!" Titus calls from outside as the door shuts. "Idiot."

Tac closes his mouth and looks around the room. His stomach starts making noises again. He hasn't eaten since yesterday.

Entering the observation room, Titus finds his partner asleep in the corner.

"Catullus!" he shouts.

His partner abruptly wakes and stands up.

"Ugh, sorry. I must have dozed off somewhere around the throwing rocks or whatever it was." Catullus says through a yawn. "Hey, did you figure out how he talks without moving his mouth?"

"No, but he's either extremely smart or extremely stupid. I haven't decided which," Titus responds.

"So, I'm assuming he still has no papers," Catullus shrewdly mentions as he steps over to the table for coffee.

"You think I'd listen to a three-hour story about bears and wolves if he had papers?" Titus, obviously frustrated, cuts him off. "We've already searched him. He has no papers or anything. This is just ridiculous. I can't tell if he's crazy or simply on drugs."

"Well, I haven't heard of the talk-without-your-mouth version of opium that's hit the streets recently. I think it's worth entertaining that he might actually be telling the truth, no matter how ridiculous it sounds," Catullus states, pouring his coffee.

Titus stares through the one-way mirror at Tac, perplexed at the situation. After a minute, he walks over to get himself some coffee. Propping himself up on the ledge below the one-way window, Catullus stares at Tac.

"I don't think he's on any kind of drugs I'm familiar with. He shows no signs of being intoxicated. He's not scratching anything. His sentences are coherent. And his body language is sound. If he *is* on drugs, it's something we've never seen before." Catullus offers.

Titus turns and takes a sip of coffee, "Man, I don't know. But whatever he is, we've never seen this before." They both ponder the situation for a moment before Titus leaves the observation room.

A loud beep sounds in the interview room as Tac turns his focus to the door as Titus enters. He trips on the threshold and falls, spilling his coffee.

"Ugh." Titus grunts as he stands and brushes the dust from his uniform. "I'll be right back."

While Titus goes to get something to clean up his mess, Tac picks up the coffee and puts it back in the cup on the table. Catullus drops his coffee and his jaw watching this.

"Really?! What is this? Spill coffee day?" Titus loudly gestures as he walks into the room.

"Duh...duh...Did you just see that?!" Catullus exclaims pointing at the window.

"Duh, duh, did I see what? You spilling your coffee? Yeah, I had a front-row seat. Thanks," Titus snidely says reaching for the paper towels.

"No! Not that! The spilled coffee just floated back into your cup!" Catullus yells still waving his index finger at the window.

"The hell are you talking about?" Titus says walking over to the window.

Titus peers through the window at the ground where his coffee should be. Sure enough, it's clean. And his cup is full and sitting on the table.

"What the hell?" he asks under his breath.

They both walk around to the interview room, but are unable to say anything. Titus slowly walks over to the table and tips the cup over.

"Why did you do that? I just cleaned that up," Tac says.

With no response, Tac lifts his hand and puts the coffee back in the cup.

Catullus makes incoherent sounds as Titus steps back from the table.

"How did you do that?" Titus asks.

"I just picked up the liquid and put it back in the cup." Tac responds. "You're pretty clumsy, you know that?"

Catullus laughs hysterically as Titus flashes at look of disapproval at him.

"What?" Catullus says clearing his throat, "He's not wrong."

Turning back to Tac, he states, "What you just did is impossible."

Tac picks up the cup and floats it around the room. Both Inquisitors stare at it in awe.

"What is so impossible about it?" Tac questions.

"Um, no one else can do that, Tac," Titus responds softly watching the cup. "Can you put the cup back on the table please? Catullus, can I speak with you outside please?"

Titus walks out the door, grabbing Catullus by the arm and pulling him along. The door shuts behind them. Titus spins Catullus towards him and grabs both of his shoulders.

"We've got to call the Governor. This is way over our heads." Titus states.

"Yeah, but it's pretty cool, right?" Catullus responds with a chuckle.

"No, it's weird. I don't understand how he does that. Couple that with the fact that he doesn't speak with his mouth, none of this makes any sense. There's no telling what this guy is capable of. So, don't piss him off." Titus states sharply.

"Ok, well, I'll go talk to him while you give the Governor's office a call." Catullus offers.

"Fine, just keep him talking about the Hive or whatever," Titus instructs, gesturing dismissal to the air.

Catullus enters the interview room to find Tac relieving himself in the corner. He notices his chains are broken, dangling from his wrists.

"Tac, we have special rooms for that," he says slowly backing out of the door and letting it shut again.

Catullus scratches his head and walks into the observation room.

"Umm…" he says.

"Yeah, that's right. One of the mounted patrols found him about 10 miles west of the detention facility this morning and brought him in for questioning," Titus states into the phone. "I interviewed him for over three hours. The guy speaks without moving his mouth and he can somehow move things without touching them. He's also got no papers."

"Titus," Catullus fumbles through his words as he glances through the window at Tac, "He, uhm, broke his handcuffs and is peeing in the corner."

Titus turns towards the window.

"Oh, shit. You guys need to hurry up. He somehow broke his cuffs and is pissing all over my interview room!" he exclaims and snaps the flip phone shut.

"Who is this guy?" Catullus asks moving closer to the window.

"I have no idea, but it's not our problem anymore. The Praetorians are on the way. No one else goes in or out of that room," Titus commands.

"Understood. What do we do until then?" Catullus questions.

"Just keep him in the interview room, I guess." Titus replies and sighs in frustration.

"Why wouldn't you be able to keep me in the room?" Tac asks.

After a tense moment, "Is he...Is he talking to us? That's a soundproof room," Catullus says with a slight inflection in his voice. "How can he hear us?! How can he speak through a soundproof wall?!" he whispers.

"I don't know," Titus replies, "Tac, just stay in the room please. We've got some people coming to help."

"The Praetorians, right?" Tac inquires.

"Yes, they'll be here soon," Titus replies as he grabs Catullus' shoulder and pulls him out of the room.

They walk outside the front of the building.

"Guards! Lock down this wing. No one goes in or comes out without my express permission," Titus commands.

Tac walks up to them. The guard draws his rifle and starts to aim it at Tac.

"Put your weapon down! He's with us," Titus shouts, attempting to disarm any situation before it formulates.

"Tac, what are you doing? I asked you to stay in the room," Titus asks.

"It got quiet and I wondered where you went," Tac responds.

"Well, we came out to meet the Praetorians. They should be here any minute," Titus states, attempting to quell the uneasy feeling in his stomach.

"Oh, okay. Do you have anything to eat? I haven't eaten since yesterday," Tac asks.

"Of course! We sure do! Follow me," Catullus jumps in front of Tac and grabs him by the arm, pulling him along. Titus sighs, shakes his head, and follows them in.

The three of them walk back inside to find the door of the interview room lying in the middle of the wing, twisted at awkward angles.

"Tac, did you break my door?" Titus asks.

"Is that what that's called? Yes. I wanted to leave and it wouldn't move for me like it does for you," he responds.

"Yeah, that's what it's supposed to do!" he quietly exclaims.

As they continue towards the observation room, Titus can't help but reflect on the last twenty-six years of service to the Empire and how this little stunt is what he'll probably be remembered for. Titus, first to contact aliens. Great. He'd be the laughing stock anywhere he went.

"What do you like to eat, Tac?" Catullus asks rummaging through the drawers and cabinets. "We've got...donuts, candy bars, foo-foos. Oh, I love foo-foos. Have you ever had them?"

"I don't know what any of that is, but I usually eat meat or soup. I don't much care for vegetables or fruit, but I'll eat them if I have to," Tac replies.

"We've got beef sticks!" Catullus shouts and retrieves one from the drawer.

Tac looks at it for a moment and bites into it.

Catullus bursts into laughter. "No! No! You've got to unwrap it first," he says with a chuckle.

Tac makes a face of disgust and spits out the first bite. Catullus peels the wrapper back for him.

"Now try," he insists gesturing at the beef stick.

Tac tries another bite and spits that one out too. "That is horrible. Is it fresh?"

"Well, I mean, it has been in the drawer for a while, but it should be fine." Catullus says as he takes a bite and hands it back to Tac. "Yeah, it's fine."

"I don't know what that is, but it's not meat," Tac replies as he tosses the half-wrapped meat stick on the counter.

Titus pulls a cigarette from the pack in his pouch and lights it. Taking a long drag, he leans up against the counter and exhales the smoke towards the hanging light above him.

"Ok, well, the only other thing we have is this cup of noodles. But it's not very good," Catullus states less enthusiastically. "I'll make them up and we'll see if you like them."

He peels back the lid and fills the cup with water from the faucet. Then he puts the cup in the microwave and presses a few buttons.

"Did water just come from that shiny rock?" Tac inquires, obviously intrigued.

Catullus is slightly confused by the question as nothing in that sequence was out of the ordinary for him.

"Ok, firstly, this is metal. It's not a rock. Well, I guess it is, sort of. But that's not the point," Catullus explains, then shakes his head to refocus on the question. "Yes, we have these running in the ground all over the place and they supply the water to us."

"Wow, we always get water from the streams and bring it back in large buckets," Tac says.

"That seems like a lot of work just for some water," Catullus states.

"I guess so," Tac replies.

"Something has been bothering me about your story. You only mentioned women once, besides your friend. What happens to the women after Commencement?" Catullus asks.

"Well, Commencement for women is fairly simple. The women with the best physical traits are chosen as Breeders, whereas the rest become Servants," Tac explains. "They don't even have to take a Test."

"Wait, all women go through this?" Catullus inquires with a grotesque face.

"Sure, everyone goes through Commencement. It signifies maturity in my culture. Not everyone makes it though. Like the quiet boy that was killed," Tac explains further.

"You know, the Greeks used to kill their own children that were deformed. Toss them right off a cliff. Sickening to kill a child, much less like that," Catullus states attempting to swallow the uneasy feeling generated by the turn of conversation. "Oh, and our women have rights here. They can be anything they want. They're not limited to cooking, cleaning, and making babies."

"Really? You let women be warriors or politicians?" Tac asks with a perplexed look.

"Sure, if they want to and they're good enough to pass the trials," Catullus explains.

"I don't think the Overlord would let that happen back home. He seems to prefer women keep to breeding or service. Maybe that's a new thing. We've been rebuilding the Hive since the Raids of the North. They almost killed us all. And they would have if Klik hadn't stopped them," Tac says.

Putting the cigarette out in the ash tray, Titus asks, "Tac, you never mentioned anything about your parents. Given what you've said about how women are treated, I think we can figure out which profession your mother has. But what profession does your father hold?"

"I have no idea what those words mean," Tac says.

"Oh, great. So, now I have to have the 'birds and the bees' chat with an alien," Titus mumbles to himself.

"Parents. Those that gave birth to you." Catullus overexplains.

Tac still isn't getting the question and makes a perplexed look.

"Tac, it's obvious that your mother is a Breeder. She conceived you with a man from the Hive. Do you know who that man was?" Titus breaks it down for him.

"No, I don't know that anyone knows that. Those who have the Overlord's blessing mate with breeders and they give birth. Those who mate with a Breeder aren't revealed to anyone. Unless, of course, he's a Barons or the Overlord. But only at Commencement would the child learn this."

"Tac, your culture is very odd to me," Catullus says pulling a chair around to sit.

"How do you think I feel about your culture? Everything about this place is strange," Tac states. "You eat strange food, you growl when you talk, and you touch *everything*. And let's not get on the moving rock you brought me here in."

"I can imagine, but that's called a vehicle," Titus confesses and lets the moment pass. "We should go out front to meet the Praetorians."

Catullus offers a confused look to him and gets a hand gesture telling him to relax. They walk slowly towards the front of the building as Titus lights another cigarette.

"So, can anyone mate with women? You said your Hive was rebuilding. But it sounds like the Overlord and Barons have a lot of say in what you can and can't do," Catullus asks about halfway to the main entrance.

"No, no one is allowed to breed without consent of the Overlord. Doing so without the consent is punishable by death for everyone involved. For the most part, it's up to the Baron to choose which of his family will breed," Tac explains. "For us Warriors, it was always the best of us. Klik still bred from time to time, but most of the time it was Frejic or one of the other better Warriors."

"And they would just pick whoever they wanted to breed with?" Catullus asks.

"Mostly. Those that were already pregnant or sick were not allowed to breed. The Baron usually helped narrow the choices down to a few breeders that were healthy and in their prime," Tac replies.

"So, you don't know who your parents are and you're not married. I'm not sure how I feel about that. It seems like you miss out a lot on holidays and birthdays," Titus states.

"What are holidays?" Tac inquires.

"You know, like Christmas and Passover," Catullus responds gesturing with his hand.

Tac holds his blank expression.

"Holidays are specific days throughout the year when you celebrate something special, like the birth and resurrection of Christ. Birthdays of your family are treated in similar fashion," Titus says.

"Oh, ok. We have season festivals and of course Commencement. We gather in the Common Hall and feast on food and drink," Tac offers.

The low rumbling of vehicles approaching causes the three to turn and face the noise.

"There are more of those things?" Tac asks.

"Many more," Titus replies. "It's how we get around. There are even some that fly like the birds."

"Wow," Tac states.

The sound grows and grows until, at last, the vehicles come to a squeaking halt in front of the detention facility. Six

Praetorians jump out of the backs of the three vehicles, stun batons drawn and quickly surround Tac.

"Is this the subject?" one of the Praetorians asks.

"Yes, this is him. Tac, go with the Praetorians. They'll be able to help you better than we can," Titus instructs.

Tac knew something was wrong with the situation. This is not how people act when they're trying to help. He slowly moves into a defensive stance.

"Tac! Relax. They're just here to help!" Titus pleads.

"Yeah? Then why do they look like they're about to attack me?" Tac asks.

"Take him down!" one of them shouts.

Two of the Praetorians charge at him rearing back to hit with their stun batons. Tac picks them up simultaneously and throws them into the vehicles, knocking them unconscious. The remaining four Praetorians encircle Tac as he returns to his defensive stance.

Tac flashes back to the abandoned village when the wolves surrounded him in similar fashion. Rage flashes across his face and he snaps two of the Praetorians necks before they can even move. The final two charge at him as he grabs them both, lifting them off the ground and throwing them into the side of the vehicle.

He turns, anger flowing from his breath, towards Titus and Catullus.

"Tac, why did you do that? They were just here to help!" Titus exclaims.

"You lied to me. They were not here to help. They were here to bind me in more chains!" Tac replies.

Titus couldn't deny the failed plan.

"Listen, you don't have to kill us, Tac," Catullus pleads.

"I don't plan to. You are not a threat to me. But I want you to see how angry and disappointed I am with you both," Tac says as he starts to relax.

Tac stares each in the eyes for several. He turns and darts down the road towards the city. Titus pulls another cigarette from his pack and fumbles with his lighter as Catullus watches Tac disappear into the distance.

"Command, this is 037. Subject known as Tac has escaped custody during transfer to Praetorian custody and is currently on foot headed for Sector 81 Prime. Subject is a Caucasian male, 6'5", approximately 250 lbs., long brown hair, blue eyes, wearing a red shirt and brown pants with tattoos covering his left forearm. Requesting immediate lockdown of Sector 81 Prime and deployment of Praetorian presence for containment," Titus shouts into his phone and snaps it shut, taking a drag off his cigarette.

"I like him!" Catullus shouts.

"Shut up," Titus scoffs and heads back inside.

Tac slows down to catch his breath. Taking in the sheer size of Sector 81 Prime, he knows needs to find food and shelter. Sirens wail and he dives into the nearby ditch just before they pass. He peeks up to see half a dozen vehicles headed for the detention facility.

He crawls slowly out of the muck and stands, brushing himself off as best as he can. His stomach growls loudly, refocusing him, and he can feel the absence of strength throughout his body. He'll have to pick his battles for the time being. He turns towards the massive city, and walks along the side of the road.

Tac reaches the outskirts shortly thereafter. The smell of fresh food causes him to salivate immediately. There is a market just outside of the massive gates to Prime. It is bustling with activity. People going every which way, buying things, the steam and smoke rising above in random places.

The sights, sounds, and smells remind him of Tes and the Market back home. In such a strange place, the market is the only thing he recognizes. Tac stumbles down the hill towards the market, with new smells invigorating every step.

As he passes trader after trader, he sees fresh baked bread, pastries, trinkets, and plenty of other things that he doesn't recognize. Being surrounded with all of this, a rough smile crosses his face.

He sees one of the traders on the far side with fresh grilled meat and pelts. His eyes light up as he marches towards her stall. He grabs one of the steaming hot skewers of meat and bites into it, juices burning his mouth. He doesn't care though.

"Hey! You have to pay for that! Three Denarius!" she exclaims.

Tac looks at her in confusion. He doesn't understand the concept of currency.

The commotion draws unwanted attention from those around him. A woman sees the predicament he's in and steps up to the counter.

"That's ok. I've got him," she said as she shells out the coinage on the trader's table.

Time seems to slow as she spins around to face him. Her bright cardinal red hair is mesmerizing as it bounces around and falls perfectly into place above her shoulders, contouring her face. She smiles and his world stops. He almost drops the meat.

"I'm sorry, they can be a bit rude at times. I'm Calida," she says.

Tac towers over her, covered in mud. *He must be homeless and starving to steal from the market,* she thinks to herself.

"Do you have a name?" she inquires with a smile.

"I'm Tac," he responds sharply.

The smile disappears from her face as she realizes he didn't speak those words. She grabs him by the arm and takes him off to the side.

"What did you say?" she asks, flustered by the situation.

"My name is Tac," he repeats, attempting to finish his bite.

"How can I hear you speak, but you don't move your mouth?" she asks, narrowing her eyes.

"That's kind of a long story, to be honest," he replies. "I'm not from around here. Honestly, I don't even really know where here is."

"Yeah, I gathered that much. You're telepathic and you steal food. But something tells me you don't know any better," Calida says, her expression relaxing.

"Can you smile again please?" Tac asks mid-chew.

She blushes and smiles, pushing her hair behind her right ear.

"If you're not from here, I take it you don't have anywhere to go," she deduces.

"The Inquisitors had me at the detention facility and called the Praetorians. So, I ran away," Tac explains, his face drawn in a disappointed fashion. "They said they would help me. But they lied."

"Well, if the Praetorians are after you, you definitely need to get out of sight. We'll get you set up with shelter and some clean clothes," Calida says as she turns and walks toward the giant wall lining Prime.

He trots quickly after her, finishing off the last of the meat and wiping his hands on his shirt.

After the short walk, Calida reaches the entrance to the storm drain. Opening the gate, she ushers Tac inside.

"In here," she whispers.

She checks to make sure they weren't followed and closes the gate behind them. Walking in the shallow water, she retakes the lead.

"You know, the detention facility is like twenty miles outside of the city. Did you run the whole way here?" she asks, pinning her hair behind her right ear again.

"Mostly. I walked the last bit. I was pretty tired," Tac replies. "But also when I smelled the food from the market, I slowed down to enjoy it."

"Ok, so you're telepathic, you steal food, and you can run really far," Calida says and chuckles. "Anything else I need to know about you?"

Tac lifts some of the water in front of her and forms a small sphere. Her jaw drops as she walks around it, fixated on the existence of a sphere of water in the middle of the air.

"How are you doing that?" she quietly inquires, not looking away.

"I just do. People here seem to touch everything with their hands in order to move it. Where I'm from, we all do it like this," he replies, changing the shape of the water into a bird.

"That is amazing!" she exclaims before remembering her voice carries very well in the tunnels. "Ok, put that down. We need to get back to base."

Calida darts off in a jog and Tac drops the water to follow her. After a few minutes, she slows down to a walk.

"How did you get here?" she asks through slightly labored breathing.

"Well, after I was exiled by the Hive, I found this weird cave with shiny rocks. I touched some of them and woke up under a tree," he recounts the abridged version.

"Shh!" she whispers, stopping in her tracks.

Tac stops too, wondering what the issue is. Calida turns around and listens intently back the way they came.

"What's wrong?" he asks.

"We're being followed," she whispers.

Calida takes off in a dead sprint.

"Keep up!" she shouts.

Tac catches up to her with ease.

"Where are we going?" he asks.

"Home base. It's where the Resistance is," she says through heavy breaths.

They reach the main door and Calida lands full force into it and starts banging on it.

"It's Calida! Open up! We're being followed!" she yells, continuing to pound away at the door.

"Freeze!" someone yells from behind them. "Turn around and keep your hands where I can see them!"

"Shit!" Calida whispers as she turns around slowly with her hands in plain view.

Tac turns with her to face the guards pointing rifles at them.

"This is a restricted area! No one is allowed down here except for maintenance crews and only with proper authorization!" one of the guards states.

"Wait a minute," the other guard says. "That's the terrorist leader!"

Calida's expression changes from frightened to disgust. Tac immediately and without hesitation, steps in front of her.

"Put your weapons down and walk away," Tac orders.

"On your faces, traitors!" the first guard yells.

Tac snaps both weapons in half and dangles them in front of the guards who don't believe what they're seeing.

"No." he sharply responds. "Now walk away while you still can."

Both guards draw pistols as Calida shields her head in anticipation. Tac breaks both of their necks in a split second as the weapons and their limp bodies fall into the shallow water. Silence fills the tunnel again.

"What did you do?!" Calida screams, walking around to look at the guards. "Now they know where we are!"

"I couldn't let them hurt you," he replies. "And they already know where we are."

The door swings open and Barius towers in the doorway.

"What the hell is all the racket?" he questions.

"We were followed by guards," Calida explains as she pushes her way past him. "We need to clean this up."

"Who the hell is we? And who the hell is he?" Barius continues asking.

"I'm Tac. I'm not from here," he replies, walking past Barius.

"No shit?" he says, mouth drawn and shuts the door.

CHAPTER VI: NIGHTMARES

"Calida!" my mother yells from downstairs. "Honey, it's time for dinner!"

"Just five more minutes please?!" I ask.

"No, sweetheart. The food is getting cold and your father had a long day," she calls back.

Ugh, why do I care? I wasn't done playing with my dolls. I throw Mr. Wiggles across the room and kick over my tea pot as I storm out of my room and down the massive staircase.

My father sits at the head of the long table in a grey three-piece suit, newspaper in hand, and smoking his pipe as usual. My mother is wearing her favorite blue dress with yellow flowers and a red bow in her hair. It's my favorite outfit too.

My favorite butler, Cassius, is already waiting for me and pulls my chair out as I approach the table.

"Good evening, Miss Calida," he says, smiling widely at me.

"Hello Cassius," I reply as I took my seat.

"What's wrong, dear?" Cassius asks with a concerned tone.

"Nothing. I was just in the middle of something. How are you?" I redirect.

"I'm just fine miss, thank you for asking," he says as he pushes me up to the table. "We have your favorite for dinner tonight."

"Please, no more chicken nuggets, Cassius," father removes his pipe and drops the paper. "I swear, I'm turning into a chicken nugget."

"Just for little miss, sir," he responds nodding in father's direction. "For you and the Mrs., we have baked salmon topped with a citrus crema and sautéed vegetable medley."

"Very well," he says with a sigh, whipping the paper back into his view.

With two short claps, Cassius summons the main courses delivered by four additional butlers.

The sun sets as we eat dinner. Father excuses himself early as he usually did. He has work things to take care of. He grabs his overcoat and hat as my mother meets him in the foyer.

"I won't be out too late tonight. Just some paperwork," father says to mother, kissing her on the forehead.

"Ok dear. I'll be waiting," she replies, stepping up to kiss his cheek.

He puts his hat on, coat draped over his arm and tells me goodnight before going out the door. Cassius walks up as the door shuts.

"Will there be anything else, ma'am?" he asks.

"Yes, Cassius. If you could tidy up my room, please," mother replies.

"Very well, ma'am," Cassius says as he turns and walks up the stairs.

"Calida, finish your dinner, sweetheart. It's almost time for bed," she instructs.

"I'm done, mommy," I say, rubbing my bulging stomach.

"I should hope so, you ate six chicken nuggets!" she says with a laugh. "Did you eat any of your broccoli?"

"No, ma'am. I had too many chicken nuggets," I reply.

"Very well. Run along and get ready for bed. I'll be up to tuck you in soon," she smiles as she ushers towards the stairs.

Mother walks into my room a short time later and finds me playing with my dolls again.

"Calida, you're supposed to be in bed," she says with a more serious tone.

"But I wasn't done playing!" I reply with my most entitled voice.

"You can play tomorrow, honey," she says, picking me up and carrying me to the bed. "But for now, you need your beauty sleep."

"Is that how you got so pretty, mommy?" I ask.

"Aww, sweetheart. Thank you. But yes, that's how I got this pretty," she says as she giggles and smiles.

"I want to be as pretty as you some day," I say, turning over in my bed.

"You will be sweetheart. You'll be prettier than I am someday," she replies, brushing my hair.

I'm startled awake to the sound of glass breaking. The dim nightlight throws shadows of my tea party on the ground. I hear voices down the hall. Loud voices. Mommy and Daddy must be arguing again. I try to pull my covers over my head to drown them out, but now I can't sleep.

I walk down the hall, Mr. Wiggles in tow, towards mommy's bedroom. The voices get louder and louder. Mommy screams and something else gets broken. I'm scared and I stop in my tracks. Mr. Wiggles falls at my feet.

"Mommy?" I cry.

There's no reply.

I peek around the corner of mommy's door. Daddy's standing there with a knife, breathing hard.

"Daddy? Where's Mommy?" I ask.

"Go back to bed, Calida. It's just a bad dream," he says not moving from where he stands next to the bed.

"I heard Mommy scream. I'm scared," I reply.

"Go *back* to bed. Now!" he shouts.

I run back down the hall and jump in my bed. I pull the blanket up over my head and start to cry.

A few seconds later, I hear footsteps coming toward my room. Father's smile appears as he pulls my covers back and hands me Mr. Wiggles, both of them covered in Mother's blood.

Calida screams herself awake to find her sheets soaked with sweat. She takes a few deep breaths and realizes she's not alone. She looks towards the door and screams again.

"I'm sorry. I didn't mean to startle you," Tac says. "But I could hear you yelling and screaming from my room and I wanted to make sure you were ok."

"It's ok Tac. It was just a bad dream," Calida replies. "Go back to bed."

She scoffs at the irony of repeating her father's phrase to him. He takes a long glance at her. After a few quiet moments, she sighs heavily, pulls the covers down and sits up in the bed.

"My father killed my mother when I was a child," she says looking at the floor. "I don't know why I'm telling you this. But that's what my dream was about. I've had the same few dreams for years now."

Calida swings her legs off the bed and turns the lamp on. Glancing at the glowing red 3:30 a.m. on her clock, "Damn, I'm sorry. Go back to bed. I'm gonna hit the gym."

"Well, I'm already up. Can I join you?" he asks.

"Sure," she replies, smirking at him. "If you like."

Tac smiles at her.

The fluorescent lights come to life with a hum, illuminating the small room littered with weights, benches, and machines.

They both squint at the blinding light. Calida goes straight for the inclined press bench. She grabs two 25 lb. dumbbells and sits down with them on her thighs. Tac is more interested in the lights than the weights.

"I've seen these before. In the cave just before I came here," he says, turning to face Calida.

Calida exhales as she moves the dumbbells above her in preparation for her set. But her mind is elsewhere. Thinking of how she could have saved her mother and Cassius. Hating that her father hadn't stayed out later and not found them in bed. Hating her mother for being unfaithful and causing this whole mess. Hating herself for not being strong enough to protect them. She discovered years ago how therapeutic physical exercise is and how it can drown out her own inner voice. So, she clings to this damp, ill-equipped weight room as her sole source of therapy to maintain her sanity whenever her thoughts overwhelm her.

Tac observes her working out, beads of sweat forming on her brow and chest. He doesn't quite understand why she is doing this.

"Is this hitting the gym?" he says.

"Yes, have you never worked out before?" she says, exhaling at the top of her rep.

"No, this is new," Tac responds. "What's the purpose?"

Starting to get frustrated, Calida says, "You lift the weights over and over again and it makes you stronger."

"Like this?" Tac says as an 80 lb. dumbbell appears over Calida.

"Shit!!" Calida exclaims as she drops her weights and rolls off the bench. She stands and looks straight at Tac, clearly agitated.

Don't get mad at him. He doesn't know any better, she says to herself.

A few seconds pass as she catches her breath and the anger dissipates. Curiosity sets in as she realizes he's been holding an 80 lb. dumbbell off the ground for about 20 seconds.

"Tac, how much *can* you pick up?" she asks.

"I'm not sure," he responds. "I can't say that I've ever tried picking up heavy things for fun."

Calida eyes the squat bar across the room with 225 pounds still loaded from someone else's set.

"Can you pick up that bar?" she asks, pointing across the room.

Tac lifts it with no effort and moves it toward the middle of the room. "Where would you like it?" he asks.

Calida walks over to the floating weights, still not sure if she believes what she's seeing.

"Can you put the rest of the plates from the stand on it?" she asks, not taking her eyes off the bar.

The remaining plates fly slowly off of the stand and slide unevenly onto the bar, overloading the right side.

Calida turns in disbelief to Tac, who stands in the same spot, unfazed by the normally impossible task she's given him.

"I still don't see how you do that." she says and then pushes the bar to see how it will react.

"I told you, this is just how I pick up things," Tac responds with a shrug. "It's how *everyone* picks up things where I'm from."

"Ok, well, set it back on the rack, gently," she says. "People are still sleeping."

The weights and the bar float slowly back to where they came from with a series of clinks.

"What else can you do?" Calida inquires, squinting her eyes slightly.

"I'm pretty good at knocking trees down," he replies. "I'm pretty good with a spear. I'm also good at fighting, but I don't really like to."

"So, you're like some sort of a superhero," she states.

"I don't know what that is," he admits.

Calida sighs and says, "Umm, a superhero is someone who has abilities others don't and uses them to help people."

"I don't know that I use them to help people, really," Tac says uneasily.

"Not yet, anyway," Calida adds.

She looks him over for a few more seconds, still figuring him out.

"Well, seeing as you may be sticking around for a while, we need to get your hair cut and find you some new clothes," she changes the subject. "You kind of stand out."

"I'm assuming standing out is a bad thing?" he asks.

"Around here it is. The Empire doesn't take kindly to those who threaten its power," she replies. "And that definitely includes a telekinetic, telepathic, super sprinter with long hair. Imagine how the Governor is going to react when he finds out you killed two of his Guards without a weapon. It won't be pretty."

"Yeah, that makes sense," Tac admits.

"Ok, well, follow me and we'll fix you right up," she says, walking toward the door.

Tac follows her out of the gym and to the shower area. Calida pulls a chair to the middle of the room.

"Sit," she instructs, tapping the back of the chair. "I'll be back in a second."

Tac sits down as she goes back to her room to grab her comb and scissors.

"We need to get your hair wet first," she says, turning the shower on and wetting her hands.

She runs them through his heavy, shoulder-length brown hair and begins trimming it to the top of his neck. Then she cuts the sides and back short to his scalp, leaving some of the hair on the top. She wets her hands again and styles his hair, bringing it to a peak in the front.

"There we go. Much better," she says abruptly and smiles, turning and walking away. "I'll be right back."

Calida walks back to her room, berating herself the whole way.

"Ok, let's not fall for the guy on the second day. You don't even know if he likes you. He may not even like girls at all. Don't get your hopes up. Even if he does, that doesn't mean he's going to fall for you. He probably doesn't even know what love is. Shit, is he a virgin?" she contemplates as she puts the comb and scissors away and walks back to the bathroom.

She returns to find Tac naked and showering. She becomes flustered as she sees his finely toned body shimmering in the light, water dripping everywhere, as he rinses the loose hair from his body. She grabs a towel from one of the bins as he turns the water off.

"Tac, catch!" she says, averting her eyes and throwing the towel at him. "Dry yourself off. I'm going to go find some clothes for you. I don't suppose you know what size you wear, do you?"

"Probably not," he replies, muffled through the towel as he dries his hair and face.

She ventures off, looking for clothes and debating the morality of her attraction to a man who probably doesn't even know what sex is. He's like a child in some respects, mentally at least. He's definitely a man physically. Her face flushes and she has to catch her breath again, the vision of Tac in the shower imprinted in her brain.

She forces her debate to the back of her mind, focusing on digging through the clean clothes for sizes that might fit him.

"You know, I really like being able to call water from the wall like that. It's very convenient," Tac says across the room.

"Uh, huh. It's great," she replies, not really listening to what he's saying.

Calida grabs a few sets of clothes and heads back to the shower to find Tac just standing there naked.

"You know, the towel is also used to cover yourself up until you can get dressed," she says, averting her eyes again. "It's not appropriate for me to see you like this."

She throws the pants at him, "Try these on," and turns around.

"They're a little big, but they'll work. Thank you," he says after sliding them on.

"And the shirt!" she exclaims, throwing it over her shoulder in his direction. She feels as awkward with Tac as she did with the boys in grade school.

Get it together, Calida!, she tells herself.

Calida turns back around after a few seconds and judges how the outfit looks on him.

How is he more attractive dressed?, she thinks to herself. *Ok, this has to stop. I need to distract myself.*

"Throw your old clothes in the bin over there," she says pointing to the corner of the room. "I'm going to try to get some sleep before daybreak. I suggest you do the same."

Calida walks quickly back to her room and shuts the door, letting all of the pent-up frustration out in a grunt as she pushes her forehead against the back of the door.

She climbs back into bed as the memory of Tac in the shower floods her brain again.

"No! Stop that!", she argues with her subconscious.

She tosses and turns for several minutes, trying to find a comfortable position to sleep in. Her thoughts keep coming back to Tac in the shower

"You've gotta be kidding me."

As she finally drifts off to sleep, she sees her father's face again. Panic and terror sets in as he has her pinned to the bed. She struggles against him and pleads for him to stop. Suddenly, she is standing in a field with a swollen belly. She cradles the unborn child and begins crying. She catches something out of the corner of her eye. She looks over to see a young woman walking in the same field, her long brown hair flowing in the wind. She looks happy and healthy. Calida glances back down at her now normal figure.

Her eyes snap open, filled with tears. She pulls the covers over her head and silently weeps for the child she'll never know. Sadness soon turns to hatred and disgust for her father. Sitting up, she wipes the tears from her eyes and checks the clock. Breakfast should be ready in a few minutes.

She quietly gets dressed and looks at herself in the mirror.

Ugh, I'm a wreck, she thinks as she starts to clean up her face.

A fresh set of clothes and some make up remove all traces of her latest nightmare. She walks out of her room and heads to the cafeteria. Soldiers greet and make way for her as she passes them in the narrow corridor. She smiles and replies with her usual "Good morning."

Smells of fresh eggs, bacon, and biscuits tease her nose as she enters the cafeteria. Groups of men and women are already in line or enjoying their breakfast. Calida walks straight for the coffee and pours herself a cup. Adding the sugar, she notices they're out of creamer this morning and molds her face in disappointment.

"Good morning, ma'am," one of the cooks say. "I saved some creamer for you. It's the last of it."

"Oh, thank you so much," she responds as she smiles. "If there's a morning I need a good cup of coffee, it's today."

Turning around, she sees Tac in the doorway. Soldiers push past him both entering and leaving. He eventually moves out of the way. Calida makes her way across the room.

"Good morning again," she says with a smile. "Did you get some sleep?"

"Hi Calida," he responds. "Yes, I just woke up. What is this place? Something smells wonderful."

"This is the cafeteria. It's where all our food is prepared and eaten. I imagine you're pretty hungry. Let's go get in line."

"Yes, I'm very hungry," he replies.

They walk up to the back of the line. Those in front of them eventually take notice and give way. When she refuses, they insist. They awkwardly walk to the front of the line.

"What'll ya have?" another cook asks as they reach the counter.

Calida takes a glance at Tac and says, "He'll have a little of everything and I'll just have some eggs and a biscuit, please."

"Yes, ma'am. Coming right up," he responds.

They travel down the line, trays in hand, as their plates are added to with various breakfast items. Calida holds her tray out at the end and another cook places the plate on her tray. Tac takes note and holds his tray out and receives two plates of food.

"Thank you," he says to the cook and turns to follow Calida.

Some of the soldiers see Calida heading for them and stand up to vacate her favorite table.

"Sorry, ma'am. We were just leaving," she says.

"That's ok. Have a seat. There's plenty of room," Calida responds.

Tac sits down next to Calida among the other soldiers and eyes his food.

"What's this?" he asks, pointing to the yellow mess on his plate.

"Those are scrambled eggs. They come from chickens," she replies, sipping her coffee.

"And this?" he asks again, pointing at another item.

"Bacon. It's meat from the belly of a pig," she answers as she reaches for the communal salt and pepper.

"What about…" he begins to ask.

"That is sausage. It comes from turkey, but the kind from a pig is better. That's a biscuit, which is made from flour," she says pointing at each item. "Those are hash browns from potatoes, that's a boiled chicken egg, and that's called toast, also from flour."

"It all smells amazing," Tac admits as the eggs start to float in front of his face.

"Tac, use the fork please," she says.

He looks puzzled at her as she gestures to the fork she picks up. He watches her scoop up some of the eggs and eat them.

"Well, that's different," he says and follows her lead.

Calida notices the others are looking at them.

"He's not from around here," she says with a giggle.

"Sorry, ma'am. We didn't mean to stare. We have to be going anyway," one of the soldiers says picking up his tray and standing. Calida nods in their direction as the others follow suit.

Tac is almost done with the first plate. Calida smiles and they eat the rest of the meal in silence. She glances over from time to time and smiles, watching Tac discover different foods for the first time and trying not to laugh when he eats the toast with his fork.

Tac finally sits back in his chair and relaxes, wiping his mouth with the back of his hand.

"That was some amazing food," he says rubbing his stomach.

Calida giggles and states, "I think you were probably just hungry. This food is not very good. But we eat what we can get a hold of. Being cut off from the rest of society has its downfalls. Access to fresh food and water is one of them. Some of the supporters will occasionally find ways to get us some good steak, but otherwise we're stuck with powdered eggs and stale biscuits."

"It's still better than the slop back home," he says.

"I'm sure of it. The cafeteria is open during certain hours throughout the day. They're posted outside the door we came in," she informs.

"Yeah, I'm not sure I get the hours thing," he admits.

She shows him her watch.

"Each day is 24 hours long. My watch has 12 positions to indicate which hour it is. Inside each hour, there are 60 minutes and inside of each minute, there are 60 seconds. So, right now, it's 6:30 am, meaning morning," she explains.

"Oh, ok," he says, trying to wrap his head around the concept.

"Speaking of which, we need to leave. I'm taking you into the field today. There are a couple of the outlying villages that have seen increased Imperial presence over the last week or so.

We need to put a stop to it. Plus, they may have supplies that we can use," she states with a progressively authoritative tone.

Calida stands and grabs both trays, emptying them in the garbage. Tac follows her out of the door and down the hallway. When they reach the war room, it is filled with soldiers.

"Attention on deck!" someone calls.

Everyone stands up straight as Calida enters.

"As you were," she says to the group. "Tac, just take one of the open seats."

Calida walks behind the podium to address the room.

"Per the intelligence brief yesterday, three of the villages neighboring Sector 81 Prime have seen Imperial troops patrolling in the area over the last week or so. They've been seen with light armored personnel carriers and automatic weapons. No reports of drone activity in the area, but play it safe. Stay under tree cover and make sure you keep your helmets on at all times," she orders. "Decuria Alpha will take the southwestern village. Bravo and Charlie will take the northeastern and southeastern villages, respectively. Clear them of any hostiles and talk with the villagers. If you find any Imperial vehicles, call it in and we'll send someone out to collect. Most importantly, stay safe. Any questions?"

The room is silent except for the shifting feet and occasional clearing of the throat. Tac scans the room, realizing they're about to go into battle.

"Very well. Good hunting!" Calida says.

"Attention on deck!" another voice rings as everyone stands and Calida walks towards the door.

Tac awkwardly looks around and after a few moments, stands with the rest.

"Tac, c'mon!" she says ushering him to follow her.

"You heard her, move out!" another voice shouts as the room fills with sounds of people standing and shuffling towards the door.

Calida leads Tac to the armory, where she grabs one of the bullet-proof vests and fits it to him.

"What's this for?" he asks, lifting his arms as she secures the straps around his ribs.

"Protection. Imperial troops carry lots of firepower, especially when they're outside of Prime. Intel has shown the troops have moved to the eastern villages and will likely be gone by the time Bravo and Charlie even get there," Calida states, grabbing a helmet from the shelf.

"See if this fits," she says, handing it to him.

"Where do I put it?" he asks.

"On your head," she quickly replies.

Tac puts the oversized helmet on backwards, causing Calida to burst into laughter.

"Ok, maybe a size smaller. Try this one," she says handing him the new helmet. "And it goes on like this."

Calida gets so close she can smell him as she places the helmet on his head.

"Much better," she says, buckling the chin strap. "Can you close the visor."

Tac reaches up and pulls the visor down until it clicks into place.

"Ok, can you still see?" she asks.

"Yes," he replies.

"To open it, grab right here with your thumb," Calida instructs as she guides his hand to the bottom of the visor. "You'll hear a click and just push it up back to where it was"

She throws her vest on, buckles it, and grabs her helmet from the shelf.

"I'm not going to give you a weapon this time. Mainly, because you haven't been trained on how to use it. But also cause you're probably better off with your mystical powers anyway," she says as she picks up her rifle and ammunition.

Calida winks and smiles at Tac as she walks past him out the door. They walk to the main door and Barius opens it. Pushing into the corridor, the bodies of the Imperial guards have been disposed of, hopefully keeping the base hidden.

The group marches down the various corridors leading out of the sewers. Sounds of weapons locking compete with boots against metal and water along the way. As they reach the exit, Calida turns around to face everyone. She is met with 'ok' hand signals from everyone. She offers an 'ok' back and drops her visor down.

She darts out of the exit to the southwest along with Tac and the rest of Alpha. Their pace slows once they reach cover of the tree line.

"Alpha, check in," Calida calls over the radio.

Each soldier calls over the radio as present.

"Tac?" Calida calls.

"I'm here," he says as she turns around to verify.

"Ok, we've got about two hours until we reach the village. Plutus take point. Darius, bring up the rear. Echelon right, people!" she says over the radio as soldiers start shuffling around and the squad forms a diagonal line.

After about an hour, they come upon the river that divides the sector. Plutus holds his fist up to order a halt as he discovers the bridge has been destroyed. Calida looks up and down the river to see if there's a point they can pass over or through the swift waters.

"From the map, there's a shallow point to the west of here where the water is calm, but it's another hour's march," Plutus states.

"I'd like to get back before nightfall. Is there another option?" Calida asks.

"I don't see any closer than that one," he responds.

Overhearing the conversation on the radio, Tac walks up to the front.

"I can build a bridge with a few of these trees, if you like," he states.

"No, we don't have time to cut them down. Plus, we don't have any rope long enough to string them to the other side," Plutus replies.

"Go ahead, Tac," Calida says, anxious to see what others think of his abilities.

"By the time we get the bridge built, we could have gone around twice," Plutus' voice drifts off as Tac punches one of the trees to the ground.

He lifts it over the river and sets it down, straddling both sides. He repeats the process with another large tree and sets it next to the first. The radio goes quiet and only the sound of the rushing waters remains as Tac finishes the bridge in a matter of seconds.

"What the fuck was that?" Plutus asks. "Are we going to address how the hell he just did that?"

"He's not from around here," Calida answers, stepping onto the bridge.

"Yeah, I figured that part out already," he acknowledges.

Calida giggles, "He's telekinetic."

"Figured that out too," Plutus admits.

"I think he's from another planet, or at least not from this one. I haven't quite figured it out. But where he's from, everyone is telekinetic and telepathic," Calida says.

The trek continues until they come upon the village. Ashes and ruins litter the once-thriving area. Bodies lay on the ground and the pungent smell of death permeates everything. Small fires remain in some areas and a sign is hung in the middle of the village.

It reads, "The Resistance is nothing but a small band of terrorists. Any support given to them *will* be deemed treasonous to our Emperor. No quarter will be given and all traitors will be executed on sight! Long live the Empire!"

Calida walks past the charred bodies of fathers and brothers amongst mothers and daughters. The weight of their deaths is crushing to her, but only manages to fuel her anger.

A long burst of automatic fire interrupts the rage.

"Contact front!" Calida yells as everyone ducks behind whatever cover they can find and returns fire.

"Tac! Take them out!" she commands.

The firefight goes on for less than a few seconds before the two guards are killed. Calida stands from behind her cover and looks for Tac.

"Tac! Where the hell are you?! I brought you along so you could protect us!" she screams over the radio.

Tac lays motionless in the middle of the road that runs through the village. Calida drops her weapon and runs to him. Blood pools from behind his vest onto the dirt path.

Snatching her visor open, "Oh, shit. Please don't be dead."

"Medicus!!! Get your ass here *now!*" she yells over her shoulder.

She rips off his vest and starts putting pressure to his wounds.

"Just stay with me, Tac. Stay with me!" Calida shouts as her instincts take over.

CHAPTER VII: RECOVERY

Tac shields his eyes from the bright light. A silhouette appears in front of him in the distance. As his eyes slowly adjust, he sees the outline change shape into a woman with flowing hair. She walks toward him.

"Hello Tac," Tes says.

"Tes?!" he exclaims.

He's confused, but it's definitely her voice. She doesn't look old and frail anymore, but strong and youthful.

"Yes. I was sent to meet you," she replies.

"Where am I?" he asks.

"There are many words for it on Earth, but this is where we all exist before life and after death," she answers.

"Oh, great. What happened?" Tac asks with dread. "The last thing I remember was walking down this dusty road in a village. Wait! Where's Calida?!"

He looks around for her.

"Relax. It's not your time yet," she explains. "And Calida is fine."

Tes finally stands in front of Tac. He sees how beautiful she is now. Her wavy brown hair floats slightly in the breeze. She smiles and Tac embraces her.

"I'm so sorry I couldn't protect you," he states, overcome with guilt.

"Little one, that was not your fault. It was my time to come home," she says, pulling back and caressing his hands. "And there's nothing you could have done to change that outcome."

"Well, if it makes you feel any better, I killed him for what he did to you," he explains.

"I know. I've seen everything," she says, smiling.

"As have I," another voice says.

Tac slowly turns his head to see another beautiful woman walking up.

"Hiya sweetheart. You may not recognize us now, but that's because these are our souls' true forms. You knew me as Shadow on Earth," she says joining the group.

"Shadow!" Tac exclaims and embraces her.

"It's good to see you too. Listen, we don't have much time to explain. The relationship between you and Calida is extremely important. You two are soulmates," Tes states.

"Ok, so what does that mean?" Tac asks.

"It means you were cast together during creation. Each of us is created in pairs. We each have our own other half," Shadow replies.

"Most of us incarnate alone on Earth as our soulmate watches over us from here. But during times of dire circumstances, both soulmates can incarnate at the same time in order to fulfill a divine purpose," Tes states.

"So, how did I get there? And where exactly is there?" Tac asks.

"First, you need to know where you come from. There are many versions of Earth. Ours was from a time far into the future compared to Calida's Earth. Our Earth has served its purpose, but Calida's Earth is being held back from evolving like the rest due to the Empire there that rules over everything." Shadow explains.

"Basically, every soul that's incarnated on Calida's Earth cannot evolve during that lifetime because of the overwhelming oppression. And this is usurping the divine purpose," Tes adds.

"Ok, so why am I there?" Tac inquires.

"When we incarnate as humans, our vision is narrowed. We are blinded by things like ego, greed, and lust. These things have a very powerful sway over our feelings and actions. As such, Earths that become this corrupt block out the divine light, preventing souls from evolving," Shadow explains.

"Ok, I am completely lost now," Tac admits.

"What you need to know, is that you were sent to Calida's Earth at a critical point in its history. Their society is an Earth-wide empire descended from one of the most ruthless ancient governments of all Earths, the Roman Empire. On your Earth, this empire collapsed early in its development, which allowed evolution to continue. On Calida's Earth, it continued to grow and has consumed the entire planet, locking all souls to repeat their lives over and over again. None of the souls can evolve. Nor can they incarnate anywhere else. The two of you will have to put an end to this vicious cycle," Shadow explains.

"That's a lot of pressure," Tac says, rubbing his chin.

"We know, but the two of you are the only two souls in a position to fix it," Tes states.

"So, what now?" he asks.

"Now you go back. You have everything you need to break the cycle," Shadow says.

"Will I see you again?" Tac asks.

"Of course, little one. When the time is right," Tes responds.

Tes and Shadow start to back away from him. Shadow smiles and waves. The light gets brighter and brighter until he has to block his eyes again. When he opens his eyes, he is staring up at a fluorescent light on the ceiling. All of a sudden, he is overwhelmed with pain in his chest. Panic sets in as he can't seem to catch his breath. As he looks down, there are bandages on him. One of them on the right side of his chest and another on the left side of his abdomen.

The oxygen mask is stifling. He removes it but finds it impossible to breathe. He puts it back on and breathes as deeply as he can and tries to sit up.

"No, sir! You keep that mask on, sweetie. It's helpin' you breathe. Do you know where you are?" the nurse asks in a thick accent.

"No," he answers softly, labored by the injuries.

"You're in the Resistance medical ward. You got shot up pretty good. You figured you'd go see the good Lord in surgery, so we had to zap you a few times 'fore you came back 'round. You're lucky she got you in when she did," she states. "Just lay back down and keep that mask on. You're gonna need some time to recoup 'fore you're up and at 'em again."

"Where's Calida?" he asks, grunting and adjusting himself in the bed.

"She just went down the hall to get some coffee. She'll be back soon," the nurse replies. "You need some meds for the pain, honey?"

"Yes, please," he replies.

"Ok, I'll go check with the Medicus and I'll be back in a jiffy," she says.

Tac tries to relax and focuses on his breathing. The television in his room is muted, but shows a reporter at a desk talking about something to do with a so-called failed attempt to overthrow the Empire. The video shown clearly depicts Imperial troops valiantly defending against two terrorist attacks. He recognizes a few of the bodies as some of those that went out on the last patrol.

Calida opens the door and stands in the threshold, "I'm so sorry, Tac."

"What? Did you not get me any coffee?" Tac replies with a smile.

Calida giggles as she walks over to his bed, "Don't ever do that to me again," and hits him in his shoulder.

"Ow! Ok!" he promises, rubbing his arm.

"Did they tell you what happened?" she asks in a more serious tone as she pulls up the chair.

"Just a little bit. Apparently I was shot and died or something. I'm not sure. Her speech is rather odd and hard to follow at times," Tac replies.

"Oh, yeah. Emma Lee grew up east of here, in the backwoods as we call it. She's a sweetheart, but sometimes she has to repeat herself so that others can understand. You'll catch on," she snickers. "Long story short, the Imperial troops we came across were issued armor-piercing ammo. That's why your vest didn't work. The first bullet went into your stomach, slowed by the vest. It caused a lot of internal bleeding. The second one pierced your right lung and collapsed it. Hence the oxygen mask."

"Will I get better?" he asks.

"The Medicus was able to repair most of the damage, but he had to take a small part of your stomach out because it was mangled beyond repair. He says you'll likely fully recover. It's just going to take some time," she admits, her face taking a remorseful shape.

"I saw on the thing up there about Bravo. What happened?" Tac asks.

Calida looks at the ground for a moment before sighing heavily, "It wasn't just Bravo. Charlie was wiped out too. All three villages were ambushes. Traps set by Imperial troops. And I led them straight to their deaths."

Calida stands and turns around as tears fill her eyes.

"That's not your fault. There was no way you could have known," Tac says attempting to comfort her.

"I should have known better," she replies, still facing away.

"You have to forgive yourself for things that are out of your control, Calida," he says as he grabs her hand.

"I don't know," she says, pulling away to wipe her eyes and turning back around. "I've been thinking about leaving the Resistance. I'm just going to get all of these people killed. I almost got you killed and you've only been here for two days!"

"Running away won't help them. They'll be slaughtered without a leader," Tac states.

"Apparently, they'll be slaughtered even with a leader," Calida adds.

"The people have to have a fighting chance though. You give them that. Without you, they wouldn't be able to organize themselves, let alone fight the Empire," Tac says.

"I may not be the best leader there ever was, but I don't see anyone else who could do a better job, unfortunately," she replies.

"Exactly. We can't abandon them now," he states.

"Tac, you're in no position to fight. You're going to be in that bed for weeks. Not to mention, this isn't even your fight," she says.

"Any fight you are in, I am in. But while I recover, you need to heal the Resistance. They need you to be strong for them right now. Speak to them. Remind them why they fight," he responds.

"I don't know how well that will be received. These people have been oppressed and at war all their lives. They're tired of fighting, Tac" she says. "And what you saw on the TV isn't an isolated incident. This happens all the time. I know you're new here, but this is just how life is."

"All the more reason to change it. We need to liberate Sector 81 Prime and give these people something to celebrate," Tac redirects.

"Are you crazy? We can't even liberate the small villages outside of the walls and you want us to literally storm the castle with less than a hundred men and women with inferior weapons and armor?" she says with her eyes wide.

"That's right. Think about what that will do for the Resistance. People all around the region will realize we fight for them. Those that have been too afraid to leave their homes to join the Resistance will have less of an excuse then," he continues.

"But what you're talking about is physically impossible. Sector 81 Prime is guarded by no less than five hundred guards at any given time, not to mention the Praetorians," Calida says.

"I know it sounds impossible. But you have one thing that the Empire doesn't have," he states.

"And what is that?" Calida asks.

"Me," he replies. "I have abilities that no one else here has. I can kill multiple Praetorians at a time. I've done it. Remember how I said I escaped from the detention facility? That's because I killed the six Praetorians that tried to take me prisoner."

"Yeah, well, you're not invincible," she retorts, poking him in the stomach.

"I think I have a way to fix that for next time. But we will need people of like mind to fight alongside us. We can't do this on our own," he says.

"Ok. I'll talk to them. Get some rest. I'll come by later," Calida says, working her way toward the door.

Emma Lee walks in as Calida leaves.

"Ok Tac, this will burn a little, but it will help ease the pain," she says.

Tac relaxes as the medicine takes over. He drifts off to a deep sleep where he dreams of running through the woods back home with his brothers. They are curious as to where he has been living in exile. So, he leads them to the abandoned village. Then he takes them to the cave he found and leads them to the bottom with all of the flashing lights. His brothers try to talk to him, but suddenly, he can't understand what they are saying.

He wakes to find the room and hallway dimly lit. Calida sleeps sitting up in the chair across the room. Tac shifts his weight in the bed and the rustling wakes her.

"Hey, you ok?" she asks.

"Yeah, just rearranging," he responds. "That chair looks painful. Why don't you go home and get some rest?"

"Cause I want to stay here with you," she replies.

He slowly and methodically moves over in the bed, "Well, at least don't sleep in the chair," he says as he motions her over.

She grabs her blanket and shuffles over to the bed. Climbing in, Tac wraps his arms around her, pulling her close.

"Are you warm enough?" he asks after a few moments.

He listens to her heavy, slow breathing and realizes she's already asleep. He pulls her tighter and lays his head down with a smile. He wakes much later to find the lights on and an empty bed. Squinting, he looks around the room, but doesn't see Calida.

A different nurse wakes him a short while later.

"Tac, good afternoon. It's time for your therapy," he says.

He grunts himself awake and slowly slides his legs over the edge of the bed with a yawn. The nurse stands in front of him to brace him.

"Ok, now, very slowly, let's stand up and grab a hold of the walker," he instructs.

Calida calls an assembly of all non-essential personnel in the cafeteria in order to address the failed operations and plan the next steps.

"Good afternoon everyone. As many of you know, the last few days have proven very difficult for us. Several members of the Resistance were killed in action as we attempted to liberate some of the local villages from Imperial rule. Before we could get there, the villages were ransacked and turned into ambushes.

Imperial media blames the destruction of these villages on us. And worse, shows the bodies of our fallen on the news in celebration of their victory. The media is painting us as terrorists," she says as she scans the room. "We're fighting a losing war right now and we have to change directions, or there won't be a Resistance much longer."

Calida closes her eyes and takes a deep breath to calm herself.

"I have begun preparations to invade and secure Sector 81 Prime," she states boldly.

Gasps and whispers echo throughout the room.

"I know what this sounds like, but if we do not address Prime head on, we will eventually all be killed and those who have laid their lives down for us will have died in vain," she explains.

She sees a few nods in her direction and continues.

"We must remember why we fight. We seek a world free from tyrannical rule and persecution. Where lovers can enjoy each other's company without being harassed by the Church. Where every person is afforded equal rights under the government, not just those in power.

If we can liberate 81 Prime, we can show the Empire that we are *not* afraid of them. We will show those who think they have too much to lose that it is okay to fight for what you believe in!

And our victory will offer us a foothold in the larger fight against the Emperor. We will be able to return to our homes. We will have modern medical facilities, clean running water, proper schools for our children, and better ways to defend ourselves.

We must secure Prime. So our children may have a better future than our past," Calida says and walks toward the door.

"Attention on deck!" a voice calls out.

"As you were," she hurriedly states.

She's greeted with awkward stares and obligatory applause. She knows they'll never follow her into the city. She nearly runs out of the cafeteria in disgust.

She keeps the façade going until she reaches her room where she slams the door shut and immediately begins crying. She's at a lost for direction and pleads with God to show her the path. Calida falls asleep with her face in her pillow, tears still streaming.

Calida holds her newborn son in her arms. He's so fragile. As her awareness expands, she looks around the unfamiliar room to see Tac sitting in the dining room talking with their daughter. He looks up and smiles at her. She's not sure why, but she smiles back and begins rocking in the chair.

Calida wakes back in her bed. She lays staring at the ceiling for a while, but cannot shake the dream. She walks down the barren corridor to the medical ward. She passes the nurses and walks into Tac's room, shutting the door behind her. Tac wakes to see her shadowy figure moving across the room. As he scoots over, she climbs under the covers with him. Tears silently fall on his chest as he pulls her in close.

They both fall asleep, but neither dreams. It is just a restful sleep. They are awoken by Emma Lee making her morning rounds.

"Good mornin', Tac! We've got to get them staples out and get you back on your feet," she says, propping the door open. "The Medicus will be by in a few minutes. Good mornin', Miss Calida. How are you, honey?"

"Better. Thank you. How're you?" she asks.

"I'm glad to hear it. I'm doing just fine, miss. Thanks for asking," Emma Lee replies. "Now, I need you to get up outta that bed or the Medicus will have my hide."

They smile at each other as Calida slides out of the bed.

"Tac, I'm going to go get a shower and get us some breakfast. I'll be back shortly," she says.

The nurse continues to check the chart and smiles at Calida as she exits. After a few moments, she closes the door.

"How much do you know about her?" the nurse asks.

"Not much," Tac replies.

"Welp, I've known Calida prolly most of her adult life. I met her right after she ran away from home the first time. She never did say much about where she came from. She just showed up one day at the hospital I was workin' in, umbilical cord in hand. Due to the circumstances, I had to report it to the authorities. She talked with the Inquisitors for a while, but I don't think anythin' came of it.

I saw her from time to time after that, whenever she would get so hungry that she couldn't stand it any longer, she'd come into the hospital complainin' of stomach pains. She was just a bag o' bones by that point. She was starvin' to death. Each time I'd bring her food until she stopped eating and passed out in one of the beds. Next day, she'd be gone again.

One day, after a couple months of not seeing her, she just shows up. This time, not looking like a bag o' bones, but very healthy. That's when she explained that she was leading the Resistance and asked me to come here.

In all my years, I've never seen her take to a man like she's taken to you. I guess what I'm trying to say is be careful with her. Please don't break her heart. I don't know she can take much more disappointment," the nurse explains.

"Wow," he replies after a few moments. "I had no idea."

"Yeah, she's had it pretty rough," she states, patting Tac on the knee. "Just, don't tell her I said nuthin'. She's very touchy about her childhood. I'll go see if the Medicus is ready to remove your staples. I'll be right back, honey."

"Thank you for telling me," he says.

She smiles and leaves the room. A few minutes pass as Tac tries to process the information Emma Lee gave him. He's interrupted by the charismatic Medicus that enters the room.

"Good morning! How's my favorite patient this morning?" he asks.

"Ok, I guess. Eager to get back on my feet," Tac responds.

"Well, I can certainly understand that. How's your breathing today?" he asks as he places the cold stethoscope to Tac's chest.

"Much better. I don't need the mask as much," Tac responds after a sharp breath.

"I agree. It sounds like you're healing up nicely. And much faster than expected," he says, draping the instrument around his neck. "Ok, let's take a look at those wounds and see if the staples are ready to come out. Go ahead and lie back for me and lift up your gown."

His voice gets lost as Tac drifts off in his thoughts about Calida and the newfound information. A sharp pain interrupts him. The Medicus has snipped the first of seven staples in his chest. He grabs the sheets and holds on as the others are cut free.

"Alrighty then! Halfway done!" The Medicus looks up and smiles at Tac.

The pain moves to his abdomen where the remaining 6 staples are removed. Before long, his wounds are being rebandaged and both the nurse and the Medicus have left. Tac examines the wounds and shifts around in the bed to try and get comfortable. The nurse returns shortly with more pain medication.

"You're gonna hafta relax, honey. You ain't gonna get any better bein' all rambunctious," she says as she injects the syringe into his IV.

"I have no idea wha…" Tac says as he drifts off quickly to sleep.

He walks the same dirt road with Alpha. He realizes what is about to happen, but he can't do anything to stop it. He screams and tries to flush the Imperial troops out with rocks from the side of the road. But nothing moves and no one flinches. They just keep slowly marching toward the village. Panic sets in as they get closer. Tac picks up more rocks, anticipating the ambush.

He sits up and throws the mask off. For the first time since the injury, he can fully breathe on his own without it. The freedom invigorates his spirit and he stands through the pain without the assistance of the walker. Dragging his IV stand, he walks out of the room and down the hall.

He sees no signs of Calida and he doesn't recognize the nurse at the station. He continues walking, each step causing pain and strengthening his resolve. Tac notices the guard by the station and turns around before reaching him. He's not really in the mood for conversation.

He shuffles back to his room and falls back on the bed, panting. He's angry at his lack of mobility and the dream. He pictures Calida walking in the room and crawling into bed with him. He puts the mask back on as he lays down to catch his breath.

Tac wakes later to bright lights and voices. He feels rested and no pain. His focus turns from his wounds to the people in the room.

"I've never seen anything like this," the Medicus states, examining Tac's wounds.

"Me neither. That's somethin' special right there," Emma Lee agrees.

Tac removes the mask and sits up, "What are you guys talking about?" he asks.

Emma Lee faints and the Medicus' eyes go wide.

"What? I've been taking the mask off since yesterday. I don't need it to breathe all the time," Tac explains, still confused.

"How…exactly are you talking with your mouth closed?" the Medicus stumbles to ask as he gets closer to Tac's face.

Tac sighs as he pulls away from the Medicus' invasion of space, "Everyone here speaks the same way you do. Where I come from, how I speak is normal. No one speaks with their mouth back home."

The Medicus checks around and in Tac's mouth with his small flashlight, but finds nothing unusual.

"Shouldn't you check on Emma Lee?" Tac asks.

"Hmm? Oh, right!" he says as he remembers she fainted.

The Medicus picks Emma Lee up and puts her into the chair.

"Look, I need to get out of this bed. I have to train. I was completely unprepared for the ambush and it costed too many lives, and nearly my own," Tac explains as the Medicus fans Emma Lee.

"Well, your wounds are completely healed, which is what we were talking about when you woke. So, I can go ahead and get your discharge paperwork done and get you back to the field," he replies, still fanning the nurse's face, "if that's what you want."

"Good. We need to start planning out the liberation of Sector 81 Prime. I need to be ready," Tac states as he slides his legs over the edge of the bed and stands up.

The Medicus spins and meets Tac at the side of the bed, "Are you insane? That place is a fortress."

"I know what it looks like. That's what the Empire wants it to look like. I am much stronger, faster, and more deadly than anyone else in the Resistance," Tac states.

"Right, because that strength and quickness is how you ended up in that bed," he retorts with a sarcastic tone.

"Just get me out of here, please. I know what I'm capable of," Tac replies.

"Fine," the Medicus turns and walks towards the door. He stops for a moment and turns back around, "You know, I've been where you are before. In fact, I ended up in one of these beds on my first mission too. Ever since I was a child, I wanted to fight the Empire. They killed my parents when I was 8. I joined the Resistance when I was just 15. Far too young, but that fire just kept raging. I wanted to punish them for taking what wasn't theirs to take. It nearly killed me too. I was shot twice but managed to hide in a bush until I was rescued by one of our patrols many hours later."

They stare at each other for a few seconds.

"After I recovered, I dedicated my life to the medical field. I knew I wasn't very good at combat, but I still believed in the cause. So, you see, you don't have to fight. There are other ways you can be useful to the Resistance," he says.

"When I was a child, I was bullied constantly. When I reached adulthood, I was part of a brotherhood that fought to protect those weaker than us. So, I've been on both sides of the proverbial fence. If I don't stand up for those weaker than me, who will?"

After a few moments he replies, "I'll be right back with your paperwork."

Emma Lee wakes up and stares at Tac.

"Are you ok?" Tac asks, "I'm sorry. I didn't mean to hurt you."

"Yeah, honey. I'm ok," she says, adjusting herself in the chair, "Just a little taken aback. I wasn't expectin' that."

"Well, the way you speak is just as weird to me as the other way around, if that makes you feel any better." Tac explains.

"Yeah, I'd expect so," she replies with a smile as she slowly stands, "I'm going to go get your clothes from the nurse's station. I'll be back in a moment."

A short while later, Tac knocks lightly on Calida's door.

"Cali, are you in there?" he asks.

There is a rustling on the other side of the door and after a few moments, it opens. Calida stands in the doorway, evidence of the tears fallen strikes Tac.

"What's wrong?" he asks as she turns her back and walks back to the bed.

Calida crawls back into bed as Tac shuts the door, removing the rest of the light from the room. Feeling his way around, he slides into bed next to her and rolls her to face his chest and wraps his arms around her. The tears immediately begin to fall again as she silently sobs into his shirt. He can feel her heart break and pulls her closer.

He wakes later and groggily looks at the clock. Ugh, 4:00 a.m. Calida isn't there, but he's pretty sure he knows where she is. As he approaches the gym, he hears punches landing and loud grunting. He stands in the doorway watching her for a few minutes. He knows she doesn't need anything from him right now, but he wants to check on her anyway.

Tac props himself up against a nearby machine as Calida throws punch after punch into the bag. Sweaty and exhausted, she finally drops her hands, panting to catch her breath. What started as a way to vent her frustration has succeeded only in making her emotions stronger. She's visibly frustrated but too tired to throw another punch. She's thankful at least the tears are indistinguishable from the sweat at this point.

After a minute or two, she finally makes eye contact with Tac, who waits patiently for her to finish. This only makes her more emotional and she looks away. She wants to fight something, anything, to take the focus off her emotions. He can tell how frustrated she is with herself and walks over to embrace her. She relaxes into his arms again and closes her eyes as the tears form again.

"I don't know what to do, Tac," she says nasally.

He kisses her forehead and replies, "It's ok. We'll figure it out together."

She wraps her arms around his back, gripping as best she can with the heavy gloves still on.

"Ever seen a girl cry while punching a bag?" she asks with a chuckle.

"I can't say that I have," he replies as she looks up into his eyes.

Their smiles slowly dissipate as the moment becomes intimate. Tac leans down and gently kisses her on the lips as both close their eyes. Calida's heart skips a beat and electricity spreads throughout her body. Tac feels more connected to her than before. Something has changed in this moment.

"I think I'm going to go get cleaned up and get some breakfast. Would you like to join me?" she asks.

"That sounds good," he replies with a smile.

She grins ear to ear and heads out the door, still removing her gloves.

CHAPTER VIII: LOYALTY

"Good news, my lord," Quaestor Gallius says while shutting the door behind her to the Governor's office.

Axius doesn't respond but just sits in his office chair, staring out the window at the night sky. Gallius pauses at the doorway for a moment, before walking up to his desk. She places the report on top of the stack of other papers in front of her.

"My lord?" she inquires softly.

The chair slowly spins around. Axius' face shows signs of age in the reflection of the single desk lamp. He stares at her for a few moments, making her uncomfortable.

"Ahh, my dear Cecilia. Have I told you how beautiful you are today?" he finally asks.

Abashedly, she drops her head and looks away, "Yes, my lord. Only every time you see me."

"Well, for such beauty, I feel I must repeat myself," he says as his eyes slowly drift down her body.

"Now, what 'good news' do you bring me?" Axius asks after a few seconds.

"We've raised taxes another 15 percent this month without major incident," she responds, still looking down at the ornate rug, letting the intricate deep blue and gold patterns distract her.

"Excellent, my dear!" he exclaims, rising from his chair. "But you know my old ears don't work so well. I need to see your face."

Gallius swallows the lump in her throat and after a brief pause, raises her eyes to meet with his hollow, evil eyes.

"Also, we've killed 18 terrorists in the last week. But the best part is, we were able to use the media to make it look like they had destroyed a few of the local villages and we came to the rescue," Gallius adds.

"Wow, I'm truly impressed!" he replies, walking around the desk to her side.

He grabs her shoulders and spins her to face him.

"I believe that deserves a bonus for you, my dear," he says as he unfastens his belt.

"Are you hearing this shit?" Bruttius says with a disgusted tone.

"Of course. I know you're new here and all, but don't get it twisted that morals apply to people like him," Lurius replies.

"It's just, she's half his age and he's just taking advantage of her because of who he is," Bruttius explains further.

"Dude, I get it. It's fucked up, no doubt. But that's how things go around here when you're the Governor. Everyone wants to please you. You'll get the hang of it," Lurius clarifies.

"I guess we got the shit-end of the stick. We're out here in this heavy ass gear standing guard for a dude that's getting off to a woman that could be his daughter," Bruttius groans.

"Could be worse. I've seen people executed for less. Our own guys too," Lurius says, shifting his weight.

"What? How?" Bruttius inquires, turning his head to look at Lurius.

"A couple of years ago, the Quaester in there was in love with a lawyer, about your age. But the Governor had his sights on Gallius and refused to let it go. She wasn't Quaester then, just a young girl. Turns out, her boy got mugged one day going home from a client's house. And when I say mugged, I mean he was shot in the back of the head," Lurius explains.

"Now *that's* fucked up," Bruttius replies.

"Yep, but he's the Governor. He can do whatever he wants so long as Rome gets their money," Lurius agrees.

"Wow, what the *fuck* did I sign up for?" Bruttius ponders out loud.

Lurius chuckles, "All that training in the Praetorians and this is what you end up as, huh? Yeah, we've all come to that realization. The best way to deal with it is to just look the other way. What the Governor says or does is none of our business. Our job is to protect him. That's it. Let karma sort it out."

"Yeah, cause karma's a real thing. The only thing karma…"

Lurius interrupts Bruttius, "Oh shit, someone tipped off the Lieutenant."

Both stand at attention as Lieutenant Vettius approaches.

"Is that little whore in there?!" she exclaims as she gets to the door and bursts through, catching Gallius bent over the Governor's desk.

"For fuck's sake, Tiberius! What is your malfunction?!" she yells, leaving the door wide open.

"Shut the door! Shut the fucking door!" Lurius yells under his breath to Bruttius.

He grabs the handle and quickly, but quietly shuts the door behind the Lieutenant. Lots of yelling and things breaking are heard in the moments afterward.

"What the hell is going on around here?" Bruttius inquires.

"Welcome to the Praetorian Guard," Lurius replies with a low laugh.

"This is like a bad tv show. How the hell did the Lieutenant know? And what does she have to do with any of this?" Bruttius asks further.

"Dude, this is one big dramafest up in here. Everyone is sleeping with everyone else. Vettius used to be the Quaester before Gallius, but she was demoted. So, Vettius has been in Gallius' position before, both literally and figuratively. We think she's a bit jealous. See, it's like being in a room full of wolves.

Just let them do their thing, don't make any sudden movements, and you might just get out with your nuts intact," Lurius explains with a chuckle.

The door opens and a messily dressed Quaester walks out. The two Praetorian Guards say nothing to her as she closes the door behind her and walks away. Yelling and screaming resume behind the door.

"Well, just tell me it's not like this *every* day," Bruttius says.

"Not *every* day, but a lot of the time," Lurius replies, cutting his eyes.

The door suddenly opens from the other side and a visibly upset Vettius emerges, screaming and hollering as she exits.

"She's a *child*, Tiberius! And you know damn well why she agrees to it! Try thinking with your slightly smarter head!" she shouts as she slams the door.

Turning to Lurius, she shouts, "Quaester Gallius is to be escorted by at least one of your guys whenever she is in there. And the door stays open!"

"Yes, ma'am!" he replies, standing at attention and saluting.

After Vettius storms off, Bruttius asks, "Can she actually do that? I thought we reported directly to the Governor."

"Ha! No, as a measure of separation of powers, we report to Lt. Vettius. She's in charge of all Law Enforcement in the sector," Lurius replies. "And that includes guard duty."

The tires on Vettius' cruiser screech as she comes to a halt in front of headquarters. She exits, slamming the door. Praetorians scramble to get out of her way as she ascends the wide marble stairs leading to the front door.

Sounds of telephones ringing, papers being printed, and conversations pierce her ears as the familiarity of the mundane redirects her focus. Praetorians and criminals alike dodge her as she makes for the staircase leading to the offices.

Finally engulfed in the sanctity of her office, she unfastens and removes her heavy armor and lets it fall to the floor. She loosens her tie and walks around her desk, opening the bottom drawer and retrieving a half-full bottle of 6 year-old scotch and a glass.

She downs a half of a glass immediately and starts pouring another when there is a light knock on her door.

"Come in!" Vettius barks.

A slender man enters the dimly lit office, shutting the door behind him.

"Sergeant, what can I do for you?" she asks before he can get to her desk.

"Ma'am, just a sit rep on our mystery guy," Pontius explains as he walks towards her.

Vettius downs another glass and says, "You're going to have to be more specific, Pontius."

"Sorry, ma'am. The mystery man who killed six Praetorians outside of the detention facility and possibly two more in the sewers," he elaborates, now standing in front of her desk.

He sets the report down in front of her along with pictures from a security camera. She sets the glass down briefly to examine the photographs.

After carefully examining each photo, she asks, "So, why haven't we picked this guy up?"

"He seems to have disappeared into the sewers with this woman," Pontius replies, setting down another set of photographs showing Tac following Calida into the sewer entrance.

"This is why we think he's responsible for the other two murders as well," he elaborates.

"Ok, well, this guy is now public enemy number one. I can't have a man running loose for murder of multiple Praetorians. Pin these two pictures to the board," Vettius orders as she hands him two selected photos, one of Tac and one of Calida.

"Yes, ma'am. Also, one of the Inquisitors from the detention facility has more information on him. I've asked him to come in for questioning," Pontius adds.

"Very well. Schedule it for tomorrow. I think I'm going to wrap up here and head home," Vettius orders.

"Yes, ma'am," he replies as he makes his way for the door.

Vettius swishes her glass of cheap scotch around on the desk as she reads through the report. After a few pages, she sighs and closes the file, stacking it on top of the massive mound in her inbox.

She shoots the last bit of scotch and puts the empty glass back in the drawer. With a heavy sigh, she stands and fixes her tie, grabs a handful of files from her desk and makes towards the door. The scotch finally kicks in halfway down the stairs and she almost giggles at herself as she has to grab on to the railing to steady her balance.

The three-minute drive to her house is an uneventful one. Even with vehicles being restricted to government employees only, the traffic on this Friday night is almost non-existent. When she gets home, her husband is waiting for her at the door.

"Hiya, honey," he says as she walks in the door.

"Hey, what's the occasion?" she asks as he clinks two glasses in one hand and an expensive bottle of scotch in the other.

"Oh, this old thing?" he replies looking at the bottle, "No reason. Just got that promotion at work and I thought we could celebrate."

"You got anything else to go with that?" she asks, smirking at him.

He sets the scotch down on the console table and pulls a small sack of white powder from his jacket pocket.

"Oh, you know me so well. Wanna have some fun?" he devilishly inquires.

"I thought you'd never ask. I need to change clothes though. Give me five minutes," she demands.

"I'll be waiting," he confirms.

Sabina Vettius wakes up naked at the foot of the bed to the sun beaming in the poorly closed curtains in their master bedroom. Her husband snores loudly. The combination of sound and light irritate her immediately. She slides slowly off the bed, grabbing a pair of sweatpants and a t-shirt on her way to the bathroom.

She locks the door behind her and turns the shower on, taking account of last night's damage in the mirror. Memories of her erotic, drug-induced night start to come back as she uses the toilet. She rubs the bridge of her nose as she finishes and gets into the hot shower.

As she applies the pomegranate-scented body wash, there's a knock at the door.

"Honey?! You okay in there?!" her husband asks loudly.

"Yeah! Just taking a shower!" she replies quickly.

"Ok! I'm going to get the coffee started and make breakfast!" he announces.

"Ok, I'll be out in a few!" she shouts over the running water.

She steps fully into the hot stream and lets the water run all over her body, washing away any insecurities along with the remainder of the body wash. Her mind starts to drift back to work as she lathers up the floral-scented shampoo. This mystery man intrigues her. There's not much information on how he was able to kill six Praetorians at the same time, much less how he's been able to avoid detection and capture.

She ponders multiple ideas on how he achieved this, from martial arts master to advanced weaponry. As her thoughts subside, she finds herself washing the last of the conditioner from her hair. Finally, she sighs and turns off the water. She lets the water drip from her for a few moments before she exits and wraps a towel around her.

After pulling on her clothes, she walks back to find her phone has two missed calls. She picks up the phone and calls Pontius back.

"Good morning boss. Sorry for the early call, but Inquisitor Titus is waiting in your office," he informs her.

"Shit, ok. I forgot he was coming in today. I'll be there shortly," she replies, closing the phone.

She grunts loudly in frustration, strips her comfy house clothes off, and throws on a fresh uniform. She barely has time to throw her wet hair into a bun. She'll have to do her make up in the car.

Walking by the kitchen, she says grabbing her cup of coffee, "Sorry honey, work just called. I have to go in."

"Oh, okay," he hesitantly replies, "Any idea when you'll be home?"

"I'm not sure, but I'll call you later," she replies as she shuts the front door behind her.

The short commute was filled with the same questions she asked herself in the shower. No answers revealed themselves though. The situation truly puzzles her. Praetorians were far better trained and equipped than any resistance force currently known. They should have been able to subdue him without incident.

She drags herself up the stairs to her office, only hurried by the remnant of her hangover coupled with the loud ringing of phones and voices. Once inside her office, she sighs heavily, removing her sunglasses and turning to her desk.

"Good morning, Lieutenant," Titus says, turning from the sun-filled window behind Vettius' desk.

"Good morning, Inquisitor. I apologize for my tardiness. I completely forgot I asked you to come in today," she replies, shielding her eyes with her hand.

"No consequence, ma'am," Titus retorts and closes the blinds.

"Thank you," Vettius says.

Silence resumes as they both take their respective positions at her desk. Vettius pulls the top drawer open and retrieves her bottle of aspirin.

"Ok. So, this mystery man that we've been seeing on footage. Who is he?" she asks, dumping two pills into her hand.

"Well, firstly, he told us his name is Tac. Just Tac. No last name. He had no papers with him and refused to give us any other viable information. I've prepared a preliminary report on the investigation so you can reference the data," he says, setting the report in front of her. "The most notable qualities about him are that he is telepathic and telekinetic. I had to look those terms up, so I hope I'm pronouncing them correctly."

Vettius takes a sip of water and throws her head back, washing the aspirin down and resumes her unamused look.

"At least eight good men and women were killed by this terrorist so far. I certainly hope that our crack Inquisitors have more information on him besides his first name and a couple of medical terms," Vettius realigns the conversation.

"The majority of the interview was spent listening to his elaborate story about his home...wait. You said eight Praetorians," he says astounded.

"That's correct, Inquisitor. Six outside of your detention facility and at least two more in the sewer, which is where we think he's hiding," Vettius confirms.

Titus clears his throat and says, "and I'm assuming you want to know how he did it?"

"Of course I do. But more importantly, I want to stop him. Praetorians have the best weapons, gear, and training in the world. For a single person to dispatch a Praetorian is an oddity and worthy of an investigation. For a single person, who should have been in handcuffs if you hadn't let him escape, to kill eight Praetorians in at least two separate engagements is not an oddity, it's a threat. The survival of the Empire depends on our ability to keep the peace and enforce the law. With someone like this running around with superpowers, that puts all of us in jeopardy," she states sitting back in her desk chair.

"Yes, ma'am," he replies.

"Now, why wasn't this information in your report?" she inquires.

"I recounted the entire interview process through the point where he escaped. I felt I had already explained his abilities thoroughly enough without stating the obvious," Titus replies.

"Ok, fine. Let's talk about where you found him," she directs.

"One of our patrols found him passed out next to a tree near a village suspected of inciting terrorism. After the cleansing, they found him and brought him in for questioning," he replies.

"And you witnessed his escape, yes?" Vettius inquires, finally looking up from the report and stares at him.

"Yes, ma'am. Both Catullus and I were present," he confirms.

"And yet you failed to even attempt to apprehend him," she states, looking back at the report.

"Failed is a harsh word. The man can literally snap my neck from ten yards away before I could draw my weapon. What exactly was I supposed to do?" Titus responds colorfully, visibly frustrated with the turn in the line of questioning.

"You were supposed to do your job and stop a terrorist from escaping custody, or die trying," Vettius replies.

Titus stands and states, "Well, I look forward to when you catch up to him. I'm sure you'll lead by great example. I'll be sure to speak at your funeral."

Titus storms towards the office door.

"We're not done here, Titus," Vettius states loudly.

"Since *our* goal here is to, apparently, implicate me for failing to prevent a fucking supervillain from escaping custody and you've already decided to pin it on me, you don't really need me here in order to do that. Do what you will, ma'am. I'm going home. I'm missing my 12 year-old's birthday party for this shit. And quite honestly, he's more important than this conversation. Have a nice day, Lieutenant," Titus says as he opens the door and closes it behind him.

Vettius sits back in her chair and scoffs at his audacity. Today was not the day.

Pressing a button on her desk phone, she says, "Sergeant, apprehend Inquisitor Titus and place him in one of the cells until he can cool off."

She hears a scuffle downstairs and plenty of yelling on top of it. But she doesn't care. No one disrespects her in her own office. She pulls the bottle of scotch from her drawer and drains the last of it into the dirty glass. She gulps it down and tosses the bottle, returning the glass to the drawer.

Walking downstairs to the jail, she sees Titus in one of the solitary cells. Her eyes lock with his far angrier pair. After a few tense moments, he calmly stands and walks to the bars.

"Listen, I may have overreacted a few minutes ago, but I don't appreciate being implicated for something that was obviously out of my control," he states quietly.

"It's not just for that. You obviously need a lesson in manners on how to speak to a superior officer," Vettius replies.

"A superior officer who turns her back on someone with over twenty years of service because of one incident? That's not very superior of you," Titus scoffs.

"Well, if you can't be convinced with reasoning, maybe you can take a look at who is on which side of the bars and determine on your own who is superior," Vettius replies as she turns to walk out.

"This isn't over, Vettius! I'm calling the Governor!" he shouts at her back.

"No phone calls for him," Vettius tells the guard.

"Yes, ma'am," he replies.

"You can't do that! I have my rights!" Titus yells.

"Titus, if you don't shut up, I will fucking bury you," she retorts as she leaves the jail.

"The fucking nerve of that bastard," she says to herself as she descends the stairs to her car.

Vettius floors the accelerator on her way home to bleed off the anger, but it's not enough. She tunes the radio until she finds a hard rock song and jams out. The blaring music and screeching tires alerts her husband to her return.

"Oh, shit! My wife is home! You've got to go, now!" he exclaims to his girlfriend.

"I thought you said she was going to be at work all day!" she replies.

"She usually is when she gets called in! I don't know why she's home. But it doesn't matter. You've got to go for both our sakes," he explains.

But it's too late. Sabina walks in the front door and slams it behind her.

"Honey, I'm home!" she shouts, setting her purse and keys on the table.

He doesn't respond immediately, so she stops moving and hears multiple footsteps upstairs. Her instincts kick in and she draws her service weapon, moving for the stairs. She creeps up the stairs, weapon drawn, as the frantic footsteps continue.

Sabina kicks in her bedroom door to find her husband laying in the bed "asleep". One whiff of the air is all it takes for her to figure out what's going on.

Rage envelopes her as sounds of heavy breathing permeate the room. She quietly walks over to the foot of the bed and stares at her so-called husband. She watches him breathe and knows his breaths per minute are too high for him to be asleep.

"BASTARD!" she screams at the top of her lungs.

He nearly jumps out of his skin.

"Jesus, babe. What are you doing?" he asks innocently.

"The question is what are *you* doing, *babe*?" she replies.

"I was sleeping, obviously," he replies with a disgusted look.

Sabina points her pistol at his face and says, "Tell me the truth."

"Whoa! That's not funny! What are you doing?!" he yells, backing up toward the headboard.

"Where is she?!" she exclaims, "And don't lie to me again."

A few seconds pass before a look of defeat comes across his face.

"She's in the closet," he quietly says.

"Come on out, you little bitch!" she yells towards the closet.

She can hear quiet crying from inside the closet.

"DON'T MAKE ME COME IN THERE!" she screams.

Slowly the closet door opens, revealing a half-naked young woman, easily half Sabina's age.

"Come on out," she ushers with her pistol.

She slowly shuffles over to the side of the bed.

"Now, what exactly were the two of you doing?" Sabina asks.

Neither of them answers as her sniffling pierces the tension of the otherwise quiet room.

"Stop crying and tell me what you were doing with my husband," she says.

The girl mumbles something under her breath and continues sniffling.

Sabina walks over to her and slaps her hard in the face, knocking her to the ground, "I said quit crying and tell me what the fuck you were doing with my husband!" she yells.

"Babe, please. It's not her fault. Be mad at me. Just let her go," he says crawling to the side of the bed.

"Shut up, you little slut," she says pointing the weapon back in his direction.

She walks over to the girl laying on the ground and grabs her by the hair, picking her off the plush carpet.

"Well, since neither of you will tell me, I guess you'll have to show me," she says, throwing her head towards the bed.

"I'm not doing that," he says in a deeper tone.

"You either show me what you were doing or I'm going to blow her fucking brains out," she says, staring a hole in him.

He stares back at her for a second, trying to call her bluff, before Sabina cocks the pistol.

"I'm not fucking around. Either you show me what you two whores were doing or she will die. Right here and right now," she says pointing the pistol at the back of her head.

"Fine, you fucking crazy bitch. If that's what you want," he says.

"And I'm going to sit on my side of the bed and watch," Sabina says, propping herself up against the headboard.

The girl removes her jeans, assuming her position on the bed, still crying.

"Dry it up, little girl. He's not even that big," she says motioning with the pistol at her husband to assume his position.

Sabina watches them get back into position and pulls the trigger. He stops and stares as her body collapses on the bed, blood everywhere. His sharp breathing fades in as their ears slowly stop ringing.

Sabina recognizes he's in shock and waits for him to come to. About five minutes pass before he shows signs of normal brain function again. He just stares at Sabina with wonder and confusion.

"You're only allowed to sleep with me. Do you understand?" she finally inquires.

A few moments pass before he nods, sinks back, and sits on the bed.

"Good. Now take out the fucking trash and clean the rest of this mess up," Sabina says as she uses her service weapon's voice recognition feature to disable it and sets it on the nightstand. She sets her badge and watch next to it and begins undressing.

"I'm going to take a hot shower. When I get out, that whore better be in the trash out front and there better be new sheets on the bed," she says over her shoulder, trailing clothes behind her as she takes them off headed for the bathroom.

CHAPTER IX: FUTILITY

Calida and Tac are startled awake by a large explosion nearby followed by short bursts of automatic fire.

"Oh, shit!" Calida yells as she jumps out of bed and picks up her rifle from across the room.

Tac follows her to the door and she slowly cracks it open, peering down the hallway. Tac straps on his plate carrier as Calida follows suit.

"Move. I have to go help them," Tac says.

"I'll cover you," she replies.

They move slowly down the hallway when a Praetorian turns the corner, weapon at the ready. Before he can fire, Tac snatches the weapon from him and breaks his neck. Two more Praetorians follow him only to suffer similar fates.

"Ok, maybe I'll just watch," she says under her breath as she stares at the bodies on the ground.

Bursts of automatic fire ring out throughout the small complex as Tac and Calida continue down the smoke-filled narrow corridor. Tac checks the entry way. The mangled front door is blown off its hinges and small fires litter the room.

"Barius!" Tac yells.

There's no response. He'll have to deal with the remaining Praetorians first. He grimaces, his rage forcing its way back to the forefront of his consciousness. Tac turns to move down the rest of the corridor to medical. The two of them clear each room on the way, killing Praetorian after Praetorian with ease.

Calida hears footsteps behind them and spins around to find a Praetorian lining up a shot on them. She squeezes the trigger and cuts him down where he stands. Tac snaps his neck for good measure. They continue past the cafeteria.

It's too quiet at the entrance to medical. They quietly creep in, taking account of the damage. Another Praetorian waited for them behind the nurse's station. He emerges with his weapon pointed at Calida as Tac snatches it away from him and hits him in the face with it. His limp body falls to the floor in an awkward position. Calida walks over and kicks him over, removing everything from his pockets and vest.

Sergeant Pontius wakes to a very bright light in his face. He tries to block the light with his hands, but he's tied to a chair. Calida checks the Medicus for a pulse, but she already knows he's gone. Tac sees his nurse face down in a pool of blood on the other side of the bed.

"Who ordered the raid?" Calida asks Pontius from across the room.

"Decius Pontius, Sergeant. Praetorian. Serial eight-six-one…" he replies as Calida strikes him in the face with the butt of her rifle.

"That's not what I asked! Who ordered you to raid us?!" she repeats.

"Decius Pontius, Ser…" another swift crack rings out as Calida strikes him again in the face, breaking his nose.

Blood gushes down the front of his uniform into his lap as he struggles to shrug off the blow.

"Decius…Pontius…Sergeant" he sputters through the blood.

Tac stands and turns toward him, snapping his left ankle. Pontius screams in agony, but begins to recite his name and rank again. Tac breaks his right ankle. Pontius screams again in agony.

"Okay, OKAY!" he screams, spitting blood everywhere, "Just stop, please!"

"Tell us what we want to know," Tac says, putting slight pressure on Pontius' left knee.

"Okay. Lieutenant Sabina Vettius ordered the raid. I'm her second in command," he states, spitting a large glob of blood on the floor in disgust.

"Vettius," Calida whispers.

"Do you know him?" Tac asks.

"Her. I used to. She was like a big sister to me growing up. Then she got involved with the Empire after…" she states then drifts off.

"After what?" Tac inquires.

"After her father killed her mother," Pontius chimes in.

Tac looks at him with a slightly puzzled look.

"So, you really have no idea who she is, do you?" he asks and chuckles with blood-stained teeth. "Calida is the Governor's only child."

"Used to be. He's dead to me now. As I should be to him," she replies.

"Well, the nurse told me about when you ran away from home, but I don't think even she knew where you ran away from," Tac says.

"That was a very rough time for me," she replies in a defensive tone.

"Okay, but the fact that your father is the Governor is a rather important detail," he replies, visibly frustrated.

"It's not something I think about a lot," she lies.

"So, you see. Your Resistance is doomed. Your leader is blood to your very enemy. The Emperor himself will end you!" Pontius yells before a swift crack of his neck ends his life.

Tac spins Calida towards him and stares in her teary eyes. Her expression of years of pain and torture at the hand of her father melts his anger and he pulls her in to hold her. She finally lets go of her emotions and the rifle as it falls to the floor. She silently weeps in his arms, grasping around his waist.

After a few moments, Tac kisses her on the forehead. "We can't stay here any longer. We need to backtrack to the front door, grabbing supplies and survivors, if there are any," he states.

She nods in agreement, wiping her eyes. She picks her rifle back up, stabilizes her emotions with a heavy exhale, and turns to follow Tac. They check each room on the way and find three survivors. Two were hiding in the back of the cafeteria and one in the barracks. They all gear up with what they can find and follow to the front door.

The fires still litter the floor. Barius' burnt and shrapnel-riddled corpse is leaned against the far wall from the explosion. He never knew what hit them. Tac peeks out the doorway. To his surprise, it's empty. In fact, the whole sewer is empty. He fully expected to have to fight their way out, but it seems the entire force came into the base.

As they exit the sewer in the early morning hours, the rest of the world seemed completely oblivious to the massacre endured at the hands of the Praetorians. Birds wake in their roost as the five survivors pass underneath. If they were being chased, this would have been a bad route. But they're not. This time.

The further they go from Sector 81 Prime, the more Tac feels at home. The trees, flowers, grass, and birds are all slightly different than what he remembers of home, but it's close enough for him.

"Why don't we just live out here?" Tac finally inquires. "It's actually really nice."

"Because Sector 81 owns everything out here as well. They send patrols out constantly. That's why we hid in the sewer. No one bothered us down there," Calida replies. "Well, they didn't used to."

Calida secretly blamed herself for bringing Tac into the base. She doesn't typically do that unless they are sure the person is completely loyal to the Resistance. And even then, those that do come and go are very careful to not lead anyone to the base's location. It's hard to trust people in this situation. But she also blamed Tac for the events leading to the raid. She knew it was unavoidable, but if he hadn't shown up, most of the Resistance would probably still be alive today. Even if he is the best chance they have of winning, she feels like she's losing the war with each passing day. As they continue to walk, sounds of a vehicle on a nearby road break the monotonous march.

"Everyone get down!" Calida yells.

Laying in the tall grass, the sound of a single vehicle gets louder and louder. Suddenly, the engine roars to a stop as multiple doors open and close.

Turning to Tac, Calida states, "I think they're using GPS to track us."

"What's GPS?" Tac asks.

"Long story short, they can see us from the sky," she replies. "If we get through this, we need to stay hidden under trees from now on."

They dare not raise their heads to find out where they are, but sounds of footsteps and radio traffic get louder and louder.

"Calida! Are you guys out here?" one of them yells. "We're friendlies."

Calida peeks slowly from behind the grass to see two men standing at the edge of the field, weapons in hand.

"There are two Praetorians. We need to find out what these guys know. Tac, can you take their weapons?" Calida asks.

Tac peeks up quickly and back down.

"Not from here. They're too far," he replies.

"Shit. Ok," she says, quickly trying to come up with a plan. "What if we give away our position? They'd likely walk towards us, bringing them in range."

"Or they may just open fire on us," one of the survivors says.

Calida ponders for a moment before looking at Tac.

"If they can get a little closer, I can take their weapons and radios from them," Tac explains.

"Ok, if they become hostile for any reason, everyone backtrack the way we came to the tree line," she says, pointing at the thick cover.

Everyone nods and agrees.

"Hey! I'm over here!" Calida yells while standing up.

The two men see Calida and begin crossing the tall grass, weapons at the low ready.

"Calida! Thank God you're safe," one of the men says.

"Yeah, we heard about the raid and thought the worst," the other confirms.

"Yes, we're safe. Some of us anyway," she replies. "They killed most of my people."

"The whole precinct is on high alert after they realized some of you escaped. That and how they found Pontius. That kind of made them angry," the first man replies.

In a whirlwind, their weapons and radios are pulled away from them as they're knocked to the ground. Calida steps over one of them, pointing her rifle at his head as Tac holds their own weapons against them from the air.

"What in God's name was that for?" the other man asks. "We said we were friendlies!"

"Oh, that's a friend of mine. He's really good at killing Praetorians. Very likely the only reason any of us escaped this morning," she elaborates. "Men, meet Tac. Tac, meet two men about to meet Jesus."

"Whoa, whoa. Now, just hang on a second. We're not here to harm you," says the first guy with outstretched palms.

"Says two Praetorians carrying weapons chasing the last remnants of the Resistance in Sector 81!" she shouts, shoving the end of her barrel in his face.

"Calida, please. Give us a chance to explain. I know we haven't seen each other in a long time, but I swear on my mother's life, we come to you as friends," says Lurius, raising his visor.

Thinking she does sort of recognize him, Calida says, "You've got fifteen seconds."

"We went to primary school together. Back before, well, when your mother was alive. You didn't really speak to me then. I was the shy kid in class. But you always had this pink and purple polka-dotted pencil that you would write with every day," Lurius recollects.

"Lots of people have pencils like that. Five seconds," she strongly iterates.

"Okay, okay! I 'accidentally' kissed you on the cheek at the school dance. You went with the popular kid, I had a huge crush, it was a whole thing," he confesses.

Calida slowly lowers her weapon and asks, "That was *you*?!"

"Yeah, I'm not super proud of it either, ok? But I was infatuated with you and there was no swaying me," he continues.

"And if it makes you feel any better, we're not Praetorians," Bruttius chimes in.

"If you're not Praetorians, why are you wearing their uniforms?" Tac asks.

"Heh, he really does speak with his mouth shut," Bruttius chuckles.

Their firearms move closer to Bruttius as he resumes being serious.

"We're actually Praetorian Guard. Assigned to protect the Governor. We 'borrowed' these uniforms from supply and the weapons, gear, and vehicle from the armory," he explains.

"For what reason?" Calida asks.

"To find you," Lurius answers.

The sounds of the two Praetorian rifles being locked and loaded reinforce the seriousness of the situation.

"Anything else?" Tac asks, moving their rifles closer to them.

A few tense moments pass before Lurius chimes in again, "Look, I was your informant. Your mole on the Imperial side. I used a dead drop in one of the pipes in the sewer to pass along any information I could get my hands on. It seems, though, the information wasn't always accurate."

"Yeah, a lot of good men and women have died because of that information," Calida declares with anger, "But, we were able to do some good things because of it too."

"Either shoot us, or let us join you. I don't even care at this point. I just want to get this rock out of my back," Bruttius interjects.

Calida stands silently for a few moments as the debates internally.

"Get up. Tac, give them their weapons back," she orders, walking toward the vehicle. "But if you betray us, we will tear you to shreds."

"Understood," Bruttius states, stretching and rubbing his back.

Tac gives them their weapons back, crushes the radios, and starts after Calida.

Turning to Lurius, Bruttius says, "Well, she's a feisty one. I like her."

"Yeah, well, she's not the leader just because she's pretty," he retorts with a chuckle.

As they approach the vehicle, crackling and muffled voices come from the radio inside. Calida gets in the driver seat and Lurius climbs in the passenger seat. Tac and Bruttius ride in the back seat, with the remainder of the survivors in the back of the cab.

"So, where were you headed? There's nothing out here," Lurius asks.

"Honestly, I led us this way because there *is* nothing out here. Our base was compromised, most of my people killed, and the villages have proven to be even more dangerous, both for us and the villagers," she replies as she pulls the vehicle back on the road.

"How far do you plan to go?" Bruttius asks.

"Just far enough where we can be safe. The Resistance is done for the moment. We don't have the numbers or resources to fight. So, I figured we'd take who we could and get somewhere safer to live, at least until I figure out something else," Calida explains.

"Well, I've already disabled the GPS on the vehicle, so no one is following us," Lurius states.

"So, if you guys are Praetorian Guard, or were, what are you doing here? With us?" Calida inquires.

"Well, I was actually new to the Guard," Bruttius explains enthusiastically as he leans forward on the back of the seats, "I spent ten years as a Praetorian before that. But I got bored with it. So, an open position was posted with the Guard and I applied. You know, it's actually kind of funny. I wanted to be in the Praetorian Guard when I was a child, you know, propaganda and shit. But, as it turns out, it's nothing like what they say it is.

Standing guard outside of the Governor's office in full gear all day is not my idea of fun. Plus, I hate politics. Axius is a creep."

"Bruttius," Lurius interrupts, "you do realize this is his daughter, right?"

"Oh, shit. I'm sorry. I didn't mean to offend," he apologizes.

"No, it's ok. Creep is a compliment for him. He's far worse in reality," she informs.

"Really? What have you heard?" Bruttius says, intrigued with the possibility of gossip.

"My knowledge doesn't come from other people. This is first-hand information and I don't really want to discuss it," she cuts him off.

"Oh, okay. Sorry," he says, sitting back in his seat.

Everyone stares out the window at the passing trees and foliage. As the sun starts to set, Calida pulls the vehicle off the road and in between some heavy brush to help camouflage it.

"Ok, this should do for the night, at least," she says.

Bruttius wakes up in the back seat, "Are we there yet?"

"Yeah, for tonight, anyway," Tac confirms.

"Ok. I got a good nap in on the way up here, so I can take first shift," Bruttius offers.

"Ok, but we need to work on food and shelter first," she replies, scanning the area for a good place to set up for the night.

"We've got that covered," Lurius explains as he walks to the back of the vehicle and pulls two large containers from the back.

"What's that?" Tac inquires.

"Supplies. Food, emergency water, first aid kits, a few tents, etcetera," Bruttius explains.

"We didn't want us to starve to death and we didn't expect you had much time to think about provisions as you were running for your lives," Lurius comments further.

"That's excellent thinking, gentlemen. Thank you," Calida says, shaking their hands.

"We're glad to help, ma'am," Bruttius smiles.

Tac looks at the picture-based instructions briefly as metal poles and fabric take flight around them, seemingly assembling itself in mid-air.

"That just fucking blows my mind," Bruttius states. "I mean, I know he can do it, but my mind just doesn't want to believe what I'm seeing."

Lurius stares at a few pieces as they fly by, "Yeah, I'm with you on that one."

"Either of you good at starting a fire? I can do it, but I'm not very good at it," Tac asks.

"Sure, we've got some fire starter," Bruttius explains, pulling the small brick from one of the kits.

"Good deal. I'll see about getting some firewood if you guys want to get the food ready to cook," Tac suggests.

"Sounds like a plan to me," Lurius replies.

Calida slowly paces back and forth in the clearing. Tac walks up to her and kisses her forehead, "It's going to be ok. Just relax tonight. We can figure everything out tomorrow."

She smiles back at him and giggles, "That's not how it works, but I appreciate the sentiment."

Tac smiles at her again and wanders off into the light brush, picking up firewood and stacking it in the air. Calida takes in the sights and sounds, spinning around slowly to enjoy the beauty. Sounds of crickets and little bursts of light from the fireflies tingle her senses.

She had forgotten how much she liked being out here. Being a city-girl and the Governor's daughter, she didn't get to leave Prime very much. But ever since she joined up with the Resistance, sometimes they were required to spend the night in the field and she enjoyed every minute of it.

"Calida! Food's almost ready," Lurius yells, interrupting her recollection.

The smile disappears from her face as she turns and walks with her arms crossed back to the others.

"So, Tac. How did you get your powers? Were you in some sort of experiment?" Bruttius enthusiastically asks.

"What? No," he replies dismissively, taking a bite of food.

"Well, were you bitten by a feral creature or exposed to a lot of radiation? C'mon, man. There's got to be a story behind that," Bruttius prods muffled by food.

"Well, firstly, I'm assuming you mean when I move things or how I speak. There's no real story behind it, it's just who I am. I didn't acquire my abilities through any special event. Everyone back home has the same abilities," he explains.

"Well, that's boring. I'm kind of a super hero buff, myself. I love them all. Here, look at this website I made. It's got all the great super heroes! See, there's the Saint. And that's Wolf Man. He's a shape shifter. Oh, and there's…" Bruttius ardently explains.

"You fucking idiot!" Lurius exclaims, slapping the phone from his hand. "They can track that! I specifically told you to leave electronics behind for this reason!"

"Yeah, but I didn't think you were serious. What happens if we needed to call someone to come pick us up?" he replies.

"You can be really fucking dense sometimes. And you're testing my patience. Get rid of the phone. *Now*," he orders.

"I'll do it," Tac says as he picks it up off the ground.

"Oh, this should be cool. What are you going to do? How far can you throw it? Can you make it burst into flames with your laser eyes?" Bruttius asks, sitting back down in his seat, eager for the display of power.

Tac quickly crushes the phone in on itself and launches it deep into the woods.

"Well, that was anticlimactic," Bruttius unhappily declares, reaching for his food.

"Everyone finish your dinner and get some rest. I doubt they'll come for us tonight, but we'll need to move out early in the morning," Calida orders. "Except for you, Bruttius. You have first watch. Tac will take second watch."

"But I kind of like this spot. Plus everything is set up. Why do we have to leave?" Bruttius asks.

"Because some idiot brought his GPS-enabled government-issued phone with him while fleeing from the same immoral and oppressive government," Lurius taunts condescendingly.

"Well, I didn't think about it that way. I could have just turned location services off and we would have been fine. You didn't have to destroy the phone," he retorts, sulking in his chair as he finishes his dinner.

"That might be true, but we don't know if they have a backup chip or service on the phone to bypass the operating system. Plus, they can still get approximate location from triangulating the location from the towers. The most logical thing to do was destroy it," Lurius explains.

Bruttius ignores his reply, stands, and takes his post at the edge of the camp.

"It's ok. He'll be fine," he says to the others. "I'm going to get some sleep. Don't stay up too late kids. Early morning tomorrow."

Lurius stands and walks towards one of the tents. Everyone but Calida, Tac, and Bruttius head toward their tents for the night. Both Tac and Calida still sit around the dying fire, quietly finishing dinner.

"I don't know what we're going to do now, Tac," she says after a few minutes, interrupting the sounds of the crackling fire.

"Well, back home, exiles would sometimes move very far away from their Hive. We even knew a few that had joined other Hives. I figure, if we can get away, we might be able to do something similar here. Maybe join up with another group of Resistance fighters in another sector?" Tac offers.

"Maybe. But other sectors are just as corrupt, if not worse. We're more likely to be caught and transported back here for execution than we are to find another hidden group of fighters. Plus, I really don't want to leave. I know it sounds weird, but as fucked up as this place is and as unholy as my father is, it's still home. I'd feel like I'm giving up on it," she explains.

"I can understand that. When I was exiled, I moved in with Tes and Shadow, who were my only friends outside of the Hive.

Even though I wasn't allowed back in, the Hive was my home. It always will be," he says, poking the fire with a stick.

"Well, I guess we'll just have to figure it out as we go," she says with a heavy sigh.

"We will," he confirms, smiling at her.

A few minutes pass before Calida stands up. She walks over to Tac and grabs him by the hand.

"C'mon. Let's get some rest," she says, smiling at him.

She leads him into her tent and closes the flap.

Calida wakes up to the sounds and smells of a camp fire. She pulls the sleeping bag down and dresses.

Opening the flap, she sees Tac standing near the fire. Snores from the other tents confirm how early it is as she scans the horizon for the impending sunrise. She walks up behind Tac and puts her arms around him, hugging him tightly. He turns around and kisses her gently on the lips.

"Good morning," he says.

She blushes slightly and smiles, "Good morning."

He hands her a cup of freshly brewed coffee.

"Oh, you are a Godsend," she quietly exclaims, sniffing the stark aroma and taking a sip. "Mmm, that's exactly what I needed right now."

Tac just smiles at her and kisses her forehead.

"And that too," she says, smiling back.

Shortly thereafter, everyone wakes up and starts packing up the camp. Standing around the smoldering fire, breakfast is consumed quickly and quietly.

"I think we should ditch the vehicle. It's only got about another quarter tank of fuel anyway. Plus, we have no way of knowing if they can still track it," Lurius states.

"Well, you removed the GPS, right?" Calida asks.

"Yes, but with the radio, they may still be able to triangulate our approximate position, if they care that much. Plus, they already know we spent the night here because of the phone incident. And, by now, they've probably figured out that we defected and are likely looking for the vehicle. I'd rather not give them another vector to follow us," Lurius explains.

"Good thinking. That might throw them off a bit," Calida confirms.

Calida backs the vehicle up onto the road, facing down the hill. With the engine off and transmission in neutral, they push it hard enough to where it moves on its own. They turn and everyone picks up a pack as they start marching in the direction away from Prime.

CHAPTER X: VENATOR

I'm startled awake by the sound of my cell phone ringing. Slowly, I roll over and answer it.

"Magius," I groggily say into the receiver and then clear my throat.

"Venator, I apologize for waking you, but we've got a priority one alert here that needs your immediate attention," the female voice says.

"Who is this?" I ask, pushing the covers off me and sitting up with my legs off the side of the bed.

"This is Captain Quintus of Imperial Law Enforcement," she says.

"Well, Captain. I'm currently on leave. You'll need to find someone else," I reply with a yawn, wiping my eyes to read the 3:48 am on my clock.

"I understand that, and normally we would dispatch a local resource, but the order comes all the way from the Emperor's council. I've sent you a dossier containing all the information we have at the moment. I've also taken the liberty of arranging transportation to Sector 81 Prime," she states.

"Where the hell is 81?" I say as I open my laptop.

"It's in the Western Empire, in the south eastern corner of the northern continent," she replies.

I take a moment to pull up the global map and locate it.

"Holy shit. That's out in the middle of nowhere. It's not even in my jurisdiction," I retort.

"We're well aware of that, sir. But we have no one of your caliber anywhere in the vicinity and the matter at hand requires a highly skilled professional, which is why the council assigned you," she informs me with a sigh.

"Ok, so why is the council concerned with something this far remote?" I ask, intrigued by the abstract nature of the mission.

"From what I understand, the Governor of 81 has some ties with someone on the council. That's all I know," she replies, even more exasperated.

"Alright. Alright. I'll take a look at it. Standby," I say.

Sometimes, I hate being good at what I do. I pull up my email and open the unread message from the Captain. I glance over her message, picking up some of the same details she's already shared and start the download for the dossier she referred to.

"Ok. I have the dossier. I'll be in touch," I say as I pull the phone away and hit the end call button.

"Honey, what's going on?" my wife asks.

"Just work. Go back to sleep," I reply standing up with my laptop and phone in hand to go into my office.

As I set the laptop down on my desk, an email from Roman Airlines comes in.

"Oh, you've got to be kidding me," I say out loud.

I reluctantly open the email to find my airline ticket for the flight to the Western Empire. I immediately hit redial on my phone.

"Captain Quintus," she answers.

"Captain, this is Magius. Why do I have a commercial ticket in my email?" I ask, agitated.

"Sir, the priority one alert requires your immediate involvement. There are no government transports headed that way for at least a week," she replies.

"What about my private jet?" I inquire.

"I'm sorry sir, but the Atlantic is just too big for a smaller jet like that. There was no other option to get you there as quickly as possible," Quintus replies.

"Thanks," I say with a sigh as I end the call and set the phone down.

I scan the barcode with the app on my phone and it shows a 6:00 am departure.

"Dammit!" I shout. Luckily, the airport is a mere fifteen minutes away, but this is getting ridiculous. What could be this damn important?

I start going through the dossier and pouring over the limited information. None of this makes any sense. I'm way over qualified for this mission. The wall clock gently chimes, diverting my focus from my laptop. Shit, it's 5:00 am.

I hastily pack all my gear and clothes into my oversized suitcase. After taking a quick shower, I put on my best suit and get ready to head out the door.

After fixing my hair, I walk back into the bedroom to find my wife still asleep. I glance over at the clock. 5:30 am. Time to go. I kiss her on the forehead as she gently wakes up.

"Where are you going?" she asks.

"Business trip. Overseas," I reply.

"How long?" she inquires.

"I'm not sure yet. Couple of days. Maybe a week. I'll call you later and let you know," I answer as I grab my jacket, satchel, and tip my suitcase to walk out the door.

"Don't destroy the house!" I call back as the door shuts.

The drive was quicker than normal in the early hours. I pull into the nearly empty parking garage and take my normal spot by the elevator.

Walking up to the airline counter, I set my bag on the scale.

"Sir, this bag is too large and too heavy to put on the aircraft," the attendant says.

I hand him my badge and reply, "No, it's not."

"My apologies, sir," he quickly states. "It must be a calibration issue. We'll get this loaded up for you immediately. Do you need me to print your boarding pass?"

I wave my phone at him as I take my badge back, "No thanks. I've got it on here."

"Very well, sir. You're all checked in. Your flight departs in fifteen minutes from Concourse B, Gate 36," he says, increasing his speaking pace. "You'll need to hurry as security is usually backed up at this hour."

"Thanks," I say as I put my badge away and start toward security.

All four lanes are completely backed up, so I flash my badge at the guard and he waves me past the massive lines.

"Let this one through!" he shouts over the commotion to the guard patting everyone down.

I pass the second guard and look up toward the signs for Concourse B. Right, the tram. God, I hate commercial travel. All this just to sit on a plane for nine or ten hours.

I get to the gate as the attendant is shutting the door. I scan my boarding pass and the beep draws her attention.

"I'm sorry, sir. But boarding is concluded for this flight," she says.

I flash my badge yet again as she sighs and re-opens the door with her badge and code.

"Thank you," I say, pushing past her and down the ramp.

I quickly take my First-Class seat and stow my bag under the seat in front of me. To my surprise, the flight is quiet empty save for a few families behind me. It should give me plenty of time to read the dossier in its entirety and do some research.

I buckle in and ignore the stewardess as she does her safety brief. The sun is starting to rise as we back away from the gate. My eyes start to droop as I can finally relax now. The internal lights are dimmed and I drop the shade to mask the sun's rays.

I'm pushed back into my seat and startled awake as the plane's engines whine to takeoff power. The repeated shudder of the entire plane as we build speed makes me nervous. No matter how much I fly, this part always makes gets my heart pumping.

The shuddering abruptly stops as we detach from the ground and gently lift into the air, allowing me to relax my shoulders and slow my breathing.

"First time flying?" a pretty, young stewardess says to me a few minutes later with a smile as she unbuckles herself and stands.

"No, I just don't care for takeoffs and landings," I retort, looking her up and down.

"Well, we're airborne now, so sit back and relax. Would you like a drink?" she asks in a pleasant tone so close to me that I can smell her floral perfume.

"Whiskey, please. On the rocks," I reply simply, pulling my bag into the seat next to me.

She returns briefly, drink in hand and sets it down on my tray next to my laptop.

"My name is Alba. Please let me know if you need anything else," she says with a wink.

"I just might," I reply as a smirk crosses my face.

Just another perk of the badge. But definitely one of my favorites. I've enjoyed the company of many women over my career, thanks to this shiny piece of metal.

After joining her in the lavatory for some "refreshments", I return to my seat and begin working on deciphering the necessary details from the sparsely populated dossier the Captain had prepared. It smells political. Which means I'd have to mind my manners. So much for an extended tour of the West.

Finally, my eyes start to burn from staring at the screen for too long. I close my laptop and swap it out for my sleeping mask and headphones. Glancing at my phone, we should be landing in a few hours and I should probably catch a nap.

"Sir, could you please make sure your seat is all the way up? We're preparing to descend and will be landing momentarily," Alba informs me with her perky tone as the captain flashes the seat belt sign and begins his speech over the intercom.

I lift the sleeping mask as she makes her way towards her seat. I'm sure I grumble something as I squeeze the button and sit up.

I open my laptop back up and start to scan the research again. I never feel prepared enough. The more I know about my marks before I get boots on the ground, the better off the mission goes.

"Sir, please stow large electronic items such as your laptop until we've landed," a different stewardess instructs me.

I flash my badge at her, "I'll keep my laptop on as long as I need. But thank you."

"I'm sure all the ladies back home drool on your badge when you flash it around, but up here, I'm the boss. Your laptop, when not properly stowed is a safety violation as defined in the Roman Airlines handbook, section ten, subsection "f", paragraph three. Now, you have three seconds to close and stow your laptop or I'm going to have the Praetorian take it from you," she arrogantly replies.

"Fine, just understand, you brought this on yourself," I inform her as I shut my laptop.

"I'm sorry, what was that?" she coyly asks.

"I said, understand you brought this on yourself," I reply.

She cuts her eyes at me before walking back down the aisle. She's desperately in need of a lesson in manners. As soon as we are on the ground at Sector 58 Prime's airport, I make a call to the local Governor's office and have him dispatch two Praetorians to apprehend the rude stewardess.

Alba stands at the exit of the plane and smiles at me as I approach, "Thank you for flying Roman Airlines. Have a great day!" she says.

I grab her butt, look her in the eyes and say, "Thank you very much for your service. You've made this flight especially memorable."

She's taken aback and blushes immediately at the attention.

"Yes, sir. Please enjoy your stay," she says shakily as I release and walk onto the jetway.

I stand right in front of the gate as the Praetorians walk up with the rude stewardess in handcuffs so she would know it was me.

"Next time, be careful who you give orders to," I instruct.

She proceeded to flail in her cuffs and curse me out so colorfully, it could be considered art. I could do nothing but laugh. Her lesson of the day? I outrank her. Don't fuck with me.

The government chauffeur met me at the bottom of the stairs and put my luggage in the SUV.

"Good morning, sir," he says shakily. "We're very honored to have an operative of Rome visit with us today."

"Thank you, umm, I'm sorry. I didn't catch your name," I inquire.

"Pompeius, sir. Lieutenant. In charge of law enforcement here in the capital sector," he affirms as he pulls into traffic and turns his emergency lights on.

"Pompeius, pleasure to meet you. My name is Magius, Venator," I reply civilly.

"Yes, sir. The pleasure is mine. I've been anticipating your arrival. Please sit back and relax. There are some refreshments in the console to your left. Help yourself. We'll be at the airfield shortly," he mechanically states.

I wonder how many times he practiced that line in the mirror this morning. This guy would definitely shit himself in combat. How did he ever get to Lieutenant? Eh, not my circus, not my monkeys. As long as he can drive responsibly, we'll be ok.

I pull out my laptop and begin scanning the files again. Reports on Calida, Tac, and several other high-ranking terrorists, history on their base of operations, how long they've been running operations, targets believed to be of significance, etcetera.

And just like being interrupted at the best part of a book you're sucked into, we arrive at the airfield in record time. Finally, proper accommodations are made with a fully fueled government jet. I climb in and tell the pilots to take off before settling into my seat in the back. As I look out the window, Pompeius appears relieved to be rid of me. I hate boot lickers.

We took off on no delay and before I knew it, we were touching down in Sector 81. I must have dozed off. I thanked the pilots on my way out to an empty tarmac. No concierge, no vehicles, just nothing but an old dusty hanger and a shack. I pop my head back in the cockpit.

"Are we sure this is Sector 81?" I inquire.

"First time to the boonies, sir?" the pilot in charge asks.

"I'm afraid so," I reply.

"Yeah. They have no services at this airport. Hell, we even have to refuel the plane ourselves. But you can call the Governor's office and they'll send someone over to pick you up. Here's the number," he says, turning and passing a piece of paper to me.

"Thanks again," I said as I turn and deplane the second time.

I grab my bag from the first officer as he was kind enough to retrieve it from the cargo bay before his post-flight inspection. I walked over to the broken chain-link gate and pushed it open. I found it odd that there seemed to be no security whatsoever at this airfield. Gates were open, the hangar was open. Hell, the door to the "tower" was open.

This better be a quick mission. I could already hear the banjos. With phone in one hand and paper in the other, I call the unfamiliar number.

"Thank you for calling the Governor's office for Sector 81. For Latin, press one. For all other languages, press two," the feminine computer voice states.

"Why the fuck do I have to press one for Latin? It's literally the official language!" I yell into the phone as I press one.

"Thank you for calling the Governor's office. If you know your party's extension, you may dial it at any time," the voice chimes again followed by light music.

"Great, now I'm on hold. You can't possibly be that damn busy out here! There's nothing here!" I exclaim.

"Your call is important to us. Please remain on the line and the next available operator will be with you shortly," the female computer voice says, unphased by my emotional rant.

I let out a heavy sigh and rub my forehead to slow the impending migraine that the combination of the perky computer and hold music is causing. Finally, someone picks up on the other side.

"Hey, this phone is ringing and won't shut up," I hear a distance voice say.

A more distant voice says, "Well, hang it up. That phone doesn't even work half the time."

"Noooo!" I yell and then click.

I have a propensity for breaking my phone when I get angry, but this was neither the time nor the place for that. I angrily dial the number again, press one again, then spam zero to get straight to the operator.

"Hey, this phone's ringing again," the distant voice says again.

"HEY, DON'T YOU HANG UP ON ME AGAIN!!" I scream.

"Ok, well, answer it idiot," the more distant voice says.

"Ummm, hello?" he finally says, obviously with the receiver to his ear now.

"Yes, this is Pius Magius, Venator from Rome. I have been sent here on assignment and I am currently waiting at your pitiful excuse of an airfield for transport to the Governor's mansion," I quickly say.

He pulls the receiver away from his face again, speaking to the other man, "He says he's a Venator from Rome and he's waiting at the airfield. Do we have an airfield?"

"A what? Wait, I think I saw a memo this morning about that," the distant voice says.

I can hear papers shuffling in the background. I sigh at the complete lack of competence with these two. They wouldn't make it two seconds in Rome.

"Lieutenant Vettius!" the other man screams, "That Venator is at the airfield waiting on us."

"Sorry, sir," the first man says, "We had a logistical error, but we will send someone immediately to pick you up."

"Thank you," I say as I hang up the call.

Late afternoon turned to dusk as I wait under the decaying pavilion for my ride. Even the plane I came in on had already left at least an hour ago. Finally, I see headlights coming along the lonely dirt road that traverses the western hill.

I'm about to starve at this point and it's getting colder out. Two out of the three things I hate. If the driver is dressed as a clown, I'm going to lose my shit. Eventually, the vehicle pulls up to the curb. This gorgeous lady jumps out, apologizing profusely before she can even get around the vehicle.

"I am so very sorry, Venator. There was a mix up in communication on when you would be here," Vettius says quickly. "Here, let me get your bag."

"That's ok, miss. I'm sure we can find something to settle the debt," I say, flashing her a grin.

She blushes as she grabs my bag, "I'm sure we can, but for now, please climb in and let's not waste any more of your time."

The older SUV smells of stale chips and cigarette smoke. Repulsive. I take advantage of the dome light and retrieve my laptop from my bag in the back. I needed to distract myself, otherwise, this was going to get out of hand before I could even start the mission.

My wife doesn't like it when I go out of town on business. Well, not so much the business part, but the fact that I am inclined to also hunt the local women. Except that she has men over all the time when I am out of town. Women too. It is a dual standard that she is all too happy to enforce.

I focus on my work as much as I can. They weren't kidding about being in the boonies. The road to Prime had so many potholes, I'm surprised my laptop didn't go through the window at times. Vettius kept quiet most of the drive, except for small talk. Prime was pretty far away from the airfield. In fact, this airfield is apparently shared with two other sectors that border 81. It was very late when we pulled up to the Governor's mansion and I was startled awake by the concierge opening my door. It's a good thing I wasn't leaning on it.

I pulled a business card from my bag and handed it to Vettius.

"Please give me a call should you need *any* of my services," I say with a wink at her in the rear-view mirror.

"Thank you, sir. I'll will be sure to call you as soon as the need arises," she replies with a smile as I exit.

The concierge retrieves my bag from the back of the SUV and shuts the door before Vettius drives off.

"Good evening, sir. I hope you had a pleasant trip," he greets.

"Not exactly, but I'm here now," I reply.

"I'm truly sorry to hear that, sir. My name is Nerius. I am the concierge and head butler to Tiberius Axius, Governor of Sector 81. Please do not hesitate to let me or any of the staff know if there is anything you need during your stay," he recites, rolling my bag up to the large wide staircase just inside the door.

"Thank you, Nerius. Right now, I'd like to see my quarters and a hot meal, if it's not too much of a bother," I answer.

"Certainly, sir. I'll have the chef prepare you a fine meal and send it up. Please follow me. I will show you to the magnificent Lucius suite, which is by far the best available room in the mansion, second only to the Governor's quarters," he proudly proclaims as he starts up the stairs.

"Very well, Nerius. It is a welcome relief," I reply.

"Persius! Please take the Venator's luggage and follow us to the Lucius suite," he shouts down the stairs.

Nerius opens the double doors exposing a well-furnished room, complete with modern accommodations. Persius places my bag at the foot of the massive bed as I make myself more comfortable by removing my jacket and tie.

"Persius will return with your evening meal as soon as the chef has finished preparing it. Breakfast will be bright and early at 6:00 a.m. and your daily newspaper will be outside of your door no later than 5:30 a.m. Again, please do not hesitate to let us know if there's anything else we can do to make your stay more accommodating," Nerius eloquently recites.

"Nerius, what time does the Governor usually start business?" I inquire as I roll up the sleeves on my white button-down shirt.

"He usually begins his day shortly after 9:00 a.m. unless there are extenuating circumstances. Considering that he is sleeping alone tonight, I would expect he would be able to meet with you promptly at that time," Nerius responds.

"Perfect. Thank you very much," I say as I toss him a Dupondius.

His eyes get wide once recognizing the large coin, nods slightly, and shuts both doors behind him. I lounge in the oversized chair by the recently lit fire and stare at it briefly until there is a knock at the door.

"Come in!" I shout as I slowly stand.

Three butlers, including Persius enter carrying large golden trays and set them on the dining table. Each removed their cover as Persius describes the local delicacies that the chef had prepared. Honestly, I was too tired and hungry to listen.

"And with that, is there anything else you need, sir?" Persius asks me.

I toss him a Dupondius and say mid-bite into the juicy turkey leg, "No, but thank you very much, Persius."

I thought he might cry right there looking at the coin, but he recovered quickly and bowed out just as gracefully as Nerius. This meal was exactly what I needed. A smoked turkey leg, fried potatoes, a salad, some fruit, and a little bowl of chocolate. Quiet possibly the best meal I've had in a while, and from the backwoods of all places.

I rang the bell shortly after finishing as Persius enters the room almost immediately.

"All finished, sir?" he asks walking up to the table.

"Yes, thank you. It was fantastic. My compliments to the chef," I reply.

"Very well, sir. Please don't tip me this time. You've already done so much," he begs.

"Ok. Well, then thank you again and have a good night," I say as two more butlers come in and remove the golden platters and wipe the table down.

I woke early and jumped in the hot shower. The paper and extensive breakfast are both delivered on time, as promised. As I put on my jacket, there is a knock at the door. I'm not expecting anyone yet, so I comb my hair quickly in the mirror and open the door.

"Good morning, Venator," Vettius says with a smile.

"Good morning to you, Lieutenant," I reply, shocked. "What a pleasant surprise. Please come in."

"Thank you, but I just wanted to stop by for a moment. I had to drop some paperwork off and one of the butlers told me you were in this room," she deflects.

"Well, in that case, I'll take a rain check," I retorted.

"How long will you be in town?" she asks.

"Sadly, after tonight, I'll likely be in the field until my mission is over," I replied with a sorrowful tone. "However, today will be mostly meetings and interviews and I'll be here all night reviewing evidence if you'd like to stop by."

"That sounds like a plan. I'll see you tonight," she says with a smile.

"See you tonight," I say as I glance down at her chest for a moment before shutting the door.

Well, at least I have something to look forward to. I took a deep breath and composed myself before leaving to meet with the Governor. His reception area was ornately decorated with a double opposing staircase with the secretary's desk on the lower floor. She sees me and immediately meets me at the foot of the staircases.

"Welcome to Sector 81 Prime, Venator. The Governor is expecting you. Please follow me," she says before leading me up the left staircase. As expected, armed members of the Praetorian Guard stood on either side of the Governor's door.

She opens the door and introduces me as I enter and shuts the door behind me.

"Venator, welcome," the ageing Governor stands and walks around his desk to meet me. "Please, come and sit."

"Thank you, Governor," I reply as I sit in one of the chairs in front of his desk.

"Drink?" he inquires looking down his glasses at me, decanter in hand.

"Uh, no thank you," I reply.

He pours a small glass and walks back to his desk.

"Alright, let's get down to business, shall we?" he asks.

"Absolutely," I respond, opening my notebook.

"Ok, so I assume you've had enough time to review the dossier we sent over, yes?" he inquires further.

"Yes, I have," I reply with a nod.

"Good, good. So, what I didn't disclose is that Calida is my only child. She was rather rebellious after her mother died suddenly when she was young. She ran away at age fourteen and eluded my attempts to bring her back home ever since. That was six years ago. From there, she got tangled up with the wrong people, specifically a group of terrorists hell-bent on the destruction of Roman rule and order. They twisted my little girl's mind into believing that I was a bad person," he explains.

"In a last-ditch effort to get her back, I had my Lieutenant order a raid on their base of operations in the sewers beneath the city. They had explicit orders to detain Calida and ensure her no harm, but to exterminate her terrorist friends. Unfortunately, they failed to subdue my daughter and she escaped with a particularly dangerous terrorist," he says in a much darker tone.

I continue scribbling notes as he goes on to explain how one of the terrorists, Tac, has some sort of super powers and how he's suspected of killing dozens of Praetorians at this point.

"With all of that being said, I just want Calida back safe and sound. I don't care how you do it. I don't care what happens to the remaining terrorists. Just get my little girl back home, please," he pleads.

"Of course, Governor. I'll need to interview some of your staff as well," I specify.

"You have full access to anyone on my staff," the Governor asserts with his arms spread wide.

"Very good. Unless there is something else, I'll get right to it," I state, standing up.

He finishes his glass of liquor before saying, "No, that is all. Please keep me up to date on your efforts."

"Absolutely," I say as I turn and walk towards the door.

As I exit his office and start toward the staircase, one of the Guards says, "Excuse me, sir. Do you have a moment?"

"Sure," I respond.

"Well, sir. There are two members of the Guard that we believe went AWOL. They may have even gone to the aid of the terrorists. We're not really sure. But, during the course of your investigation, we thought it might be relevant," he spouts.

Quickly writing down the details, I ask, "And what gives you that inclination, Praetorian?"

"The Sergeant of the Guard noticed some missing gear and uniforms the other day. He reported it to the Lieutenant, per protocol. The Supply Sergeant also noticed an unauthorized vehicle departure the same day. She said by the direction they were heading, they'd have to be headed for where the terrorists were retreating," he explains.

"And why is that?" I inquire further.

"Well, because sir, there's nothing south east of this installation but mountains and forest for over a hundred kilometers until you reach the border for Sector 79," he clarifies.

"That's all very good information, Praetorian. Thank you. You've done the Emperor proud," I say, closing my notebook.

He smiles and simply says, "Thank you sir. I hope you find what you're looking for."

I nod as I turn and walk down the staircase. I skim my notebook for the list of names of individuals I want to interview, but with the new intelligence handed over by the Guard, I need to check with the Supply Sergeant to get a copy of the GPS log for that vehicle.

From that log, it seems the GPS was disabled shortly after departure, however, the backup GPS was still functioning. It seems a bit too easy. I'm used to flushing out fugitives on the run through undeveloped land, I can track and locate hidden contraband in their stashes, and I can even infiltrate an enemy's ranks until I find my mark. But this doesn't seem to be the caliber of missions I'm used to. Something is off. I just can't put my finger on it yet.

The rest of the interviews are rather uneventful. Random Praetorians who claim to have had contact with the one or two of the fugitives, an aspiring Venator who happens to have some good pictures of the Governor's daughter out on patrol, even one Praetorian who claims to be amongst their ranks for a short period of time as a mole. But none of his information lines up with what I've discovered so far.

These kids are running scared. They've seen the entirety of their hopes and dreams shattered at arm's reach and there was nothing they could do about it. So, now, like the cowards they are, they're running. Hoping we don't give chase. Well, I will be the bearer of bad news on that front. I will find them. It might not be tomorrow, it might not be this week, but I will find them. I always do.

As I sit in the dimly lit room, sipping on my scotch and reviewing the notes from today's interviews, a light knock on the door draws my attention. I set the glass down and glance at my watch. Who is at my door this late? I open one of the doors to find a visibly anxious Vettius in a tight red mini skirt and white blouse.

"Good evening, Venator. I hope I'm not disturbing you," she says shakily.

"Not at all," I say, simultaneously surprised and excited. "Please, come in."

She glances over her shoulder and enters quickly. I chuckle to myself as I close the door behind her.

"You seem a bit nervous," I say after a few moments.

"Yes, I don't normally do this," she replies quickly.

"Alright, how about a drink?" I ask.

"Definitely," she responds, still standing in place.

I crossed the room to the decanter and poured another glass of scotch. Turning back toward her, I motioned her over. She hesitates momentarily and then quickly walks over.

"Relax. We're doing nothing wrong here," I say as I hand her the glass.

She takes a big gulp, "Well, it certainly feels wrong. I haven't been with someone new in over ten years."

"Well, you're here now. The hard part is done," I reply, offering some sort of solace.

She just exhales sharply and scoffs, finishing the glass.

"How about we sit down for a minute?" I say as I pour her another one.

Our eyes finally lock momentarily. She's so scared. Like unreasonably so. But as expected, she finally relaxes enough for us to sleep together. She wouldn't have come here if that wasn't her intention. After about an hour or so, we take a break for refreshments and sit down at the table, scantily clad.

"I noticed we're both wearing our wedding rings. How does your wife feel about sharing you with women all over the world?" she finally asks before taking a sip from her glass.

"Oh, she gives me grief from time to time when she feels threatened by a beautiful woman, but she has more men come over while I'm gone than I care to count, so she can just deal with it," I reply. "Hell, last week, I flew home to find her shacked up with two men and three other women. I walked in and set my suitcase down right in the middle of everything."

"Jeeze. I would have lost my shit. But I guess marriage is a little different there," she says.

"Yeah, it's very different. Almost to the point that marriage is only for tax purposes. People still date, sleep with, and even have children with other partners and no one seems to care. I guess it's an Eastern thing," I reply.

"I guess so," she says, "Hey, you mind if I take a quick shower?"

"Not at all," I acknowledge, emptying my glass. "Please, help yourself."

"Great. Thanks," she says as she stands and walks cautiously to the bathroom.

My thoughts drift back to work. I'm still trying to figure out how I'm going to get Calida out of there without having to fight off the alien. Various scenarios play out in my head as I stand and refill my glass. Staring at the window, I finally had the epiphany I was waiting for. A smirk crossed my face as all the little details fell into place.

"I know exactly how I'm going to get you," I say looking out the window.

I swirl my glass, finish it, and retreat to the bedroom, laying back on the plush bedspread and propping myself up against the headboard.

Shortly thereafter, Vettius emerges naked from the bathroom.

"Ready to go again?" I ask.

She smirks and jumps into the bed with me.

CHAPTER XI: DUALITY

Mission accomplished, I think to myself. I listen to the snoring for a moment to make sure he's not faking it before rolling my head in the plush pillow to look at the clock. It reads 3:36 am. Good. Plenty of time to find what I need.

I carefully remove his arm that has me pinned in the bed and place it at his side. Slowly and methodically, I remove the covers and slide out. I stand next to the bed and watch him sleep. It was usually my favorite part. Sometimes I was just too damn good at this. He never even saw me dose his drink. A smile creeps across my face as each passing moment confirms he's down for the count.

I slowly and quietly put my clothes back on and tip toe into the other room where his laptop is. Opening it, I squint and blink repeatedly at the intense light until my eyes finish adjusting. What an idiot. He didn't even lock his computer. I must be a better actress than I thought.

I retrieve the thumb drive from my purse. Oops. That's the actual lipstick. Grabbing the correct one, I jam it into the side of his laptop as the fans spin up and my extraction program begins executing. A single terminal shows on the screen, crawling with text way too quickly to read, but I can guess based on the current directory how much time I have left. It looks like he's saved all his work to this laptop. After this, I'll have a history of all of his marks, protocols for when he gets involved, and any leverage I may need in the future.

Well, while I wait, I think a celebratory drink is in order. I look around for my glass. Definitely don't want to drink from his. As I pour the drink, I hear his snoring change tones. *Uh, oh.* I quietly set the decanter down and plug the top back in. After a few moments, he goes back to his normal rhythm and all is clear.

Stupid, Vettius. You're gonna get caught one of these days. I think to myself as I walk back over and sit down at the small dining table.

Good. We're in the L's now. About halfway done. This part is always a rush. I open his browser and go through the history, pulling up an Imperial website I wasn't familiar with. A blank webpage with a login prompt shows. *Interesting.* I click into the username field and his username and password automatically fills in. I cover my mouth to contain my quiet laughter as I click "ok".

The bright red banner across the top confirms that this is a top secret website. I pull up the site map and start navigating through. Military operations, blueprints, and all the goodies. But I knew I wouldn't get much out of here except for what I took tonight.

Finally, I come across a page entitled Operation Purge. I briefly skimmed the details after swapping back to see that my program was in the 'S' directory. Almost done. It's not good. It's not good at all.

I hear the sheets rustling as he rolls over and quickly, but quietly, close the laptop. *Please don't go to sleep.* I whisper to the laptop in my mind. *You, on the other hand,* I gesture silently to the bedroom in the air, *I need you to go back to sleep and stay there.*

After ten very tense seconds, Pius' snoring roars back and I relax. *Jeeze that's obnoxious. You should probably have that checked out.* I open the laptop back and my eyes re-adjust yet again. I tab back over to my program. In the 'V's now. Almost done.

I tab again to the website and skim the details. It looks like a last-ditch effort plan to wipe out any insurrection from spreading between sectors. Plans for stealth bombers to be launched from the region's capital to completely obliterate an entire prime in the event it was compromised. Without the prime, the surrounding villages would die off fairly quickly.

So, ruthless, I whisper to myself. I kind of admired it. But it does change my tactics a bit. If the Resistance took over, Rome would just bomb us into oblivion. That's not going to work if I'm going to replace Axius. Definitely a problem to be solved at a later time.

I tab back over to my program which sits at an empty prompt. Done. I close the browser and my program, remove the stick and replace the cap, and bury it back in my purse. I sneak into the bathroom as work off the anxious energy from my espionage.

I quietly climb back into bed, trying not to wake him. *My God, I'm going to have to smother him.* His snoring is so loud, I can't hear myself think. *Oh, shit. My clothes.* I slowly remove my clothes and try to replace which article went where on the ground before pulling the covers back up.

As I lay there, knowing I'm not going to go back to sleep with this airplane engine of a snore in my ear, I poke him hard in the side. *Ha!* This guy's been married too long. He rolls right over and quiets down.

I wake up hours later to an empty bed and quiet room. *Well, I'm not in handcuffs, so that's a plus.* I look around the room for any sign that he's still here. Nothing. Sliding out of the bed, my clothes are folded nicely on the chair. *Interesting.* On top of them sits a hand-written note using the Governor's exquisite stationary. It reads:

> *Good morning. Sorry I couldn't say goodbye properly because I had to head out early and you were sleeping so soundly. I didn't want to wake you. I thoroughly enjoyed last night and I thank*

*you immensely. I hope to do it again sometime if
I'm back in town. Please help yourself to
whatever you need from my room. If you pick up
the phone and call downstairs, they will bring you
breakfast.*

-Yours Truly-

Pius

I smile as I fold the note up and stick it in my purse. He could definitely turn out to be an ally, especially if he has no clue how much I have on him now. *Hmm, breakfast.* It does sound tempting. *Eh, why not?* I think and pick up the receiver. Within a few minutes, there's a light rap at the door.

"Enter," I reply.

Mr. Nerius pushes both doors open and ushers in another man who sets a golden platter down in front of me at the table and removes the lid.

"Good morning, Lieutenant Vettius," Nerius says. "I trust you slept well."

"Very well, thank you." I reply.

"Excellent. Mr. Magius has already covered the cost of the meal as well as a generous tip. Please enjoy and do not hesitate to call down should you need anything," he recites eloquently.

I nod toward him as I take a bite of one of the strawberries from the bowl. He quietly shuts both doors. I drop the strawberry on the plate and cross the room to check my purse, finding both my actual lipstick and the thumb drive intact.

Yep, mission accomplished.

I stroll through the lobby as another man opens the door for me. *Now to get back home and go over all the information I gathered.* I jump into my car and speed away, turning the music on.

"Good morning, babe." I say to my husband as he reads the newspaper.

"Where the hell have you been?" he interrogates.

"Working," I reply simply as I head for the stairs.

"In that?" he nearly shouts in reference to my clothes.

I stop mid-stride. I'm going to have to nip this one in the bud.

"Yes. In this. Should we call your girlfriend to discuss it? Oh, wait. That's right," I facetiously reply.

He has no reply but instead I hear him throw the paper down. *That should do it.*

Once upstairs, I pull out my laptop and stick the drive in. It takes a few minutes to import and sort all of the data, so I step into the bathroom and take a quick shower.

When I come out in my robe and damp hair, I see that my husband is on my computer.

"What do you think you're doing?" I ask.

"Where did this come from?" he redirects.

"That's not what I asked you. Why are you on my computer? You're not a government official and you're not allowed to use my computer. We've been over this too many times now," I scold.

He stands and looks at me sternly.

"Don't you dare give me any attitude. You want to keep that promotion you just got? I suggest you bite your lip and go back to whatever it was you were doing before I got home," I instruct. "And shut the door on your way out. I have work to do."

I wait until the door click shut before I roll my eyes and cross to see what he was doing. Luckily for him, he didn't do any damage.

"We need to be out of here before daybreak. I'll work on breakfast," I say.

Calida nods and we silently dress in the pre-dawn hours. I unzip the tent and slip out, closing the flap behind me. Lurius is on watch and I wave him over to the fire.

Stoking it up and throwing another log on, I say, "Good morning."

"Morning," he replies with a yawn.

"How was last night?" I ask.

"Quiet as could be, except for the damn wind. Picked up about two hours ago and hasn't let up since. Might be some weather coming through," he reports.

"Yeah, we may even get some snow. Not good in our situation for multiple reasons," I state, looking to the sky.

I start pulling some of the breakfast rations out of one of the bags and toss them at the edge of the fire to warm. The rustling inside the other tents starts as people begin to wake up.

Bruttius stumbles out in his underwear, hair a mess, and says, "Good morning."

"Bruttius, clothes, please?" Lurius stops him just outside of his tent.

"Oh, right," he says and turns back around, "Sorry."

"I don't know how the hell that man made it through ten years in the Praetorians. If he had done that in the Academy, the sergeant would have eaten him for breakfast," Lurius states, returning to the fire.

I laugh quietly, "I can't say I would know anything about that life. I was a Warrior back home, but I bet it's not the same here."

"It's probably closer than you think," he replies. "I can see some of the same disciplines in you."

"Thank you," I reply.

"So, man to man. You planning on sticking around long here?" he asks.

"That's the plan. Not that I have another option, but even if I did, I want to stay here. With Calida. I don't want to be in a place where she isn't," I staunchly reply.

"Understood. I think it's a great thing, you and Calida. You two look so incredibly happy together. But also, the way you work together, feeding off one another. It's like you were made to be together. Like two halves of a gear. Put them together and the whole picture comes into place," Lurius states.

"I think those are done now," Calida says behind me.

I'm snapped back by her words and immediately notice the sizzling of two of the pouches as they've busted open from the heat. I retrieve them and set them on the ground against one of the trees to cool.

"Sorry about that. Lurius and I were just talking," I state.

"I heard," she says with a smile.

"Well, guess the cat's out of the bag now, huh?" Lurius says, elbowing me in the side.

"What does that mean?" I ask.

"She knows your plan now. The gig is up! Might as well settle down and build a house," Lurius states playfully.

"Well, that might be a little fast, Lurius," Calida says with a chuckle. "But it's a nice thought."

We sit around the morning fire, eating breakfast and discussing random topics.

"Alright, I guess we should start packing up," Bruttius says.

"Yeah, we need to move out," Calida says facing towards the tents.

"I'll start breaking them down," I reply.

I pull everything out of the tents and pack it nicely in a few of the packs, then disassemble the tents, packing them nicely in the other set of packs.

"You know, that would take us at least thirty minutes if we had to do it manually?" Lurius states.

"Damn life saver. If only he could carry everything too," Bruttius replies.

"I probably could. We'll see if I can in a few minutes," I say.

Bruttius lights up like a child, "Sweet!"

I lift all of the camping gear and carry it about ten meters behind us as we hike the final few kilometers up to the summit of the small mountain we've been traversing. As we continue up, amongst the arbitrary rants from Bruttius about various superheroes and who is better than who, I keep seeing this thing out of the corner of my eye. Every time I look though, it's gone.

The snow is finally starting to stick and the wind grows with each step. We are definitely not prepared for this type of cold.

But these are the mountains and mother nature works differently up here. Luckily, we're just passing through.

"Ok, do we want to take a rest at the summit or push through?" Calida turns to ask.

"I vote for pushing through. This weather is ridiculous!" Bruttius exclaims.

"Yeah, I'm not so fond of it either," Lurius says.

"I'm good. I can keep going," I add.

Nods and agreements continue.

"Ok then, let's get below the snow line on the other side and we'll set up our camp early," she orders.

There it was again! The flash. Right out of the corner of my eye. I'm just not fast enough to catch it. I know I'm not hallucinating. Whatever it is, it's very fast.

"You don't have to be afraid," I finally said.

Everyone stops in their tracks and turns to look at me.

"What?" Lurius says.

"Shh," I reply as I set the gear down quietly.

"How can I hear you?" the voice asks.

"I'm not sure, but I think we can hear each other," I reply, turning towards the last place I saw the flash.

Calida creeps up to me, weapon at the ready, "What is it?"

"Relax," I say, lowering her weapon, "He's not going to hurt us."

"What do you mean he?" she asks.

A few seconds pass and he doesn't say anything else.

"Are you still there?" I ask.

Now, there's nothing but the wind.

"So, just out of curiosity, which packet did you have for breakfast? Cause I don't want to eat that one tomorrow," Bruttius states with a grin.

I laugh at his joke, "I think it was a wolf. I could talk to them back home. In fact, one of my best friends was a wolf. Until she gave her life trying to defend us."

"Wow, from what?" Bruttius asks.

"Another pack of wolves," I respond.

"Ahh. Did you get them all?" he inquires further.

"No, we killed all of them except for the alpha. He got away," I reply. "She also saved us from a four-meter tall bear."

"Wait, what?" he exclaims.

"Yeah, he was pretty big. And really strong. Knocked me clear across the village we were in," I acknowledge.

"You never mentioned that part," Calida says.

"It hasn't really been relevant until now," I reply.

"So, my man is a wolf talker now? What else can you do? Control the weather?" Lurius facetiously states.

I playfully reach up to the sky and snap my fingers, pushing the snow away from us briefly, "Sorry, that's all I got."

Bruttius bursts into laughter and points at Lurius.

Lurius didn't think it was so funny, "Ha, ha! Laugh it up."

Everyone cracks a smile or chuckles as the march resumes. I started thinking about the wolf again. I wasn't really expecting to meet another wolf like Shadow, especially this far from home. But I guess I shouldn't be that surprised.

We finally get low enough on the other side of the mountain to where the falling heavy snow turns to slush. Somewhere we can set up camp and get some rest. By now, everyone is cold, wet, hungry, and exhausted from the day's march.

"Hey, that looks like a good spot for the night," Calida says, pointing to a good-sized indentation in the side of the mountain. "Protected from the wind on three sides. Yes, it'll do nicely."

No one argues since the only thing we want to do is sit down for a minute. I prop myself up against one of the barren trees and set the gear down in the back of the indentation. Once everything is unpacked and set up, I attempt to start a fire, but all the wood is wet.

"Lurius, do we have any more of that fire starter?" I ask.

"If it's not in the bags, I don't suppose so," he replies.

I turn all of the bags over, but nothing comes out.

"Great. Well, I'll see if I can find some dry wood further down," I say as I slowly stand to my already aching feet and head down the road.

"Hang on. I'll go with you," Calida shouts at me.

I don't know why, it's such a small thing, but her coming with me makes me really happy. Just watching her walk towards me gives me a surge of energy. She smiles and I light up.

"What?" she asks with a chuckle.

"Nothing," I reply.

We head further down the mountain, looking for dry wood.

"I really wish I had met you at a different time," she finally says.

"What do you mean?" I quickly reply.

"Well, it's just we're in the middle of this God-awful war and I have so much to do, being the leader and all, that I haven't had much time to focus on us, whatever we are," she explains.

"We don't always get to dictate when we learn life's lessons. Sometimes, we need extreme situations to help us grow. Regardless of the circumstances, I am so thankful to have met you when I did. You've shown me a side of life that I've never known, and probably never would have known if it wasn't for you," I retort.

"I guess I just wish we had the security that we could just focus on being with each other and making each other happy all the time," she says with a sigh.

"I'd like that too. Maybe we'll have that kind of life soon," I reply.

We finally find some dry, soft wood to hopefully start the fire. She points at different pieces of freshly fallen trees as I pick them up. She even shows me how to get fat lighter from one of the standing trees. We gather as much tinder and dry wood as she thinks we'll need and head back up the mountain.

Shortly thereafter, we finally make it back to the camp. I don't think anyone has moved in the time we were gone. I don't blame them. We spent most of the last fourteen hours walking. Everyone is exhausted. Time to get a good fire going and get some hot food in us.

I grab a smaller piece of the dry soft wood along with a branch and fashion a quick fireboard. Spinning the tip of the smaller twig against the other wood finally results in some smoke and a few embers. I build the smallest timber up beside it and flip the board over, dumping the embers into the bundle.

The fire starts to build as I prop some of the dry wood up to catch and the wet wood around it to dry out. I'm getting better at it, but still not as good as some of the citizens back home. It's ok though. It's not a race here. The result is we'll be warm tonight and into tomorrow morning, we'll have hot food, and we'll be able to dry out our clothes while we get a well-deserved good night's rest.

It's several hours before anyone says anything coherent. Mostly grunting and struggling to remove wet clothing, shivering from the cold, stomach noises from the nutritional deficiencies, and yawning. We all sit around the fire, finishing our dinner.

"Who's on watch tonight?" I ask.

"Umm, I think I'm up first and that puts Bruttius on second watch," Calida replies.

"Yep, then Calida will be first watch tomorrow night and Tac will take second," Bruttius explains.

"Ok. In that case, I'm going to go to sleep early," I say, standing and making for Calida on my way to our tent.

I embrace her and kiss her gently on the top of the head, "Good night."

"Sleep well," she replies. "I'll see you in a few hours."

Even devoid of wind, the inside of the tent is cold. I may have to pull it closer to the fire if the temperature drops much through the night. I curl up in the ragged sleeping bag I have and drift quickly off to sleep.

I'm startled awake sometime in the middle of the night by footsteps outside the tent, crunching the frozen ground beneath. I lay there for a moment, making sure I heard what I thought I did. I hear the feet shuffle again.

The zipper finally travels around the flap and what looks like a pistol and arm quickly enter the tent. Before I can react, two muffled shots ring out and I feel a sharp pain in my chest. My vision is the first to go. Next is the ringing. I feel like my ears are going to explode. I try to stand up, but I'm so uncoordinated that I immediately fall flat on my face. And that's when everything goes dark.

CHAPTER XII: INFILTRATION

As I walk up to Sabina's front door, I glance over at her neighbor's house to find an older couple sitting on their front porch. Couples like that have agitated me ever since Nonus was gunned down nearly two years ago. Just seeing them that content with each other makes my stomach turn. I know Axius killed him, I just can't accept that it was over petty jealousy. And now I'll probably never have what they have.

"Cecilia! Welcome!" Sabina says enthusiastically as she opens the door.

I smile back at her and glance at the security camera covering the front door. Of course, that's how she saw me.

"Hello Sabina. I got this for you," I state, handing her the cheap bottle of scotch I purchased on my way over.

"Oh, how thoughtful! Thank you. We're so glad you could make it," she adds as she closes the door behind me.

"It's not much, but it's all they had," I explain.

"Oh, no. It's great. I actually needed a new bottle for work. Believe it or not, I prefer the cheaper scotches. They have this rustic feel to them that I really like," Sabina retorts.

"Well, I'm glad," I say with a smile.

"Cecelia! There you are!" I hear and turn my head to see Mr. Vettius crossing the foyer to greet me with open arms.

"Nope. Hands off, dear," Sabina says with her open hand against his chest. "Sorry, he's a little touchy."

I giggle and reply, "No consequence."

"Can I get your coat?" she asks me with her hand outstretched.

"Of course," I reply, sliding the dark evening jacket from my shoulders, revealing the strapless red party dress.

"Whoa," Mr. Vettius whispers.

"Aren't you burning something, dear?" Sabina asks him, putting my jacket on the coat rack behind the front door.

"Just brain cells at the moment," he says staring at me.

"I meant in the kitchen," she replies starkly.

"Hmm?" he asks, shifting his focus to her.

She gives him a dirty look.

"Oh, right. Dinner," he mumbles with his eyes stuck on me as he walks back toward the kitchen.

"I'm sorry," I say turning toward her, "I didn't realize this was going to be an issue."

"Oh, honey, it's not. He's like a pet. Sometimes, he just needs a little discipline," she replies with a hearty laugh as she turns and walks into the kitchen.

I laugh in return. He does kind of act like a dog. Hopefully, we can get through dinner without him humping my leg.

Not that her husband has anything to do with my business at the Vettius residence. The best way to have a meeting about something you don't want anyone else to know about is to disguise it as something social. Our choice has been to have dinner about once a month in order to catch up on our efforts to get rid of Axius.

As I follow Sabina into the kitchen, I rub my arms to knock the chill off of the night air. Something smells magnificent though. And I haven't eaten since breakfast. I always save my appetite for these nights. Mr. Vettius should have been a chef. The food he serves is absolutely some of the best I've ever had the pleasure of tasting.

"So…girl talk," Sabina says with her eyes bright as she sits down in one of the ornate bar stools at the island.

Ugh, I hate this part. But I entertain her and sit down in one of the other stools.

"How did it go with Rufus?" she asks eagerly.

"Eh, he was nice," I reply.

After a few moments she says, "Just nice? Did you take him back to your place?"

"No. We had dinner at the pasta restaurant you suggested, but I went home afterward. I just wasn't feeling up to it," I explain.

She sighs and grabs my hand, "We have to get you back out there. You're far too young to give up on love."

The fact was, I knew I was never going to find anyone like Nonus. He was like gravity to me. And ever since that day, I've been weightless, floating around like a leaf lost in the wind.

"How about a drink?" she asks.

"Ok, but none of the hard stuff you drink. Last time I was hung over for three days," I reply.

"Well, you're in luck," Mr. Vettius chimes, "Sabina picked up this nice bottle of Merlot from Naples a few weeks ago and we've just not had an opportunity to crack it open yet."

"Now we're talking," I say, re-energized.

"I will find you a guy. I've set my mind to it. And you're going to fall head over heels for him. Just you watch," Sabina says, popping the cork from the bottle.

She tries so hard. I'm not sure why though. It's not like her and her husband are living in a fairy tale. In fact, they're pretty much just like every other older couple I know. I guess your thirties can be rough when you've been married half of your life.

"Ok, ladies. Dinner is almost done. Why don't you take that wine to the table and I'll start bringing the food out," Mr. Vettius says, ushering toward the oversized marble table.

"Sure, dear," she says, grabbing the wine bottle and the decanter before heading toward the table.

"Cecilia, how do you like your steak cooked?" he asks loudly over the sudden sizzling of meat.

"Medium is fine," I shout back to him.

Sabina pours the decanter half full and swishes the dark red wine around as he brings over a silver pan full of roasted red potatoes, onions, and peppers and sets it down in front of us.

My mouth starts to salivate as I take in the overwhelming earthy aromas with a hint of garlic. I let my eyes scan over the glossy vegetables, noticing the slightly charred edges that are my favorite.

Sabina begins to pour wine from the decanter into my long-stemmed glass.

"Wow, that looks amazing honey," she says to him.

"Oh, just you wait. The main course is finishing in the oven as we speak," he says, walking over with another pan of roasted asparagus.

I wasn't really a fan of asparagus. Mainly because it was often mushy and drenched in oil. But if Mr. Vettius made it, I'd try it. The poor man had his flaws but seeing his passion for cooking as he bounced back and forth in the kitchen almost made me envy him. He still had something that excited him in life. And I just couldn't bring myself to shatter it by dumping my relationship issues on the dinner table.

Finally, he removes the steaks from the oven and sets them on the cutting board to rest. He wipes his hands on his plain black apron, removes it, and hangs it on a hook in a corner of the kitchen.

As he sits with us, Sabina finishes filling his glass.

"Wine always makes me feel fancy," he says with a grin. "I feel like we should toast to something."

Sabina turns to me, glass in hand, and says, "To young love."

"Hear, hear," Mr. Vettius chimes in.

I awkwardly smirk at them both and clink glasses to not be rude. She can be so hopeless at times. But it is nice that she tries to help me. Maybe she's right. Maybe I'll find someone new. I always shifted back and forth between disdain and hope when it comes to love. I just wanted my Nonus back.

"It certainly would be nice to see you with a man. You always look lonely when you come here," Mr. Vettius says.

Sabina slaps him in the arm, "Really?" she says to him. "I think the steaks are ready."

"I'm sorry, I didn't mean to offend you," he says to me as he starts to get up from his chair.

"That's ok. I get it from my mother all the time," I lie.

She's been dead for ten years, but it was the only thing I could think of to dispel the taint of the latest twist in the conversation.

Sabina flashes me a confused look as he returns to the kitchen. She knows how my mother passed. Hell, she was one of the Praetorians that stopped by my parents' house at the time and had to tell my father that his wife had passed in a horrific car accident. I take a large gulp of the wine.

"Alright," he says as he sets the cutting board on the table and begins slicing the steaks. He uses the carving knife and fork to set mine on my plate, followed by Sabina, and finally his plate.

Rejoining us, he states, "Let us pray."

We join hands and bow our heads.

"Bless us, oh Lord, and these thy gifts which we are about to receive from thy bounty, through Christ, Our Lord. Amen," he chants.

"Amen," Sabina and I add and then place our napkins in our laps.

"This all looks and smells utterly divine," I state with a smile as I reach for the serving spoon in the potatoes.

"Well, I'm glad you like the presentation. But just wait until you taste it," he says, flashing me a grin as he spoons out asparagus onto Sabina's plate.

I slice into the steak, and to my surprise, the knife goes right through to the plate with a light clink. I can see Mr. Vettius silently serving me some of the asparagus, but I am too enthralled with the bite of steak I'm about to consume. Gently, I place the warm meat on my tongue and remove the fork as the spices and juices coat my mouth.

I close my eyes and lean back in my chair, setting my silverware down on the edges of the plate as best as I can as I slowly chew. The savory juices explode each time, tickling all of my taste buds.

"Cecilia? You ok over there?" Sabina says with a chuckle.

I finish chewing, swallow, and sigh heavily before opening my eyes.

"Oh, I am so much better than ok," I reply, still licking the taste from my lips.

"I think you put the poor girl into a coma, dear," she says as they both laugh.

"Wow," I simply state, sitting back up to take another bite.

The cycle repeated each time I took a bite of the steak. By the time I decided to try the other dishes, they were at the perfect temperature. The salty and savory potato dish was just the right companion for the steak. And the asparagus was buttery, salty, and still a bit crunchy all at the same time. I decided I might actually like asparagus, I just hadn't had it cooked properly.

"Well, it looks like you cleaned your plate," Mr. Vettius says as he reaches for one of the serving spoons. "Would you like some more?"

"Can you not see the poor girl is already about to pass out? Let her breathe," Sabina defends me with a light tap of her napkin to his left arm.

"Thank you, but I am so incredibly full," I reply, almost drowsily. "I don't think I could eat another bite."

He wipes his mouth one last time with his napkin, folds it nicely, and sets it next to his plate and then stands to remove our plates from the table.

"Very well, shall we move on to dessert then?" he asks glancing at Sabina and me.

I request mercy through my facial expression.

"Not just yet, honey. Let's allow some time for dinner to digest first," she replies, smiling at me.

He turns to walk to the kitchen as I mouth "thank you" to Sabina.

"I must say. The man can cook," she says quietly across the table to me.

"I couldn't agree more," I reply. "I don't think there's a restaurant in Prime that could touch that meal."

"It's honestly why we never go out," she says with a chuckle. "Every time we do though, he always has to speak with the manager or the chef after the meal. It's exhausting."

I take a sip of wine. It's good that it was a red because I completely forgot about it during dinner. The tart, fruity taste is refreshing.

"Shall we move onto business?" she asks as her expression changes.

"Absolutely," I reply, standing with my glass in hand.

"Honey, we're going to go into the office to discuss work. We'll be back shortly," she informs him.

"Alright," he says wiping his hands on a dish towel and smiling at us. "Enjoy."

I follow Sabina out of the dining room and down the hall to her lavishly furnished home office. I loved her office so much. There were all sorts of books lining the walls from floor to ceiling. I could spend weeks in here.

"Ok, so," Sabina says, bracing herself. "The latest. You know what a Venator is, right?" she asks.

"I've heard of them, but I don't think I've ever dealt with one," I reply, squinting.

"Well, they're part of the department of Law Enforcement. Whenever there's a particularly dangerous or elusive fugitive, they are dispatched to apprehend them. They excel in being able to track and subdue people that don't want to be found," Sabina expounds.

"Ok, so they're basically called in to hunt people down, yes?" I inquire.

"Exactly. So, we had one dispatched to hunt down the two fugitives that are on the run in 81. I'm sure you've seen the wanted board," she says.

I nod in agreement and take a sip of wine.

"Well, I spent the night with him," she says.

"You what?" I almost shout as my eyes go wide in shock.

"Shh," she says. "My husband doesn't know."

I motion the action of a zipper across my lips and take another sip of wine.

"It's not the first time, and it won't be the last," she retorts with a dismissive hand gesture. "Men want sex and as long as I can get close enough to drug them, I get access to whatever they have. Which is the case here."

"What exactly did you get?" I inquire curiously.

"Well, I ran an extraction program on his laptop and pulled up all of the files he's been assigned to for the past eight years. Every mark, every result," she states, spinning her laptop toward me on her desk.

"Wow," I say.

"He hasn't missed a mark in that time period and his average time to collect is less than two weeks," she explains further.

"I'm not sure I see the problem," I cautiously state.

"He's going to catch Calida and Tac, soon. I've built the Resistance up from nothing over the last four years to try and diminish the confidence Rome has in Axius' ability to govern," she states sitting down in her plush leather chair and setting her glass on the desk. "But it seems that either I've failed or maybe Rome just doesn't give a shit."

"Maybe we need to give the Resistance more time to recover?" I inquire.

"I wish it were that simple, but with the Venator hot on their trail and the rest of the Resistance demolished in the raid Axius forced me to authorize, I'm afraid we're at the end of the proverbial rope with this option," she rationalizes. "Plus, I gained access to a classified website that put the final nail in the coffin."

Intrigued, I ask, "How so?"

"It seems Rome has a contingency plan for if they lose control of a Prime. Basically, they'll bomb it back to the stone age," she says defeatedly.

"Well, shit. What do we do now? He can't stay in that office. I can't work for that man much longer!" I say, my tone becoming progressively more dire.

Sabina holds her hand out to keep me from overreacting, "Relax. I don't think we can coerce Rome to do our bidding any longer."

"What does that mean?" I ask aggressively.

She sighs heavily and then says, "It's time for us to take matters into our own hands."

Chills ride down my skin as I know the time has finally come for me to get my hands dirty.

"Ok," I simply state. "What did you have in mind?"

"I think we're just going to have to kill him. I don't see any other way," she replies with a shrug.

My breathing quickens as I imagine sticking a knife in his throat.

"I'll do it," I say sharply.

"What? No arguing?" she asks with a chuckle.

"Sabina, he killed Nonus. It's the least I could do for him," I remind her.

She purses her lips and simply nods.

"Well, this isn't exactly your area of expertise, so we'll have to plan accordingly," she finally says.

"I'm ok with that. Whatever I need to do to kill that bastard, I'll do," I state firmly.

"Ok," she agrees. "I think you should spend the night."

"Alright," I say.

"How does dessert sound?" she asks.

"It sounds good to me," I reply with a smirk.

Wine always gives me hangovers. It's why I don't drink very often. I quietly slide out of bed and pick up my clothes off the carpet. Apparently, it also impairs my judgement significantly as I turn to see them both still asleep in the bed.

I begin dressing as Sabina wakes up and groggily says, "There are some sweats in the third drawer," pointing across the room.

I cross and find a set of grey sweats that I think I can fit into.

"Do you mind if I take a shower?" I ask quietly.

She motions with her hand to go ahead and I step into the bathroom. I silently shut the door and lock it, exhaling all of the tension. After a quick shower, I dry off and throw on the sweats, which are still too big for me. But they'll do.

I open the door to Sabina standing awkwardly as I carry my clothes out.

"My turn!" she shouts and runs in and slams the door.

Mr. Vettius still snores away. I hope last night doesn't cause any issues. But I can't stay in this room right now, so I head down stairs to the kitchen. My headache has been softened by the hot shower, but I still need water.

I fill up a small glass from the tap as Sabina comes bouncing in.

"Good morning!" she shouts, startling me.

"Morning," I say, reeling from the increase in volume.

"How about some coffee?" she asks.

"I would love some," I reply, downing the glass of cool tap water.

"Aspirin," Sabina states as she opens a drawer from the island and sets the bottle down on top.

"Thank you," I respond as I refill my glass.

"No, thank *you*," she says, "Last night was awesome."

"I agree. I really enjoyed it," I lie, knowing damn well I have no idea what happened after dessert and the two bottles of wine. But I can guess.

"Ok. This morning we're going to focus on how you're going to get in to Axius' quarters. I think you should sleep with him again," she says bluntly.

I almost gag the aspirin back up, coughing the water out of my mouth.

"Or not," she reconsiders, patting me on the back.

"It's not that," I say with a cough, "It's just repulsive every time and you caught me off guard."

"Well, maybe you could just pretend to want to sleep with him," she suggests as she pours coffee grounds into her oversized coffee maker.

"It would get me close to him, but how do I kill him?" I ask.

"Well, we're going to have to be careful about that. We don't want fingers to get pointed the wrong way," she says as she ponders the question.

The 'brew' button lights up on the coffee maker and she presses it before turning around to face me.

"So, guns and knives are out. As much as he deserves a painful death, we need it to look natural," she says, crossing her arms and leaning against the counter.

"Well, we're only going to get one shot at it," I state. "If I'm caught, he wins."

She looks at me with desperation, "That's not going to happen, Cecilia. I'm way too good at this and we're going to do it right. When we're done, I'll be Governor and you'll be my right-hand woman. We're going to change the world."

"I believe you. I'm just having a hard time seeing it," I reply honestly.

She walks over and grabs me by the shoulders, "I believe in *you*, Cecilia. If I didn't, you wouldn't be here."

I nod and sigh to bleed off the nerves as she walks over to the cupboard and retrieves three coffee cups.

"Does he have any food allergies?" I ask.

Sabina spins and looks at me with eyes wide, "Genius!"

I flinch at her volume.

"Sorry, but you are a genius. He's deathly allergic to all forms of shellfish," she says as a grin creeps across her face.

Her reaction gives me chills.

"But how to get it in him? He only eats from his private chefs and they are very aware that he cannot have any kind of shellfish," she ponders, dropping sugar cubes into each of the cups.

"I'm sorry, I didn't ask you if you liked sugar in your coffee," she says looking over her shoulder at me.

"I like my cream and sugar with a little coffee," I reply with a chuckle.

She simply smiles and pours the coffee.

"I think we could condense some stock made with shellfish down into a potent enough concentration to do the job," she states, topping off the last cup.

"And I just pour that into his drink?" I ask, naively.

"He'll taste it and know what's going on before it takes effect. No, we'll have to put him to sleep first. I've got just the thing. It's the same thing I used on the Venator. It's tasteless and odorless. He'll never know what hit him. Then, all you have to do is pour the stock down his throat and that should be all she wrote," she elaborates as she carries two cups toward me and extends one.

"I'm sorry, do you have any cream?" I ask.

"Oh, sorry," she says, returning to the fridge. "All we have is half and half."

"That will work perfectly," I respond.

As I stir my now appropriately colored coffee, I inquire, "So, we're really going to do this?"

"As long as you're ok with it," she anxiously replies.

"Yes. I think it's a well-defined plan and, as long as everything goes accordingly, we should succeed. Once I'm sure he's no longer breathing, I can just call the guards in and play damsel," I allude.

A smirk comes across her face, "This is why I brought you in. You remind me so much of myself when I was younger."

I smile at the compliment and enjoy the first sip of my coffee.

"Good morning, ladies!" Mr. Vettius struts into the kitchen in his tight white underwear.

"What the fuck do you think you're doing?" Sabina retorts.

He stops dead in his tracks and the smile disappears. I almost snort my coffee.

"What? It's nothing she hasn't seen before," he replies.

She just gives him the look. After a second, he sighs and goes back to their bedroom to dress.

"See, told you. Dog," she says.

We both explode with laughter.

"I heard that!" he yells from down the hall, which only makes us laugh harder.

"Ok. I'll see about getting the right shellfish and start making the stock," Sabina says. "Go home and do everything you normally do. Try not to think about it too much."

"I'll do my best," I reply, gulping down the last of the coffee.

Tonight was the night. I couldn't shake the nerves. Axius was throwing a gala at his mansion for a few selective guests to mark the celebration of Christs' birth. Sabina somehow got us both invitations. This was way over my paygrade. But look at me, huh. Rubbing elbows with generals and the like.

"This is for you, Nonus," I say under my breath.

We ascend the marble stairs out front, holding our dresses at the knee, up to the Praetorian Guards.

"Quaester Gallius, Lieutenant Vettius. Good evening ladies. Please make your way inside," he says.

"Thank you, gentlemen," Sabina responds as they open the door for us.

The inside of his mansion takes my breath away. Marble and gold as far as the eye can see. Deep purple rugs line the transition to the intricate staircase. Violins bring a warmth to the ambiance as I see various old people dressed in their best, shaking hands and eating hors d'oeuvres.

Sabina walks us through the light crowd to the bar and picks up two glasses of champagne, passing one to me. I take a heavy swig.

"Cheers," she says with a chuckle.

"Sorry," I clink my glass with hers.

"Relax, everything will go according to plan," she affirms.

"I know. I'm just nervous. I'll calm down in a few," I reply, hoping that instills some confidence in her. In actuality, I'll just be tipsy in a few and everything will be fine.

We make our social rounds, Sabina introducing me to various guests. Some of the men, looking us up and down. *Dogs,* I thought to myself but I smiled back. They had no idea what was going on.

Soon, the Governor, himself graced us with his presence. I watched as people started to kiss his ass before he could even get to the bottom of the staircase. We waited for our turn.

"Ok, you're up," she says quietly to me. "Good luck."

"Thanks," I say as the lump in my throat rises a little higher and I throw back the rest of my champagne. I set the empty glass on the platter of a passing butler and began to cross the room toward Axius.

Ok, just like Sabina said. Laugh at his jokes. Touch him when appropriate and let him see what he wants.

"Cecilia! My dear!" he shouts at me from across the room.

Whew, ok. Here we go.

I shrug off the garnered attention from the room and walked over to his side.

"Cecilia, I'm so glad you could make it. This is my favorite time of year and what a way to celebrate it with my favorite Quaester," he states.

"I'm your only Quaester, sir," I reply as laughter burst from the small circle.

"That you are, my dear. That you are," he says with a chuckle and turning back to continue his conversation.

I look around for Sabina who is quietly watching from the bar. She silently nods as I slightly smirk back at her.

"Cecilia, you don't have a drink?" he asks.

Axius snaps his fingers at one of the butlers passing nearby, getting his attention.

"Son, make sure this woman has a drink in her hand at all times," he orders, pointing at me.

"Yes, sir," he replies as he turns to me, "What is your drink of preference, ma'am?"

"Champagne is fine with me, thank you," I reply with a smile.

Before long, he is introducing me to people who are mingling with him. Each time he does, he pulls me in a little closer and even puts his hand on the small of my back. Even though it makes me gag on the inside, I can't fight it. I knew this coming in, but it's different standing here trying to smile at random people while he is feeling me up.

Ugh, will this party ever end? I ask as I look around for Sabina again. I see her as the doorman is putting her jacket back on her. She doesn't make eye contact with me before heading out the door.

I'm on my own now. Breathe Cecilia, just breathe. I do my best to hold it together. I watch as people leave the party, one by one.

"Would you care for a drink from my private collection, my dear?" he finally turns to ask me.

"Ooo, a private collection. I like the sound of that," I reply as I put on my best interested face.

"Say no more, my dear. Follow me," he replies as he turns to walk up the stairs.

The upstairs is just as impressive as the rest of the house. The guards open the door to his master suite as we approach. My eyes fixate on his bed as a wave of calm washes over me suddenly. The hard part is done, now all I have to do is drug him and pour the vial down his throat when he falls asleep.

"My dear, do you like scotch?" he asks when he reaches the massive bar across the room.

"I don't mind it at all," I lie, taking my hair down and fixing my dress.

It doesn't matter what he gets me to drink. Just so long as he drinks his. I take in the stunning intricacies of all the marble, mahogany, and silk seemingly littered throughout the room.

"Here you go, my dear," he says, passing the golden leaf-inlaid tumbler to me.

"Thank you, sir," I reply with a smile.

"I must say. That dress is absolutely stunning on you," he states, his eyes drifting down my body.

"I'm glad you like it. I picked it out especially for you," I lie again.

He gets close to smell my hair and I know this is my chance. I quickly reach under my left breast and remove the small clear pill and drop it in his glass. *So easy,* I think to myself.

I watch his glass as the pill instantly disappears into the liquid.

"You smell absolutely divine, my dear," he says.

"As do you, sir," I reply, then mouth *what the hell*.

He begins to kiss my neck as he sets his glass down on the bookshelf.

"How about a toast, sir?" I ask.

"What?" he asks, interrupted, "Oh, ok."

"May tonight be the wildest night of our lives," I state with no effort.

Wow, that sounded good! I didn't even practice that! I think to myself as I smile at him, clink his glass, and throw the scotch back. *Ugh, God. That's horrible.* I think, trying not to make a repulsive face.

He sets the glass back down and we resume our tango over to the bed where I push him on his back and climb on top. *How long did Sabina say this took to work?* I ask myself as I start to undress. Before I can even pull the dress over my head, he's out for the night. I actually have to look twice to make sure.

But sure enough, he's out, just like she said. The smile disappears from my face as I reach under my right breast and retrieve the vial of overly concentrated seafood stock.

This is it! It's actually going to happen! I squeal to myself.

I open the vial and pour the contents into his agape mouth as he gargles it and inhales. *That's for Nonus, you son of a bitch!* I think as his breathing gets progressively shallower before stopping. Then he turns blue. It's working.

Suddenly, the doors burst open, Guards have their weapons trained on me. *Ok, time for drama.*

"Help! I don't know what happened!" I shout as I climb off of him, clutching the vial in my dress close to my chest to cover my underwear.

"Get on the ground!" one of them shout at me with their rifle in my face.

"Please, get him help!" I scream, fake tears flowing down my face.

"Medicus to the Governor's quarters! Code blue!" the other guard shouts into his radio.

Shortly after, the Medicus and two other EMTs enter, bags in hand. They work on him for a long two minutes. As they do, I slip the vial in between two books. Not where I planned to stash it, but it is my only option at this time. Finally, they relax.

"Ok, he's breathing. I've got a good pulse," the Medicus says. "Let's get a stretcher in here and get him down to my office."

How the hell did they do that? I ask myself.

"Is he going to be ok, Medicus?" I ask through sniffles as he passes by.

"Yes, he'll be fine. It looks like anaphylactic shock, by my first guess. But we'll need to run more tests to make sure," he says.

Two more guards enter as Axius is being carried out of the room.

"Ma'am, place your hands behind your back," one of them states.

"What for?" I ask defensively.

"Attempted murder," he says.

"But I didn't do anything! He just stopped breathing!" I plead with them.

"We have hidden cameras all throughout the compound, ma'am. We saw you pour something down his throat," he replies.

Uh, oh. I think as they put me in handcuffs and drag me half naked out of the room.

My mind goes wild with tangents on how I can get out of this. The squad car pulls up to headquarters with a screech. I still don't have my clothes on. They could at least let me dress.

One of them pulls me from the back of the car and leads me up the stairs by my arm.

"Ow, you're hurting me," I say.

He doesn't respond.

Whistles and cheers pound my ears as I'm pulled into the lobby where Praetorians and criminals alike stop to look at me. Finally, the elevator dings open as we enter and head to the basement.

The Guard shoves me into a cell and removes the handcuffs before shutting the cell door. More cheers and whistles from the inmates.

The Guard on duty retrieves a white jumpsuit for me. I quickly throw it on in the corner of my cell. That should keep them quiet for the moment. My mind continues to run wild for a few hours. I think it has been a few hours. I look at the small opening at the ceiling to see the colors of sunrise populating the sky.

I guess it has been longer than I thought. Sabina bursts in the door and a wave of relief comes over me.

"I need to speak with that one, alone," she says. "Now!"

Something doesn't feel right.

The Guard puts cuffs back on me and walks me to one of the interrogation rooms. I've only been in here once for a demonstration. The dark room scares me as he sits me down and latches the cuffs to the table.

"Turn the cameras off too," she instructs.

"Yes, ma'am," he says.

The door shuts behind him as she turns back to me.

"What the hell happened?" she asks.

"Everything went according to plan, but they had cameras in the room!" I say as I burst into tears.

"Shit. So they saw everything?" she inquires further.

"I'm guessing so," I reply, sobbing heavily.

She comes around the table and hugs me.

"Sabina, you gotta get me out of this," I cry.

"Honey, I don't think I can. They've got you on camera," she replies.

"What am I gonna do?" I ask, looking up to her sorrowful expression.

"The only thing that's left," she says. "If they have you on camera, they're going to publicly execute you."

She stares into my eyes for a few moments before reaching in her pocket and pulling out a small white pill.

"What's this?" I ask as she hands it to me.

"The only way out," she says coldly. "Put that in your mouth and keep it in your cheek. When you can't last any longer, bite down on it and it'll take away the pain."

"So, you're just going to leave me here?" I ask wildly.

She kisses me and retreats to say, "I have no other choice. Otherwise we'll both be dead."

The realization hits me and a wave of relief washes over as I realize there is no getting out.

"Thank you for all that you've done for Nonus and me. I'm sorry we didn't succeed," I say to her.

"I'm sorry too," she replies softly. "Guard!"

I slip the pill into my cheek and the door opens.

"Take her to the square by the entrance to Prime and execute her," Sabina orders.

The Guards enter and carry me outside as instructed. I look up at the brilliant hues in the sky as the sun begins to come up. Such beautiful colors.

I feel the eyes watching me as they put me into the back of the squad car one last time. Before I know it, they're pulling me out again.

"Strip her down!" one of them shouts.

Two of them rip my jumpsuit and underwear off as I stand in handcuffs. I look back up at the sky as the oranges disappear and the brilliant blue resumes. Suddenly, I feel a sharp pain pierce my right hand.

I scream in agony as I look to see a large spike being hammered into the middle of my hand. Another sharp pain on the other side. *The pill. Where is the pill?* I ask myself. I search for a few agonizing seconds and finally find it. I bite down on it hard as everything soon goes to an overbearing white light.

Nonus appears from the light with a smile.

CHAPTER XIII: LOSS

The sun beams in the front door as I open it, home from work. Calida looks up from preparing dinner and smiles brightly in my direction.

"Hi, honey. I'm home!" I say.

Little Junia runs up to me, thrusts her arms up, teddy bear still in hand, and squeals, "Daddy!"

"Hello, Pumpkin!" I reply, setting my briefcase down and picking her up. "How was school today?"

"Good," she replies with a smile.

"Good?" I ask again.

"Yeah," Junia says.

I exaggerate a kiss on her tiny cheek as Junia smiles even wider and giggles.

"Alright, go play," I instruct, putting her back down.

"Da da, da da!" tiny Caius says as he waddles as quickly as he can towards me.

"There's my little slugger!" I shout picking him up. "How is daddy's favorite little man?"

Gibberish flows from his mouth as I play along.

"Oh, really? You helped mommy out today? Well, I'm sure your mommy appreciates your help," I say carrying Caius in one arm over to Calida.

I kiss her on the cheek and takes a deep sniff of the meal she is preparing.

"Oh, it smells great in here, honey. Is that Tes' meat stew recipe?" I ask.

A few seconds go by without reply before I try to draw her attention, "Honey?"

She still doesn't say anything. She continues working in the kitchen, moving between cupboard to drawer and back to the stove as I dodge her.

"Is something wrong?" I ask, increasingly concerned.

She and the kids suddenly disappear into thin air. The cookware and smells of a hearty dinner disappear to reveal a dimly lit kitchen that reeks of mildew. I'm thoroughly confused and go room to room calling for Calida and the children, whose names I now cannot remember.

Each room is just as empty as the next. I start to panic as there are fewer and fewer rooms they could be in. I search the whole house and end back up in the kitchen.

I wake up face down in the tent. Confusion initially sets in for a few seconds before the pain from the darts still in my chest finally break me free of the dream. I roll over, shivering and removes the darts. The wind howls against the tent as the half-opened flap blows in the wind.

I slowly try to stand, still reeling from the effects of the serum. It's freezing in here. I throw my clothes on and unzip the tent, walking out into the fresh powder. There's no movement in the camp and the fire has indeed gone out. I check the other tents to find the frozen corpses of Lurius, Bruttius, and the rest of the survivors, each with a dart in their chest. All except for Calida.

Wait a minute, Calida was on watch last night. Maybe she's still up there.

I walk up the hill to where she was huddled up. Her weapon lies under the tree, partially dusted with the new snow. But she's not there. At least there's a chance she's still alive. The question is where is she?

"Calida!" I desperately call out.

The howling wind through the trees is the only thing that can be heard besides my breathing.

"CALIDA!" I shout again louder, my inner voice breaking in despair.

Again, no answer. Maybe she's buried somewhere underneath this snow. I frantically brush the snow around with my feet. Maybe she is just passed out like I was. But I only find dirt and exposed tree roots.

I start walking beside the road back to Prime, distraught with my mind running wild trying to make some sort of sense of the situation, hopefully leading to where she is. Shortly down the road, I notice some of the snow is disturbed. As I gets closer, I can see there are fresh boot prints in the snow.

Did she stumble away from the camp in confusion? I call to her again, but still no answer aside from the howling wind. Someone definitely came this way. There's two tracks, one leading toward the camp and another leading away. I guess whoever shot me and the rest of the group must have taken her, or at least knows where she is.

As feeling and coordination returns to me, I move faster up the side of the mountain, following the tracks through the snow. The wind comes straight at me, fighting each step I take down the barren snow-dusted road.

After about an agonizing hour of walking headlong into the blizzard, I finally reach the top of the mountain where I find vehicle tracks off the side of the road where the footprints end. The thin air and exposed skin is starting to take its toll and I begin shivering.

I know if I don't get warm, I'll be in no place to move soon. I head into the woods and starts making a fire. The wood is all soaked though. I'll have to find some dry wood before I can build a fire. I wince as I stand, still reeling from the effects of the darts.

I have to decide whether to go back to the camp for supplies and to warm up or continue down this side of the mountain and hope I get to a decent altitude with dry wood before I freeze to death. I have no idea how much time Calida has, if she's even still alive, so I begin making my way down the mountain through the thick brush and trees towards Prime, and hopefully Calida.

The trek back is much slower than before from the blizzard and icy conditions, but the wind is almost bearable and the snow doesn't fall as thick on this side. I've got to hurry up. This cold is starting to make my hands and feet go numb. Unfortunately, due to the snow and ice, I know I can't run without potentially slipping and falling. This is not the time or place to get injured.

Finally, it seems the snow storm has let up momentarily and the wind dies down. I find some drier wood half way down the mountain and pick up enough to hopefully last the night. I return to the side of the road and continue down the mountain side. Most of the snow hasn't accumulated here and travel is a little faster.

This is the first time I've really been alone since I got here. Being out in the snow like this reminds me of the winter back in Tes' hut. Except there is this burning drive to get back to Calida. I have no idea who has taken her, or if she'll even be in Prime. But that's the first place I'm going to look.

My stomach starts making noises to remind me of how long I've gone since eating last. I gather up some of the fresh snow and eat it. It won't provide any lasting effects, but it's not a great idea to be hunting with a noisy stomach.

It's still going to be a day or maybe two before I can make it back to Prime, depending on the weather. I'll have to find shelter, water, and food. If I had thought about it, I would have just taken the camp apart and brought what I needed. Whatever was in those darts really affected my judgement and had me unstable for a while.

First thing is first, I need a fire to get warm. Then I can work on shelter, food, and water. I start a friction fire with some of the drier tinder I found. It takes a long time to get two tiny little embers, but I manage to get them into the bundle and blow on them until they light.

Sitting there, carefully laying slightly larger tinder on the infant fire as it grows larger, I have time to reflect on last night's events and collect my bearings. I do feel guilty for leaving them all behind. I normally wouldn't do that, but that serum had me all messed up. After this is all over, I'll go back and build pyres for each of them, if I'm still alive.

As the fire starts to engulf the larger tinder and finally a few small logs, I can move on the next item on the list: food. I have no modern weapons with me, so I'll need to fashion a spear.

If Klik taught me anything when looking for a new blank, he made sure I knew to always use green wood. Unlike dead wood that you use for burning, green wood is more flexible. It flies better and has a lower propensity to breaking and chipping. Plus, it's denser, meaning more mass which translates into more momentum when it strikes your target. That leads to further penetration and a better chance of scoring a kill.

I scan the trees overhead for a proper specimen. I snap off a large limb from one of the trees. I made hundreds of these during armory duty as a Warrior, but it's been more than two seasons since I've made one for myself. I fumble through the process of stripping the extraneous twigs and branches off. I hold it up to my eye so I can see down the entire shaft. It's not a bad specimen. It's a little off kilter and heavy on the back end, but it should work just fine for what I need. I'm not exactly going into battle with it. Well, not yet anyway.

I repeatedly strike one rock against another, forming a makeshift knife. Then, I use the knife to taper one end of the spear and set it in the fire to harden. My mind wanders as the moisture boils out of the tip of the spear. I miss Calida. I miss her smile. I miss her laugh. It hurts in my chest to know that I failed to protect her. I have no idea who took her or what he's doing to her. But I swear when I find him. He will pay…dearly.

I pull the spear out and grind it down further on a flat rock nearby until I have a hard point. At this point, I'm prepared to go hunting, at least the spear is. I can't stop thinking about her. I hate myself right now. I don't know if she'll ever forgive me. But it doesn't matter. I promised I would protect her. The least I can do is track her down and free her if she's still alive.

I've got to get out of my head. I stand up and move away from the camp toward the tree line. Maybe focusing on hunting will help distract me for a short period of time. Birds are all over the place, but it defeats the purpose to even throw my spear, too little meat for the effort. No, I need something bigger.

I wander around for what seems like hours, attempting to track whatever so-called footprints I've found, but to no avail. I've always been horrible at tracking. I sit down at the base of a tree, frustrated and defeated.

I must have nodded of a minute. I'm woken by the low grunts of a whitetail. I look at the sky and wonder why they would risk being out at this hour. Not that it matters. It's his mistake. After searching with my eyes for a few seconds, I finally notice the signature tail flick of a good-sized buck around fifteen meters away.

Damn, he's close, well, for a white tail. They're very skittish normally. I float the spear behind the tree I'm against and position it horizontally so I can launch it as soon as he looks away. I'm pretty sure I'm upwind from him, so it is only a matter of time before he smells me.

He looks down to graze and I launch the spear. I missed. It sails straight over his back, less than a half meter above him. I jump up and retrieve the spear as he takes off in a dead sprint to my right. I take a moment to estimate how far I have to lead him and release the spear again. It sticks him right in the heart as his forward momentum coupled with the impact of my spear causes his body to flip end over end into the low brush.

A wave of relief comes over me and I immediately start salivating. I have to internally scold myself so I can focus on carrying the carcass back to the camp. I retrieve the spear first. 'Defend yourself first, always' Klik used to say. Ok, so he used it in a different context, but it still applies here. Where there is prey, there are predators.

With my spear at the ready, I lift the white tail up and carry him back up the hill to my camp. I must have slept longer than I thought. My fire is out, but still warm. No matter. I slit the white tail's throat and hang him upside down from a nearby tree to drain while I build the fire back.

I repeat the process with the friction to embers to tinder and finally get it back to a stable fire. I search for and find a large, flat rock that I can cook the meat on and place it in the fire, building small logs in a semi-circle around it to help pre-heat it.

As it builds further, I retrieve the deer and start cleaning it. I throw the entrails and skin down the hill, making sure to dispose of them where the wind won't blow the scent back at me. Using my makeshift knife, I carve some thin slices off the shoulder and toss them onto the stone. They sizzle immediately, causing me to salivate again and my stomach to churn with anticipation.

I roughly slice off a few more pieces and flip the first ones. Finally, after what feels like an hour, but was more like minutes, the first pieces are done and steaming in the chilly air. I pick one up and touch it with my hand. It's too hot. I float all three pieces around as I throw the next three on the stone. I bite down hard into the first piece and lean back against the big rock in pure bliss. This is the first fresh meat I've had since I got here, nearly three weeks ago. It literally brings me to tears as I chew and I'm totally content for most of the meal.

By the time I'm full, I've eaten most of the shoulder and some of the hindquarters. The sky lights up in brilliant colors signifying dusk. I know I won't make it back tonight. She'll be alone again tonight. My anxiety returns as all I can do is stay warm and wait. I finally decide that I should try to get some sleep. I anticipate a fight when I get back to Prime and I'll need my strength and a sharp mind.

I hang the carcass way up in one of the nearby trees to keep predators away and curl up next to the fire. I try to quiet my racing mind and fall asleep, but I have a lot of trouble with such a simple process. It shouldn't be that hard. I've done it thousands of times. I change positions several times before I find one that is comfortable.

Something startles me awake in the middle of the night. It's near pitch black with the dying fire and clouds above. I don't move and try to control my breathing. Something is out there. Maybe it hasn't discovered me yet. I slowly feel for and grab hold of my spear, preparing an ambush.

Then I hear the familiar grunts and sounds as it gets closer. It's definitely a bear. Probably attracted to the white tail in the tree. I knew I should have buried it. Now I have to fight a bear in the dark. I slowly and quietly lift my head to try and see it. To my surprise, I can actually see the outline of a very large bear about ten meters away from me.

In a flash, I leap up and launch the spear at its heart. The blinding white light pierces my entire body and time stops. I shield my eyes with my hand, eventually adjusting to show a large brown bear eclipsed by my spear, seeming to hover in front of it.

"Hello, my child," the bear says.

"Am I dead?" I reply, extremely confused by the unexpected turn of events.

"No. Tes and Shadow have been watching your journey and asked me to come speak with you," it says.

"Your voice sounds really weird. It's like a male and a female speaking at the same time. Who are you?" I inquire.

"My name isn't important. All you need to know is that I mean you no harm," it says as my spear floats back in my direction.

"Wait, you spoke with Tes and Shadow?" I say shortly after catching on.

"Yes, they currently reside on the other side with me," it replies.

"How are they?" I ask.

"They are great. But they worry for you. I've seen your soul Tac, and you carry a great deal of unnecessary guilt and shame with you. It is keeping you from doing what you are here to do," it replies with a maternal tone.

"Well, I have a great deal to feel guilty about. Most recently, allowing whatever happened to Calida to happen. I was supposed to protect her and I failed," I reply with conviction. "Almost the same way I felt about Tes and Shadow. I was supposed to protect them too."

"That was not your fault, child. Tes and Shadow have already forgiven you for that. Calida will forgive you too. But I can tell you that she is alive, for the moment. You will find her where her father resides," it explains.

"Ok, thank you very much," I say.

My eyes snap open. *Wait, was that a dream?* I ask myself. The sun has already broken the horizon. Time to go. I pull the carcass down from the blood-stained tree and toss it near the tree line. Something will be along soon for a free meal. Kicking the snow and dirt over the fire, I pick up my spear again and start moving to the road.

The snow is starting to recede and before long, I'll be able to run. It shouldn't take more than two hours to run the last sixty or so kilometers, but I plan to take a quick break halfway through. As I begin my hike, a wave of peace comes over me that I haven't felt in a long time. My anxiety about Calida is gone and I know for sure where I need to go to save her. I just hope I'm not too late.

Before long, I'm below the snow line and I start on a light jog to keep from burning all of my energy in the first part. I make really good time for the first thirty kilometers. I find a stream running under the road and stop for a drink. The snow last night held up well, but I've sweat most of it out by now.

I let my body cool down a little bit and the water settle before I take off for the last thirty kilometers. I have no idea what I'm going to do when I get there. All I have is a shoddy spear and my anger. They have automatic weapons and armor, and a lot of them.

I start to worry again. My mind wanders to devise a way to get Calida free. There are hundreds of Praetorians in Prime and at least a dozen Praetorian Guard in the Governor's mansion. They take his safety very seriously and have much better weapons and armor than normal Praetorians.

Either way, this will not be easy. The best idea I can come up with is to stroll in the front door and start breaking necks. I have a feeling that Prime thinks I'm dead. Which is a good thing. They don't know I'm coming, which gives me the advantage of surprise.

The closer I get to Prime, the more invigorated and angrier I get. I want answers. I want them to suffer. But most importantly, I want my Cali. I want her back safe.

It's midday by the time I reach the outskirts of the city. The market I walked through when I first arrived is bustling again with activity. As I approach, I slow to a walk, as to not bring attention to myself. I try to enjoy the smells and sights. It reminds me so much of home. I kind of laugh to myself of how far I've come since that day in the market with the bully. I was afraid of him for some reason, but now I'm about to storm a heavily fortified base with hundreds of Praetorians. My how times change.

I get inside the main gate and walk towards the central plaza. I can't read any of the signs, and I have no idea where the

Governor's mansion is. But as I'm trying to figure out where to go, something catches my eye in the distance. It's a large cross sticking out of the ground. I get closer and I can tell that there's a person suspended on it. It's a rather odd sight. Suddenly it hits me, my stomach drops, a lump forms in my throat, and I freeze in place. It's a body, of a woman. And she has red hair.

CHAPTER XIV: CAPTIVITY

I come to with a massive headache. The room is dark. No, there's something over my head. The carpet beneath my feet feels oddly familiar. I try to move, but my arms are tied behind my back. I can barely feel them, so I try to move my shoulders and fingers around to get some blood back to them.

I can see shapes through whatever is over my head and I notice my nightlight in across the room. 'Oh, God,' I think to myself. My breathing quickens as I realize I'm in my childhood bedroom which means my father is nearby and is the culprit for all of this.

My mind starts racing. If I'm here, that means Tac wasn't able to stop whoever took me. If he wasn't able to stop him, he's probably dead along with everyone else. The Resistance is truly dead, and I am probably next. Tears form in the corner of my eyes and I inhale hot air as I start hyperventilating.

The hood is snatched off my head by a man I don't recognize. He doesn't say anything but looks down at me, devoid of empathy. It's quieter in the house than I remember. Memories of the night my mother was killed flood my mind. Ugh, I can taste metal. I vomit at my feet, which only makes my headache worse.

"It's the tranquilizer. You'll be ok in a few hours," he says.

I try to steady my stomach and my eyesight to focus on him and say, "Who are you?"

"My name is Pius Magius, Venator for Rome. Your father employed my services to retrieve you, unharmed," he replies.

"And the others?" I ask, fearing the worst.

"They're all dead," he replies after a few seconds.

Tears flow steadily as I hang my head and watch them fall to the ground.

"Are you sure?" I ask shortly thereafter.

"We have a specialized weapon we use in situations that require stealth. It fires a small dart and is nearly absent of sound. I shot you with a tranquilizer dart. I shot each one of your Resistance with a dart that contains a poison specifically bio-engineered to stop the heart. It's strong enough to kill a horse. And then I shot your boyfriend with two of them, just to make sure," he says coldly.

My heart implodes and I ugly cry right there in the middle of my room. What mascara I had on before, now streaks across my cheeks and dots the beige carpet in front of me. I know it's only been a few weeks, but he was the kindest, sweetest man to me. And now, according to this so-called Venator, he's gone forever. So are all of my friends. I'm alone, again, a scared little girl in my room fearing the moment my father walks in.

Everything I've done for almost a decade has been to make sure I never end up in this room again. Now, it just seems foolish that I even tried. I was always going to end up back here. By fighting it, I've caused the deaths of hundreds of people. For what? In the name of a Resistance movement that had no chance in hell from the beginning? Selfish and ignorant. That's what I am, a selfish and ignorant little girl.

I haven't felt this alone since I was living on the streets. All of the crying and snot running everywhere is making my head split open. Just more pain on top of everything else. Why not. Pile it on. I deserve to be punished for what I've done to all of these people. They trusted me to lead them and protect them. And I could do neither properly.

"Dry that up," Tiberius says throwing the door open. "Dry it up right now, you little bitch."

Oooo, I do *not* like that word. I fiercely look at him through my tears.

"Fuck you, you bastard!" I scream.

"Just like old times, huh, sweetheart?" he asks facetiously.

"Why am I here? I've told you, I'm not your daughter and you're not my father. Did you conveniently forget our last conversation?" I inquire.

"And at what point did you think that anything you say holds any weight? Not only am I the man of the house, but I'm also the Governor of this district. You couldn't prove anything, even with video evidence and a signed confession from me. I'm untouchable. And you *are* my daughter and you will be for the rest of your life," he replies.

"You're just as prideful and stubborn as before. Tell me, do you still rape little girls for fun?" I ask, staring him in the eyes for his answer.

"I can take what I want from people who don't have value," he coldly replies.

"Fuck you. Did you tell the Venator to kill Tac too?" I ask angrily.

"I told him that I didn't care what happened to the rest of your little group, just that you were brought home unharmed," he retorts. "But now that I think about it, it is the best outcome. I'll probably give him a bonus for that. Technically, there *was* a bounty on both your heads."

My anger turns to rage as I try to break free of the bindings holding me to this chair. I scream unintelligibly and spit at him, void of anything of consequence left to say.

"Please, just leave me alone," I say quietly after giving into the restraints.

"That's more like it. You might just get dinner tonight," he turns to walk out of the room. "And don't forget to dress up pretty."

He shuts the door and the room goes silent except for my rhythmic breathing. Over the next hour, I try my best to break free, but whatever my arms are tied behind my back with is very strong.

Two Praetorian Guards burst into the room and shut the door behind them. They say nothing but start to unshackle me. Now I know that it's a pair of handcuffs with another chain to the floor which keep my arms in place. No wonder I couldn't break free.

One of them crosses to the closet and pulls a random outfit. *Yeah, like that's going to fit. I haven't been in this room for almost ten years, guys.* He tosses it on the bed along with a pair of shoes. The second guard removes the other two cuffs from my ankles. I don't immediately resist cause it's nice to feel my hands and feet again.

"Get dressed. Makeup is in the vanity drawer," he instructs.

They both then turn and walk out. I hear the lock on the door engage shortly after it's shut. I stand up and take a status of my body. I get dizzy and almost fall over. Using the bed as a brace, I slowly straighten my body. My left arm is in a lot of pain, just below the shoulder. I rub it to try and loosen it. That's when I find the entry wound for the dart that bastard used. Other than that, I seem unharmed.

I walk to the back of my room and pull the curtains back to reveal bars covering the window and two cameras panning the back yard. *Fuck, I'm trapped here.* I turn my face in disgust and shut the curtains quickly. I start looking around the room for possible weapons. There's not a damn sharp object in the whole room. How long has he been planning this?

The door opens again and one of the Guards walks a few steps in before asking, "Why aren't you dressed?"

"I'm not dressing up for that pervert," I reply without looking at him.

"Governor Axius commands your presence at dinner and he commands you wear appropriate clothing," he replies mechanically.

"I don't give a fuck what he 'commands', he doesn't own me," I shout defiantly, hoping he'd hear. "He's taken me prisoner against my will, yet again!"

He crosses the room and stands behind me, "He commands you get dressed."

"Fuck you, you little patsy," I turn around and tell him.

He swiftly punches me in the stomach, knocking the air from my lungs and sending me to the ground.

"He commands you get dressed. And be quick about it," he reiterates.

It takes a few seconds before I can breathe again. Now, I'm just pissed off.

"A sucker punch? Is that the best you have? Get your ass back in here so I can send you to the Medicus!" I yell.

The door opens and two Guards enter and cross the room. I take a swing at one's face, but he dodges quickly and punches me again in the stomach. I winch, but I was ready for it this time, as I kick his legs out from underneath him, sending him crashing on the flat of his back. Just as I'm about to move in to beat this little fucker's ass, everything goes dark.

When I come to, I've been dressed in the outfit that was picked out and laid across the bed. My left cheek hurts and from what I can deduce, the other Guard must have knocked me out when I wasn't looking. I slowly get up and cross to look in the vanity. Yep, I've got a good shiner going. I poke my cheek and flex it, checking the inflammation. That's really going to sting in the morning.

Then I recognize with horror the outfit I'm dressed in. It's my mother's favorite dress that she was killed in. He didn't even bother to sew up the knife holes. Some are even still stained by my mother's blood.

The door opens and both Guards enter before shutting it behind them. They both walk up to me and handcuff my hands behind my back again.

"Which one of you little bitches hit me?" I ask.

"That'd be me," one of them answers. "Maybe you'll think twice before…"

I immediately kick him in the testicles. As he falls, everything goes dark again. I wake sometime later, again laid out on the bed, but with leg shackles with chains attached to the other leg and my handcuffs. I'm probably going to look like a racoon tomorrow, but it was worth it.

I slide down and off the bed and shuffle back over to the vanity. My nose is rather swollen and the dried trickle of blood from it tells me all I need to know.

The Guards enter yet again, just like before. They pull a chair up to the vanity and force me to sit down. I damn near break my fingers doing so. Another Guard, female this time, enters and crosses the room to me. She sighs and pulls drawers open, pulling different types of makeup out.

"Please don't make this more difficult than it has to," she says to me. "I know this is probably going to hurt, but I was ordered to fix your makeup for dinner."

"Whatever. I'm getting tired of this game anyway," I reply.

Fuck that's tender, I think as she applies foundation around my eyes and cheeks. I wince and move away from her hand as she tries her best to smooth out the creamy foundation that's obviously two shades lighter than I am. I look like a fucking ghost. This is stupid. Or was that his intention between the makeup and my mother's dress. He's such a sicko.

She puts the foundation down and does my eyeliner and lashes in the same fashion. Finally, a bright red lipstick completes the look. I hate bright red lipstick. It just looks weird on me.

"Finished?" one of the Guards asks.

"Yeah," she responds.

Each of the male Guards take an arm and lift me out of the chair to my feet. She stands in front of me with a brush and works my matted hair to a sheen finish. I hate feeling like I'm being prepared for a ritual sacrifice. When I get free, I'm going to kill all of them.

She steps aside as they push me forward into a clanging shuffle toward the door. One of them drops away to shut the door as the other pushes me toward the stairs. As I awkwardly descend, I can see him sitting at the table. He's wearing his suit as usual, smoking his pipe and reading the paper.

I take a deep breath as I continue toward the table. He takes notice and stands, removing his glasses.

"Calida, so glad you could join me for dinner," he says.

I say nothing in return and make for my usual seat. My course is corrected to the right side of the table.

"Now, now, you're the lady of the house. You sit next to me," he says in a sinister tone.

Someone pulls the chair out for me as I'm thrust into it and pushed under the table.

"Can someone take these cuffs off me? Eating is going to be difficult without the use of my hands," I say.

"Oh, my dear Calida. You apparently can't be trusted to keep your hands to yourself. So, the handcuffs are going to stay on," he says. "I'll feed you dinner."

The butlers come through the side door, just as they always have, carrying silver platters with food. One of them sets a tray down in front of him and one in front of me. Removing the silver dome, I see chicken nuggets and French fries.

"Ahh, your favorite," he says.

"When I was six," I reply.

He picks up a nugget with his fork and moves it to my mouth. If I weren't starving this would go completely differently. It's been at least a day since I've eaten anything. I open and take the entire chicken nugget, chewing quickly and swallowing.

"Oh, ok. So, you *do* have a bit of an appetite. Good," he says picking up another.

I take that one and start chewing.

"Maybe tonight after dinner, we can have some Daddy-Daughter time, like we used to. That used to be your favorite," he says picking up another nugget.

I know what he means by Daddy-Daughter time and it's not fucking happening. I spit the mouthful of food in his face. He pauses for a second as his demeanor changes from pleasure to rage. I forgot how quickly he gets upset. I hope that's the only thing I inherited from him.

He backhands me in the nose so hard that my chair scoots back a few centimeters. My eyes tear up immediately and blood gushes into my lap. I exhale loudly from my nose to clear it.

"That wasn't very nice," he finally says.

"Fuck you," I retort with a swollen nose and a mouthful of blood.

He waves his hand as the Guards pick me back up and drag me across the floor toward the stairs. Damn, I'm really hungry now. My stomach anticipated much more food. Maybe next time he won't be a complete creep.

"Daddy will be up in a minute to tuck you in, sweetie," he calls as they carry me up the stairs.

"Take your time, bastard," I call down facetiously.

We stare at each other in disgust until I'm out of sight. They open the door and toss me in on my stomach. The impact forces more blood out of my nose and knocks the wind out of me. I roll to my side as the door is shut behind me, trying to catch my breath.

I finally sit up and look around the room. I've got to find a way out of this hell hole. I push my knees up to my chest, sliding the handcuffs and chains over my feet. I stand up slowly, wiping my nose on the back of my hand.

I waddle over to the window, drawing the curtains back again. I start banging on the window, which has been replaced with bulletproof glass.

"Fuck," I say in distress.

There's got to be a way out of here. I quietly shuffle back over to door and jiggle the knob. It's locked from the outside. Tears form again as I realize I'm in serious trouble. There's no other way out of this room. I shuffle slowly, defeated, back over to my bed and sit on the edge.

Shortly after, the Guards burst in followed by Tiberius. They walk directly over to me and start unshackling the chain from my legs and attach it to the headboard. I know what's happening and I start flailing my legs trying to get away.

"NO! NO!" I scream over and over again as they each grab a leg, unshackle the chain between them and pull them away from one another.

I can see his pleased face as he approaches me, removing his jacket and loosening his tie. I struggle to no avail, they're holding me too tightly. He slowly undoes his belt and pants, sliding them down to his ankles, drawing the anticipated horror out longer than necessary.

He climbs on top of me as I continue struggling and places his hand around my neck, squeezing my throat until I can't breathe. I flail harder until he lets up slightly and I start panting. I stare up into his face with pure hatred as this devilish smile spreads across his wrinkled face.

No matter how hard I try, I can't move and his grip gets tighter again. My vision starts to go. He loosens his grip and tears stream down the sides of my face as I gasp for air before he climbs back off the bed.

Silence ensues aside from the jingling of the chains as the two return the configuration to normal. He refastens his pants and belt, fixes his tie, and picks up his jacket from the edge of the bed. The Guards lead the way out as he backs slowly away from me. I quietly sob.

"Now you're mine, forever," he says before turning to leave.

The door shuts and locks again as I burst into tears. I wish Tac were here. He could have stopped all of this. I cry myself to sleep late in the night.

I wake early in the morning to overwhelming nausea. I roll to the side of the bed and vomit on the floor.

Remembering last night, I whisper, "No, not again," and vomit again.

I roll out of the bed and shuffle to the door, "Help, please. I need to go to the restroom," I call through the door.

A few moments pass before I feel it again and vomit in front of the door. It opens and I'm grabbed by my hair and led outside and down the hall to the bathroom. He pushes me to the ground in front of the toilet. I pull myself up and vomit three more times into the bowl, finally with mostly liquid.

Ugh, it's all in my hair and on my hands, I think as I flush the toilet. Another Praetorian comes in the bathroom and helps stand me up. The two strip my mother's dress and underwear from my body before they push me into the shower and turn the water on.

"Fuck! That's *cold* you assholes!" I scream at them as water goes everywhere with the open shower curtain. I turn away from them to hide as I stick my head under the water and remove the vomit. About fifteen seconds later, the water sudden turns off as I'm pulled backwards out of the shower by my wet hair.

I lose my balance and fall to the ground, being dragged out of the bathroom. The carpet in the hallway starts to rub me raw.

"Please. Let me at least stand up," I say.

He pauses as I seize the opportunity and stand. He then grabs me by the handcuff chain and pulls me back to the room and shoves me inside, slamming the door behind me.

"Could I at least get a fucking towel, you barbarians?!" I scream through the door.

Someone has already cleaned up the vomit. At least there's that. Shortly after, both Guards come through the door with a towel in hand. One holds my chains as the other dries me off.

"You want to keep those hands?" I ask threateningly.

"Shut up. There's nothing you can do about it. You'll just sit there and take it like you did last night," he replies.

I wait until he's moved on, continuing to dry me off. He stupidly places his face right where I need it. I quickly turn and elbow him as hard as I can in the nose. I laugh loudly when blood goes everywhere and he screams in agony. I know I'm about to get knocked out, but I don't care.

I wake up shortly after with a busted lip and dressed in a similar dress as the one they just ripped off of me. It confuses me. I sit up on the bed and shuffle over to the closet. As I open the doors, the closet reveals, to my horror, a dozen nearly identical dresses as the one my mother was murdered in. This sick fuck has had all of these dresses made for me just to rub it in that I'm following in my mother's footsteps. At least I'll fight back.

I shut the doors in disgusts and waddle back over to the bed. I'm going to have to lure one of the Guards in here and knock him out somehow to get the keys. That's the only logical way I can see to escape now. I'll have to make sure I'm quiet. The other Guard will likely be right outside and I'd like to have full range of my arms and legs when I deal with him.

Before I can figure out the details of my escape plan, both Guards burst into the room.

"Time for lunch," one says.

"I'm not hungry," I sharply reply.

"That doesn't matter. Your father is on the way home and you are expected to be downstairs and in a presentable manner by the time he gets here," he explains.

I think maybe I can see a little more about what I'm up against once I get outside the house, so lunch doesn't seem like a horrible idea. I'm starving, but my stomach is not playing nice at this point. I'll play along in exchange for valuable intelligence on an escape route and expected resistance.

I nod at them as they cross and drag me to the vanity again. The same female Guard comes in to do my makeup. She scoffs at my freshly cut lip as she fills in the split with antibiotic cream and covers it with the same red lipstick from before.

I'm escorted down the stairs toward the table. I can see through the sheer curtains there are multiple armed Guards on the front lawn. I look through the kitchen at the back door. It doesn't seem to be altered, so I may be able to get out that way and use the house as cover. I'll still need a weapon though and the Guard weapons are DNA and voice activated. Even if I were to get a hold of it, it wouldn't fire for me.

They sit me down in the chair as we wait for Tiberius. The Guards stand behind me on either side and the main butler waits on the other side of the table. The only sound in the room is the grandfather clock ticking away the seconds until I have to deal with him again.

Finally, the front door opens to an angry Tiberius on his cell phone chewing someone's ass for something. He sets his briefcase and jacket down on the floor, where the doorman picks them up to place them in a proper place. He struts toward the table, loosening his tie and shouting into the phone.

"I don't care who is responsible, get it fixed!" he shouts finally slamming the phone shut.

The butler pulls his chair out as Tiberius unbuttons his suit coat and hands it to him.

"Sorry, dear. Business as usual. Have you been waiting long?" he says, scooting his chair up to the table.

I simply stare at him with a blank face. He takes notice of the split lip and grabs my chin. I pull away and turn my face.

"I see we're still having to work on your manners. That's ok. We are very patient. You'll behave as you should soon," he says nonchalantly, summoning the butler to begin service.

He sounds the bell again and two more butlers emerge from the kitchen with their trusty domed platters.

"What do we have today?" he asks.

"For you sir, we have a lemon-baked salmon, fresh garden salad, and steamed vegetables," he replies as he removes the dome.

"Excellent. I'm starving," Tiberius states as he picks up his fork and digs in.

My dome is removed to another handful of chicken nuggets and French fries. *You've got to be fucking kidding me.*

"I'm sorry, I'm not six years old anymore. Can I get some real food please?" I say to the butler.

"I thought those were your favorite?" Tiberius says to me.

"Please? Just a garden salad with vinaigrette will do just fine," I say, ignoring his comment.

My plate is domed again and removed. I wait in awkward silence as Tiberius noisily chews his food, making satisfied sounds. After a few minutes, my salad comes out and they went pretty overboard. There are tomatoes, iceberg and romaine lettuces, cucumbers, red onion, croutons, chunks of what look like chicken or turkey, and a boiled egg. The acidity of the vinaigrette tickles my nose and I begin to salivate.

I reach for the fork, but my arms won't reach with the chains. I cross my legs in my seat. I quickly pick up the fork and shove a large bite in my mouth.

"That's not how a lady sits at the table," Tiberius says.

"Oh, I'm sorry, *father*, it's just chains are all the rage nowadays," I facetiously reply with a mouthful of food.

He backhands me again, but this time I'm able to turn so he hits my cheek instead of my nose.

"Bitch," I say, still eating.

"Young lady, I will not have that language in this house!" he shouts, throwing his fork across the room.

"Then let me go!" I scream, unrestricted. "Fucking let me go."

He waves his hand at the Guard, "Take her back to her room if she is going to be devoid of manners."

I quickly shove another bite in my mouth as they grab me by the arms and drag me up the stairs and lock the door. I finish chewing and sit on the edge of the bed. I need to wait until he leaves to go back to work before luring the Guard into the room.

I slowly shuffle around the room, looking for anything I can use as a stabbing weapon. Everything in here is made out of plastic. All of the makeup containers are plastic. The brush is plastic. The hangers in the closet are plastic. The window is bulletproof glass. And there's no other furniture in here except for the bed and the vanity.

I sit down on the edge as it creaks. Wait, there are springs in here. Springs are metal. I quietly push the mattress off to the side just enough so I can reach the box spring. I need something to cut the fabric. I go back to the vanity and retrieve one of the blush containers and tear off the clear plastic top, cracking it in half. It's no knife, but it should cut through this thin fabric.

It barely cuts through enough for me to get my fingers in there and rip it open. I reach into the box spring, feeling around in the dark for anything that can come loose. Shit, everything's welded in place. The doorknob starts to jiggle and I rush to throw the bed back together and sit down just as a Praetorian enters.

This is my chance. I may not get another like this. I have to take him down. I quickly try to think of a way to quietly disable him. I need his keys and a weapon I can use if he has one.

"The butler asked me to bring you the rest of your salad," he says.

"Oh, thank you so much. I'm famished!" I reply, turning on the best charm I can, given the situation.

He gets right in front of me and I stand to take the bowl. I knee him in the testicles and wrap the chain around his neck when he bends over, forcing him to drop the bowl and grab at the chain. We fall over to the ground as he frantically tries to free himself. After a good twenty seconds, his hands and arms fall limp. I keep my grip for an extra ten seconds, just to make sure.

I quietly release him as I realize just how loud that entire debacle was. It wasn't the smartest or best thought-out plan, but it worked. I feel in his pants pocket for the keys and unlock my hands first. My wrists are near raw at this point. I push him off me as I reach down and unlock the shackles on my feet as quietly as I can.

Ok, step one done. Now I need a weapon. He's got a small pocket knife and a stun baton. I take the baton in my right hand and the knife in my left and creep toward the door. I knock twice to signal the guard to open the door. He does as expected and I poke him immediately with the stun baton, causing him to fall on the floor, convulsing.

I peek my head out to make sure no one saw or heard it before moving toward the stairs. I tip toe down the wooden stairs, checking to see if anyone is in the living or dining rooms. The coast is clear. I sneak across the living room rug, headed for the back door. I know I'll still have to scale the two-meter fence, but I can't face a half dozen Guards right now.

I open the back door and glance quickly before noticing there's a Guard walking the perimeter. Shit. At least it's only one. I should be able to take care of him.

I open the door and stick my hand out, inciting him to come closer with my index finger as I whistle quietly. He takes notice and storms towards the door, pushing it open and taking the stun baton to the throat, falling face down and flopping around on the ground.

I push past him and make for the west side fence. The gate usually sticks open and I might be able to bypass having to climb the fence. As I reach the gate, it's been welded shut. *Fuck*. Okay. I guess I'm going over. I turn the baton off and drop the knife. I wedge my bare feet in between the siding and the wooden fence as I push my back up the corner. I reach the top and grab on, spinning around flush to the fence and pulling myself over.

I drop down, pulling the baton out from my dress and turning it back on. If I can make it to the neighbor's yard without being seen, I'll have a much better chance of getting out of here. I slowly get to the corner of the house and peek around to see another Guard walking toward me.

Shit, here we go again. I wait until he clears the corner and shove the baton in his side between his armor plates. The electricity causes him to pull the trigger on his weapon, letting a three-round burst rip into the house behind ours. *Fucking great.* I check again and the coast is clear, so I make a break for it. Dashing across the grass and almost to the neighbor's fence, I feel a sharp pain in my back and everything goes numb as I collide full speed with the fence and black out.

I wake hours later, sore as hell. I'm back in my room, chains and shackles back on, lights still off except for the lamp on the vanity. I sit up slowly, taking account of the damages. It doesn't feel like anything is broken, so that's good. I carefully cross to the vanity once more to look at my face. The side that hit the fence is a little swollen, but all my teeth are here and no real new damage. I got pretty lucky.

The door opens as the Venator enters and the door shuts behind him.

"Your father thought you might run, so I've stayed a few extra days until you settle into your new role," he says.

"Well, if that's the case, I know a great real estate agent in the area, cause I'm not settling into shit here. Either I will eventually get away or I will die trying. This is not my house anymore and that sick fuck is not my father!" I exclaim.

He says nothing as he turns and walks out, locking the door again. I start contemplating new ways to get out, but I'm not coming up with anything of merit. Most of the ideas will probably just get me killed. I pace as best as I can back and forth, begging for a good idea to pop in my head.

The door bursts open as the two Guards enter followed by Tiberius. He shuts the door behind him and locks it.

Turning back to me, "Your little stunt today cost you dinner."

He remains silent for a few moments. I'm not sure if he is waiting to see if I would argue with him or what. Either way, I say nothing.

"You're a little quiet tonight. What's wrong? Congested?" he asks.

I just stare a hole in his forehead.

"Hmm, ok. I guess I'm going to have to clear that congestion. Put her on the bed, feet at the headboard," he commands.

My eyes widen as the two Guards march towards me. I start swinging and kicking as best as I can, but I'm don't do much. They pick me up and do as instructed.

"Push her head off the side of the bed," he instructs as he undoes his belt and pants again. "We'll see after this if you can manage to answer a question posed to you."

I struggle to get away as the Guards pin me down in the bed. He forces his way in after slapping me enough times to make the room spin. I start to flail as I realize he's trying to choke me to death, right there. My vision starts to go as I know I'll pass out soon.

CHAPTER XV: RESCUE

Panic sets in and I dart toward her. *I'm too late.* As I get closer to the suspended woman's corpse, the familiar smell of death pierces my nose. I don't even recognize her. They beat her to a bloody pulp. Her face is swollen and her skin from head to toe is marked with dried blood from her wounds. Her naked body is limp, suspended by spikes through her hands and feet. Blood pools at the base of the freshly cut wooden cross. *They bled her dry*, I think to myself as I swallow the lump in my throat. I don't understand how someone could do something like this to another living human being. What kind of evil does it take to follow through with this kind of execution?

It takes a few minutes of combing over the details of her mangled face and body to make sure that it's not her. What I initially thought was Calida's red hair is actually blood-stained blonde hair. No, it's not her. With a heavy sigh, I glance around to get my bearings. I notice there are many people around staring at me. I was explicitly trying not to draw attention to myself. I'll have to slow down and use my hands on everything like they do. I can't afford to have a showdown with every Praetorian in the city.

As I search the horizon for the Governor's mansion, I regret not at least trying to learn some of their written language. Knowing a half dozen or so words might really help in this situation. Shortly thereafter, I see a house set at the center of the city. Well, it looks like some of the others, but it's taller, wider, and trimmed in some sort of shiny metal. Given everything that I know about the Governor, that's got to be where Calida is being held.

I begin walking slowly up the long road, trying my best to copy the people around me, when loud sirens wail from somewhere in the middle of the city. They're getting closer and closer. I notice people are walking on the raise platforms on the sides and not in the middle. Attempting to blend in, I follow their lead and walk slowly over, keeping pace with them.

The three vehicles come to a screeching halt in front me where a dozen heavily armed Praetorians jump out, pointing their weapons at me. People scream and scatter away from me.

"Freeze! By order of the Governor of Sector 81! You are under arrest!" one of them yells.

Calida's face flashes before my eyes and I feel the anger rise again. My hair stands on end. In a split second, I collapse all three vehicles, along with the Praetorians, into a giant ball of metal and flesh. The screaming only lasts a second before the only sound left is the giant metal ball rolling around on the street.

The anger dissipates along with the threat and I begin noticing the people around holding their phone out and whispering amongst themselves. *I should probably say something to them.*

"Citizens of Sector 81 Prime!" I shout. "Do not be alarmed. I will not hurt you."

More people join the others lining the streets. People come out of their homes to join them.

"I come from a place far away, so most of what I do may seem abnormal to you at first. But I assure you, I mean you no harm." I say.

"He doesn't move his mouth when he talks! He's a demon!" one person shouts.

"No, he attacked the Praetorians with his magic powers. He must be the Messiah come to free us!" another retorts.

The crowds start to panic and some run away, others drop to their knees and chant with their hands in front of them, a few brave souls start running toward me with whatever weapons they can find.

"No, I'm neither of those!" I shout.

Shit, I think to myself as I gently knock the attackers on the ground and take their weapons. *This is not how this was supposed to go. I need to get out of here and away from the mob.*

I sprint quickly toward the center of the city, turning to take the street parallel to the one I was on to keep out of sight. I slow back to a walk once I'm certain I'm out of view of anyone that could recognize me.

What a weird bunch of people. If they're going to react like that, I really should avoid all contact with them. Not only would their panic-induced stampede put them at risk of being hurt, but they'll also give my position away, which would cause more Praetorians to show up.

Either way, I need to stay out of sight. I walk past stores and small food shops, oblivious people try to sell me anything they have. Since they tend to freak out when I speak, I simply use hand gestures to decline their offer or ignore them completely. No need to cause a riot just yet. These are the people that are slaves to the system. They just don't know it yet. They are not the enemy.

I see two Praetorians walking towards me on the sidewalk. This could prove to be useful. I quickly dart to the left down the alley where I wait for them to walk by. As they do, I throw a rock and hit one in the shoulder. They both stop and begin to investigate the alley, shining their flashlights around, looking for the source. When they're close enough to the dumpster I'm hiding behind, I snap both of their necks, pulling their bodies to me and out of sight.

I strip them of their uniforms, mixing and matching until I have a complete uniform that somewhat fits me. The best part is the helmet fits perfectly. Complete with visor, this should keep me hidden until I can get to the Governor's mansion. I complete the look by equipping their weapons as I walk toward the exit of the alley. I try to walk like they do, wider steps and excessively accentuating their shoulders, making them appear bigger than they actually are. It's a very awkward experience, but it beats trying to blend in without the disguise.

The radio crackles and pops in my ear with conversations between other Praetorians. People saying random numbers and codes over staticky radios. Someone calls over it and asks for a status update on the code three response to the south. It's so hard to decipher most of this. What I do notice is the change of tone. When one of them doesn't respond like they're supposed to, the Praetorian calling them starts to get upset.

"Unit 53, you better not be with that hooker again. What happened to the code three you were on? Come back," the male voice calls.

Silence follows before he calls back.

"Unit 53, respond!" he yells after a few seconds.

"Unit 117, check into the status at Axius and Maximus. Unit 53 responded Code 3 to a wanted fugitive about fifteen minutes ago, but he hasn't provided a status update or responded to any calls. Cameras in the vicinity show possible multiple 187s," he says. "Units 121, 47, and 201, provide back up for Unit 117."

The voices are too distracting. I rip the helmet off and toss it to the side of the road. I hear more sirens in the distance, but they seem to be going somewhere else for the moment. The quicker I can get to the mansion, the quicker I can get Calida free and out of here.

The good thing about wearing this uniform is people get out of your way. The clunking of the heavy boots on the sidewalk coupled with the unique jingling of their equipment they carry serve to announce your approach. Citizens here have trained themselves to identify these sounds and to move out of the way, even if they cannot see the Praetorian. It is a welcome caveat.

I hear even more sirens a few minutes later going in the same direction as the previous ones. Whatever they're after, there's a lot of them. This could be the opening I needed. I didn't intend to create a distraction of this level, but it sure works to my advantage. I lightly jog and over accentuate my legs and breathing to try to mirror how these people run. It's so slow and ineffective. I feel like an idiot doing this, but I have to get as close to the mansion as I can without alerting anyone.

I finally get to the inner city and slow to a walk. Squad cars drive up and down the streets, lights and sirens blaring. Even though I wear this uniform, I know I'm exposed. About a block before the mansion, one of the vehicles screeches to a halt as it drives passed me in the opposite direction. I keep walking and dip my head down to keep from being recognized.

"Hey, rookie!" one of the Praetorians yells from the stopped vehicle.

I turn my head to see him waving me over from the passenger seat. I walk over to the vehicle.

"What are you doing in this district?" he asks.

Think of something to say!

"Just doing my patrol, sir," I reply, turning to point away from them so they can't see my mouth.

"The Guard has this district, you know that. You want to tell me what's going on?" he inquires.

I pause for a few seconds before leaning down into the vehicle, "Ok, but remember, you asked for it."

"Holy shit!" he says, reaching for his weapon.

I snap both of their necks quickly. The vehicle starts to roll forward towards crowds of people. I turn the wheel to point it into the alley where it crashes into a wall and stops.

Looking down the street, I quickly check to make sure no one saw it before turning to continue to the Governor's mansion. This is taking too long. I dart down the rest of the street to the mansion. There are no patrols here. I take the ridiculous Praetorian gear off, revealing the now dirty pants and shirt Calida got for me.

As I walk in front of the main gate, spot lights and a voice says, "Stop where you are! This is a restricted area! Go back the way you came!"

I shield my eyes from the bright lights to reveal four Guards slowly moving in my direction. There are two on the ground and two on the second-floor balcony.

I snap the necks of the two on the ground and post up behind the brick wall surrounding the mansion as automatic fire echoes throughout the compound. Just as I get ready to peek around the corner, a loud bang at my feet makes my ears ring and a bright light nearly blinds me.

When I come to, I've been handcuffed and I'm lying on the street. I quickly roll over and snap the other two's necks and break free of the restraints. Hopefully, that's the last of them.

I dart up the stairs leading to the front door and burst through it. Doing so startles one of the butlers so much that he falls backwards and knocks himself unconscious. Another butler comes out of the back to investigate the noise.

"Where is she?" I ask sternly.

He points to the second floor and I take off up the stairs. I see a door with her name on it and knock it off its hinges. Sure enough, there is Calida, lying on the bed with blood all over her face. The Governor is screaming as blood covers the floor beneath him and the two Guards are confused and shocked.

Calida rolls over and spits something out on the floor as she begins to cough and spit in the same general area.

I quickly snap both of the Guards' necks and throw the Governor against the wall as hard as I can. His body is crushed against the wall and falls to the floor, face down. I rush over to Calida and break her chains off.

"I'm here. Are you ok?" I ask. "Why is there blood everywhere?"

"Yeah, I'm ok. The blood is all his," she says, pointing to the ground.

"Wow, remind me not to make you mad." I retort, half afraid and half amused.

I hear a voice behind me, "Freeze Tac! And don't even think about turning around or using your fancy superpowers. I hold in my hand a mark 24 fragmentation grenade with a no-delay fuse and a spring-loaded dead man switch. If you kill me, you kill us all."

"Who are you?" I ask as I stand fully, back still turned.

"My name is Lieutenant Vettius. I'm in charge of the Praetorians for Sector 81. And you two criminals are Tac and Calida and you're coming with me," she says.

"Sabina, please, you don't have to do this. You know better than anyone what I went through with this shithead," she says, pleading.

"Calida, somewhere along the way, you fell off the wagon. Now, I know fully that everyone has their own coping mechanisms but joining a terrorist organization and assassinating the Governor shouldn't be one of them," motioning to the half-naked corpse across the room.

I slowly turn around to see her holding something in her hand. Her radio crackles and an unintelligible voice says something into her earpiece.

"What the fuck?!" Vettius screams.

"What is it?" I ask.

"The Venator called Rome to tell them they'd lost 81 Prime and they've activated Operation Purge," she says. "He's killed us all because of you two!"

"What is Operation Purge?" I ask, fearfully.

"Long story, short. They're going to bomb Prime with us still in it," she expounds aggressively.

"How long do we have?" Calida apprehensively inquires.

"Five, maybe ten minutes. These are supersonic bombers from the Western Capital. Hell, the operation itself is highly classified," she says.

"We have to get as many people out of here as possible," I say.

"The only chance we have to save anyone is to get them into the sewers. It was originally built to double as a bomb shelter from the Old War. We have a legacy contingency plan for air raids. There is a siren on the top of headquarters that, when sounded, indicates there's an imminent threat of a bombing. It hasn't been used in nearly a hundred years, so who knows if it works or if the people will even know what it means, but that's our best chance," she explains.

"Ok, but what are you going to do about the grenade?" Calida asks.

"I think I have something for that," I reply. "Where is the switch you have to hold?"

"Right here on the handle. That has to stay in," she says pointing to the trigger.

I reach out and grab the grenade, making sure to keep the trigger down.

"Got it?" she asks, slowly releasing.

"Yes, I have it," I reply as I push it towards the window.

I knock out the window and push the grenade into the ground below before letting go. We dart down the stairs and out of the front door.

"Over here!" Vettius yells from her vehicle.

We run to and jump in the vehicle as she slams on the accelerator, spinning out and heading back towards headquarters, with lights and sirens blaring. She slams on the brakes and we slide up to the front of the building, not bothering to turn the vehicle off and jumping out.

"Hurry!" She yells, running up the stairs.

We follow as quickly as Calida's legs will take her. Vettius darts down a hallway to a door at the end of the hall.

"You guys have got to hustle, we only have minutes to get them below," she says.

Inside the dark room, Vettius flips a switch causing several machines to whir and come to life. A few antiquated buttons pressed, a large lever thrown, and a low growl is heard throughout the building. It gets louder and louder until it's screaming and we have to cover our ears.

"Come this way!" Vettius yells as she heads out and down the stairs into the basement.

She runs to open the jail cells.

"What the hell is going on, Vettius?" Titus says, concerned.

"No time to explain, Titus. Just get into the sewers with everyone else," she instructs.

The detained all run out of their cells, headed for the massive door at the other end of the hallway. Titus recognizes and gives Tac a disgruntled look as he passes.

"Quickly, we've got less than few minutes!" She yells, shuttling us down the dusty stairs.

We make our way to the vault in the center where hundreds of men, women, and children are gathered. Families take count of their members and rejoicing when more join them. They all look so frightened. A few of them stare at me. I recognize some of them from the first incident with the Praetorians. I don't think they mistake me for their Messiah anymore, so that's good.

Soon, loud explosions rock the city, causing dust and debris to drop from the ceiling. Everything these people have, everything from clothes to family heirlooms, are being incinerated as we speak. It infuriates me that they would do this to their own people. I thought the Governor was bad. Well, he was, but these people are much worse.

We sit there for hours as the bombings continue, shaking the very foundation to its core. The lights flicker briefly a little each time an explosion goes off and more dust falls from the ceiling, forcing parents to shield their children from the debris.

Finally, they stop. We stay in place for at least another half hour to make sure. Some of the Praetorians that made it try to push the vault door open. It breaks loose and then stops, blocked by something. They push for a good minute before collapsing. It won't budge.

I stand and cross the room, "Step back, please," I ask them.

I reach back and punch the door, which budges slightly as gasps and whispers ensue. I reach back, over and over again, throwing everything I have at this door when it finally breaks free, pushing the massive amount of concrete out of the way. I walk into the sewer to see most of it has collapsed.

I turn to catch a glimpse of Calida. She nods her head and I turn back to start moving the rubble out of the way. We spend the next hour or so digging out. Once we finally break through into the clearing outside of Prime, it's nighttime and we can feel the heat emanating from the nearly molten city. This isn't going to be easy for any of us now. It's a wakeup call that most in this group were not ready for.

We start moving for the tree line, often taking glimpses back at what once was Sector 81 Prime. Most are still in shock and disbelief. Some mourn lost loved ones that didn't make it to the shelter in time. Some just stare into the distance. They've been thrust to the front lines in a war they never volunteered for.

The Resistance died yesterday, snuffed out by a single Roman Venator. After tonight, the Retaliation has been born. Cast in the fire by the rash decisions of officials in a far-off land. It will take time to regroup and collect ourselves before we begin. But make no mistake, these people are angry. I can see it in their eyes. They want revenge. And the Western Capital will pay dearly.

Made in United States
Orlando, FL
19 November 2023